Spike

John Burns

Spike

MACMILLAN

First published 2000 by Macmillan
an imprint of Macmillan Publishers Ltd
25 Eccleston Place, London SW1W 9NF
Basingstoke and Oxford
Associated companies throughout the world
www.macmillan.co.uk

ISBN 0 333 77951 7

1 3 5 7 9 8 6 4 2

A CIP catalogue record for this book
is available from the British Library.

Phototypeset by Intype London Ltd
Printed and bound in Great Britain by
Mackays of Chatham plc, Chatham, Kent

*This one's for Conor who forced me
to turf out the boring bits.*

Chapter One

He came out when I was just about to give up hope.
It was knocking on three o'clock in the morning. The
front door flapped wide open when I was lighting my
last cigarette. I stuffed it in my right-hand pocket so
he wouldn't see me. For a second or so he stood in
the doorway, looking like a cardboard cut-out. He
peered up into a starless night and pulled the overcoat
collar tight and snug around his jowls. He glanced
back into the narrow hallway. There was no sign of
Daisy Dropsy-drawers. He walked towards me down
the mews with long, strong strides, his leather soles
kissing the cobbles a moist goodnight. Splock *splack*
splock. I could hear him breathing down his nostrils
as he passed me. He was that close. You couldn't see
much of his face for he had his head down and the
only street lamp was on strike. But as a trained
observer I observed from my damp corner that we
were wearing matching Crombies. Only his looked
warmer and newer than mine. It probably didn't have
a cigarette burning hell out of his pocket either.

I watched him shoulder his way through the drizzle
to a Range Rover, parked on the double yellows. He
hadn't copped a ticket. His sort never do. The driver's
door shut with a beefy clunk and the engine kicked

in at the first go. It was a mist grey Range Rover. It slid off into the gloaming with a soft hiss. It was invisible. He'd forgotten to turn his lights on.

That left the mews desolate, apart from me, halfway between hypothermia and rigor mortis, and the lemon light from the lounge of Number Eight. The rest of London was safely abed and snuggled up beside its wife. Except for him. And her. And me.

I'd nothing better to do so I dragged out the cigarette, puffed it back to life and watched the lemon light. After less than a minute the lemon called it a night. Twelve seconds later the apricot came on in the upstairs bedroom.

I imagined the next bit. He was driving back through the empty shining streets to the flat in Dolphin Square. He'd stuck something stringy and quavery on the CD. Sometimes he hummed along with it, for he was in fine form and he didn't know that I knew.

Then I imagined her. That was more difficult because I had never seen her. But I pictured her upstairs in the glow of the apricot lampshade, untousling her hair. It was long and blonde, maybe more blonde than nature intended, but nature sometimes skimps on the fine detail. She had a full-length mirror glued on her wardrobe. She didn't glance in it, but I did. She was wearing a white lacy Victorian thing that went all the way from the nape of her neck to the tips of her little pink tootsies. It was wide open. Shameless hussy.

She sat by her dressing table and brushed and brushed her hair until it lay flat and clean and silvered. She pursed her lips and frowned at herself in the

2

square mirror. Yes, she was still beautiful. The frown disappeared under a dollop of vanishing cream. She dabbed away the stains of the day with lilac and lavender tissues plucked from a box all covered in dinky little flowers. A lazy smile bloomed on her lips as she remembered his eyes, lit by her loveliness. She turned to the bed and saw the rumpled sheets. They were apricot too. Her pointy little tongue flicked her teeth in mischievous memory.

My cigarette went out.

Her wrist jangled bracelets. She pressed down lovingly on the sheets, caressing away each and every fold of the night. Her hand was pale and delicate and she paused as she smoothed so that she could approve the fine fingers, the milky cuticles; the stroke of a mistress.

Then she shrugged herself free of the dressing gown affair and she climbed into the still tepid sheets. Now she was naked as sin. For one rich warm moment she was back in his big shouldered embrace and remembering the luxuriant power of sex, the language of their passion. She breathed a throaty sigh. She turned to one side and switched off the apricot light.

All this I imagined. For I have a terrific imagination. That's what they pay me for.

What I didn't need to imagine, what was honest-to-God fact, was that Howard Lanche had just spent seven hours in the secret company of a woman who was not Mrs Lanche. I could have knocked out the story right there and then. Stick a slick headline on top, say *LOVER BOY'S LANCHE PAD*, and there's another kick-'em-in-the-pants tabloid front page.

But somewhere deep in my bones I'd the feeling

this one would never make the paper. You don't turn over people like Howard Lanche unless you know what you're getting up to. And I didn't.

I turfed away the cigarette and ambled off in search of a prowling taxi. Back home there were Bensons by the drove and a litre or two of untapped Gordons crying out for me. Also it was warm and dry there. I walked faster.

I'd spent seven sopping hours door-stepping Number Eight Turnbull Mews, and I was still laying bets that my story would end up on the spike. So why was I doing it?

That's another story altogether.

Chapter Two

Wind back about forty or so hours. I was sitting at my desk, fiddling my expenses and not doing anybody any harm, when Jools shimmered up and helped herself to my Bensons.

'Tony Belker wants to see you,' she said happily. 'Where's your lighter?'

I said, 'Tell me what the Beast wants first.'

'No.'

I thumbed my Hong Kong Dunhill. She whuffed and whiffed on the cigarette.

She said, 'I don't like these. They're too strong.'

I said, 'I'll remember that in future.'

Jools wobbled over to the window and gazed down ten floors to where February was drilling holes in Old Father Thames. She forgot me and watched the river worm through the ebb tide mudbanks, ploughing ever onwards to strange and exotic places. Somewhere out there beyond the hail were Gravesend, Greys and the Isle of Dogs. Adventure stirred the very soul. Jools forgot about me and I got on with the serious biz of distressing a forged taxi receipt. It's easy when you know how. First you give a cab driver an outlandish tip, thereby prompting him to hand you a book of blank receipts. You find yourself a pen which has *not* been supplied by the office. I'd nicked mine from the lottery desk in Waitrose. You write a whacking great figure on a bill, say fifteen quid, which is what I'd just done. You do this with your left hand, unless you're left-handed. In which case you use the right one. If you're ambidextrous you could always try it with your toes. Now you scribble Winnie Mandela's initials on it, or alternately, Michael Winner's. The reason you choose them is because the letters run together and if you do it right it resembles the signature of an illiterate megalomaniac. Now you have what looks like a kosher twenty-four-carat taxi bill. Perfect. Except it's too *new* looking. So you flick your cigarette over it, slop a drop of office coffee atop, rub it in, rip off one corner, scrunch the whole thing up in a ball and unfold it. And there it is. A lovely little work of art. It's almost a shame to part with it.

Jools woke up. 'Max. Tony wants you.'

I said, 'You still haven't told me why.'

She shrugged her shoulders, demonstrating that her Wonderbra was still working wonders. 'How should I know?'

I said, 'You're his secretary.'

Her eyes went all Clint Eastwoody. 'And what does *that* mean?'

It means, Jools, that we've all heard the whispers about you and the Beast and the office car park and the security video: the video that had to be wiped.

I said, 'You work with him, sweetie pie. You must have some idea what he's up to.'

Jools said, 'I don't.' She returned to the window and her study of current affairs.

And maybe she didn't. I brooded. Why should Tony

Belker, our vile executive editor, want to see me? I hadn't done anything wrong recently, except for forging this taxi bill. Maybe the fat git was gifted with telepathy. And why not? He certainly wasn't gifted with anything else.

The Beast is one of those freaks that nature throws at us from time to time, specimens like Stalin, Vlad the Impaler and any old Arsenal player you care to think of.

I said, 'He wants me now?'

'He wants you ten minutes ago.'

I said, 'I've forgotten where he hides during the hours of daylight.'

Jools stubbed out my cigarette. She'd smoked less than half of it. Not even two-fifths. She sighed, pushing her chest in and out. 'Follow me.'

She bobbed off and I chugged along behind her on invisible strings of desire. Jools is a tall girl whose devotion to work-out tapes is plain for all to nearly see. She's late twenties now. When she gets to be fifty there'll be a bit more of Jools to share around. So that's something for us all to look forward to.

We padded down the grey tunnel to the lair of the Beast With Two Bellies. I was curious why he was even in the place today. It was a Sunday. Normally the acting editor on Sundays is drawn from the dross of dysfunctional drones whom editors hand-pick as their trusty lieutenants. That way the Editor gets to look half intelligent.

I shouldn't have been in today either. But I was six weeks adrift with my exes and two months down on my Amex bill. I'd counted on having a quietish couple of hours for Sundays are not as other days in the life of a tabloid newspaper. It's funtime in the asylum as the entire Z team of deputy editors get to play with the train set. This is why your Monday morning red top is knee deep in glitterati non-stories and bloodless follow-ups to the News of the Screws' STAR IN SECRET SEX SWOP OP or similar tosh. Here's a tip for the economy-minded: cancel your Monday paper. You won't miss a thing.

Jools shunted me off outside Belker's door and wandered away in search of a mirror. I rapped the mahogany veneer firmly and pushed in, pretending I didn't really have a hangover. Surprise No. 2 greeted me. 'Ah, Max,' said Surprise No. 2, aka the Editor.

The Editor? What had prised him out of the Cotswolds on a day that belonged in Siberia?

I sat down and stuck my eyeballs back in. Belker was sitting opposite. He had his sleeves rolled up to tell the world he was a busy man. He flicked a glance at a cheap digital watch, the size of a satellite dish. The Editor, in a pullover his auntie must have knitted, was standing behind him off to one side.

Belker shoved a piece of paper at me. 'Read this.'

Sometimes these newspaper execs have trouble with the printed word.

I said sweetly, 'What? Out loud?'

The Editor squeezed off a frown to let me know he was not amused. So I just looked at the piece of paper. It was a sheet of bog standard A4. There was no letterhead, only about twenty lines of single-space typing at the top of the page. I read:

Howard Lanche is having an affair with a young woman who lives in Turnbull Mews, W2. She is probably living in No. 8 or No. 10. This affair has been going on

*for some time although he is married and has grown up
children. The woman is probably as young as one of his
daughters. He is said to be infattuated with her and sees
her every time he can get away from the House. He has
his own flat in Dolphin Square as well as the Old Manor
Farm in the Constituency. He is very discreet so you might
find it hard to firmly pin him down but if you put a good
man on it he'll probably 'dig up the dirt'. The affair is
going on unbeknownst to his wife and to all intents and
purposes he is still happily married. If he is tackled about
it he'll probably deny it unless you have firm evidence to
tackle him with.*

That was it. No name. No signature. I read it again
and slid it back to Belker. He pushed it right back at
me.

He said, 'Well, what do you think?'

I think for starters that the writer is not Charles
Dickens. He splits his infinitives and dangles his prep-
ositions at you. He can't spell 'infatuated' and he's
probably over fond of the word 'probably'. Also, he's
knocking on a bit. Nobody calls it W2 any more. They
call it Bayswater. He's involved in politics, one way or
the other. Note the casual reference to the House.
And the constituency, with a capital C. Normal people
don't talk like that.

I said, 'Hmmm.' That was politer than saying so
what.

The Editor polished his specs on his woolly thing
and said, 'Very interesting, yes?'

No. The only interesting thing about it was why
they were interested. And why were they asking me,
their heroic chief crime correspondent. Then I remembered that crack about putting a good man on the

story. A fuzzy alarm bell jangled way down in my head. It told me I was that good man.

Belker opened his maw. 'It's a belter of a story. We want a proper turnover job on this one. Everything copper-bottomed and nailed down. It needs solid investigation.'

I translated, 'You want me to doorstep him.'

They nodded together except Belker's nod was one beat out of synch.

Hacks like me don't do doorsteps. We leave that sort of jollity to the apple-cheeked youths and youth-ettes we snatch from outside universities. They come to us all starry-eyed at the imagined glamour of hackery. First chance we get, we plonk them on a doorstep for hours and hours until their intended victim tells them to naff off, or calls the Old Bill to do it for him. Half a dozen doorsteps soon knocks the wide-eyed wonder out of the would-be journos. Three months later they're swearing like fish and drinking like troopers. They still have much to learn, but they're getting there.

I got there – and way beyond – a long, long time ago. Therefore doorsteps are not in my line of busi-ness. I explained this to the Editor. He wasn't listening.

He said, 'It's a highly sensitive story. It requires someone with your . . .'

'Experience,' Belker supplied.

'Expertise,' the Editor corrected.

So I was stuck with it. I said, 'Are we going for the jugular on this one?'

The Editor and Belker looked at each other. There was a pause in the proceedings.

The Editor said, 'Let's just see what comes up before we decide to run the story.'

That was no answer at all. I took another shot. I said, 'How hard do you want me to hit Lanche?'

The Editor looked pained. He said, 'I told you, Max. This is a sensitive area. It is absolutely vital he doesn't know you're investigating him. But I want the story as a matter of urgency. That's why I've come in today.'

Belker waited till the boss man was through before chipping in, 'You've got two days, three at the outside. Lanche is in his constituency over the weekend but you can make a start by going through the library stuff on him. He makes a big play of family values, as you know.'

I didn't know. There were an awful lot of things I didn't know and didn't want to know about Howard Lanche. I said, 'I'd better talk to our Parly boys.'

That triggered a couple of heart attacks. 'Oh no, no, *No!*' said the Editor, doing his squeaky bad Thatcher take-off. 'You mustn't speak to *anyone* about this. Just Tony or myself.'

So we were in secret squirrel territory here. I tapped the sheet of paper. 'Who's this from?'

The Editor smiled like the Mona Lisa in bifocals. He said, 'A source.'

That's all. I let my eyebrows slide into my hairline. The Editor ignored them.

Belker flapped his flippers together. 'Right, Max. There you have it. Do a bit of snooping, but don't face up Lanche until the Editor gives the okay. Got the picture?'

I hadn't even got the negative. That reminded me. 'Do I use a monkey?'

The Editor said, 'No. No photographers. Not at this stage. We'll just see how it develops.'

He didn't mean to be punny. I hung around, waiting for them to tell me what this was all about but they were bored with my company. The Editor was going home anyway. I picked up the sheet of paper and trooped back to my desk.

My brow had more lines than Clapham Junction. There was something not connecting here. Our mighty organ is noted for its tolerant attitude to MPs who take off their trousers in the wrong bedroom: tolerant as long as they're true New Blue Labour that is. So why were we hell-bent on monstering one of Our Own? The Editor would never get his yearned-for knighthood that way.

The thought cheered me up.

Chapter Three

The story had all the makings of nothing. But you don't expect editors or news executives to come up with bright ideas. And you most certainly don't rubbish their pitiful efforts. That is the very first rule you learn in our lark.

I had it all spelt out to me on Day One down in the bar. A creased and crumpled old hack turned his harvest moon eyes on me and he said, 'I will give you an invaluable piece of advice.'

He did this largely because I was buying him drink.

He said, 'Max, one of these days the Editor or News Desk is going to say they've got a great story that needs your special talents.' He stuck his fingers up to semaphore quotes around 'special'.

'They'll tell you somebody's just found Hitler's bones in a Kentucky Fried Chicken bucket down the Old Kent Road. They'll believe it, so you'd better believe it too. You will not tell them this is crapola, because News Desk don't like to be reminded they're not as smart as us. You will say, "Ace story. I'm on my way." And they will think, "Smart kid, that Max Chard." Meanwhile, you will go out, find a quiet boozer and give it an hour. Then you ring News Desk, while you're still sober, and tell 'em, "The story doesn't stand up.

13

The bloke who says they're Hitler's bones is fresh out of a padded bedroom at the Maudsley. Anyway, he's eaten them." News Desk will say, "Never mind, Max. You gave it your best shot. Go have a drink. You earned it." They will love you, for you have just saved them from making fools of themselves. Our purpose in life is to make them think they're clever. So, Max, *mein liebchen*, whenever *They* think they have a bright idea, you will applaud their genius. For that is the law of the jungle. Got a spare fiver?'

The old hack's beery counsel came to me today. He was bang on. If I told the Editor that his brilliant story was not worth felling an acre of Finland for, he might take offence. He might also take a closer look at my exes. And that would never do.

A raggedy Sunday headache which had been playing a snare drum solo since first light switched to the cymbals. I called the Doctor. His name is Oscar and he's not a doctor. He's a feature writer. We call him the Doctor because we once used to run to him with our complaints and he prescribed a cure. The normal remedy was two large Bloody Marys. And most efficacious they were too.

Oscar is a great man who used to wreak havoc with the vodka bottle himself until the vodka bottle got its own back. Now he lays waste to nothing more lively than Buxton mineral water and he's stopped prescribing. But he's still one of us. Oscar on this particular day was working up a page ten lead on the various girls waiting to get their grabs on the princes William and Harry. Honestly. So Oscar was grateful for the interruption. He kindly offered to meet me in the dive bar of the Stone.

14

We were the first customers of the day and we had to hang around a bit because the priggish barman thought this was no time for decent folk to be drinking. I weighed in with a pint of lager as cold as the weather. Oscar stared morbidly into his Buxton water. They were out of lime and he's too poncy for lemon. He was wearing a canary yellow sweater, knockabout jeans and white trainers with a purple go-faster stripe. That's another odd thing about Sundays – everyone tools up at the office in fancy dress. Except for me. Reading from north to south, I was clad in a Hugo Boss jacket, oyster white button-down shirt, silver and blue-black tie, navy trousers with a pleated front and black brogues. You could have taken me anywhere, and you probably would.

Oscar was not talkative today. I reasoned that the task of knocking out 800 words on fantasy Royal romances would put anyone off their Buxton water, especially a soul as sensitive as his. Oscar is a rare animal. He's a terrific hard-nosed hack and he's also a red-hot writer. He's got the key to the cupboard where we keep the three-syllable words. Naturally in our calling we have little need for such genius. But we wheel Oscar out every time we get a good tragedy. Imagine there's some kid who's popped her clogs after years of suffering. You pick up the *Mirror* or the *Star* next morning and you read:

A mother wept last night after tragic tot Bessie-Ann Bloggins lost her brave battle for life.

Oscar would go more on the lines of:

Her smile was sunshine, beaming defiance through a black cloud of pain.

Last night Bessie-Ann Bloggins smiled one last time

at her beloved mum, and then the little girl who touched a nation's heart was gone.

Actually he'd do it much better than that. He'd have choirs of angels hymning her broken body to rest and all sorts of tricks. Things they don't teach you in journalism school.

We return to the present. Oscar said, 'Whate'er ails thee, knight at arms, alone and palely loitering?' He reads too much.

I chewed over what I should say. All hacks are natural-born gossips. They come fitted with motor-mouths. Oscar has the turbo version. If I told him what I was really up to, he'd have it round the office in five minutes from a standing start. And five minutes after that, the Editor would haul me in and scream and shout.

Therefore I lied. 'It's an Editor's Must. He wants a huge drag on Battered Britain.'

Oscar stirred the Buxton water with an artistic finger. He said, 'And of course this bears no relation to your celebrated spread last month – The Sick Society?'

I said, 'Neither does it resemble my three-day Frightened City exposé which played to packed houses a month earlier.'

Oscar shook his head in sorrow. 'What's the line this time – teeny tearaways, crack barons, latter-day Fagins?'

I waggled my head. 'All that, and all the rest. The Editor's given me the names of people he says are worth talking to.'

I went through a shortish list, sticking Howard Lanche's name somewhere in the middle. I asked Oscar, 'What do you know about them?'

I left him to think about it while I ordered another pint. The bar was filling up. There was a glum bunch of groin strains from our Sports Desk stuck in a corner, all dressed by Oxfam. We exchanged grunts.

Oscar had been doing some pondering. I let him ramble on without listening until he got round to friend Lanche. I faked a yawn. I said, 'Is he as pure and virginal and Cliff Richardy as he makes out?'

Oscar said, 'Even purer. I did an election profile on him. He's straight out of the Bible, or the *Reader's Digest* anyway. Loves his wife – who's an old boot, drools on about his daughters – they're worth a tumble. Thinks divorce should be outlawed. He's certifiable.'

Oscar collects divorces. He's bang on course for his fourth.

I said ever so casually, 'These pillars of society always have skeletons kicking about in the background.'

Oscar shook his head. 'Lanche is the genuine article. I think he lacks the imagination.'

I offered Oscar a cigarette. He loftily waved the pack aside. He's given them up too. Next thing he'll be packing in the cheese 'n' onion crisps. I said, 'Does Lanche have any pretty Commons researchers, any nice young men hanging around him?'

'Sure. But every MP has them. They come free with the job. Like stupidity. He's not slipping his secretary one, if that's what you're thinking. But I did.'

That sent Oscar skipping off down mammary lane, recalling in shameless detail the girls he hadn't got round to marrying yet. Considering the amount of drink he used to knock back, it's amazing he can remember anything. I accompanied his memoirs with a couple more pints, after which my head was sufficiently appeased to let me go back to the office.

At my desk I lit a cigarette and had another look at the memo from the Editor's mole. It was only then I noticed it. Way down in the bottom right-hand corner the author had typed a date. January 20. Today was February 19. That's what? I counted it back. Nearly five weeks ago. So the Editor had been sitting on a potential splash for twenty-six news days. And yet he'd just told me the unmasking of Citizen Lanche was a rush job. He'd even yomped through the slush to brief me. Strange.

My brain wasn't up to coping with it. Instead I got down to the tiresome task of finding out all I never wanted to know about H. Lanche, MP and spare-time Romeo. I turned on my terminal, typed in the password *crippen*, and whistled up the on-screen library. It told me there were 124 cuts on the fool. The prospect of grazing through 124 stories on a black and green computer monitor was more than mortal man could stand. I shuffled off to the library and yelled for help. The duty thugee made it clear he didn't love me. 'Everything we've got on Lanche is on screen,' he lied. My hangover was worse than his so I stayed there glowering until he began burrowing in the files. In the meantime I trawled Kelly's street directory, our reverse phone books and everything else to hand. Eight Turnbull Mews was listed to a D. &. R. Probin. Someone with so many z's in his name he read like a snore lived at number ten. At least that's how they were in the two-year-old directory. I ran a library check on both names. Nothing. Anyway, Lanche's doxy might be a tenant and not listed. I took down the phone numbers because that's the sort of thing you do when you're acting investigative. The librarian returned grumbling under a bunch of manilla folders bordered with the bites of drink-starved hacks. I dutifully signed for them, leaving my friendly archivist to get back to watching the Everton and Spurs synchronized diving teams.

I'll skip over the next few tedious hours during which I laboured at the cuttings. It was ten minutes short of opening time when I sheathed the Bic and read over my findings. For those who don't know the score on Howard Lanche, here's the SP:

The money came from his old man, a monument in the architecture racket. He was a whizz at knocking up hotels and derelict office blocks. He designed his only son in the summer of '49. Howard was born on 18 April 1950 at Maidenhead. Nothing much happened for many a year and then in May '76 Howard made his first newsworthy appearance. He turned up at Birmingham Crown Court court charged with dangerous driving, thereby causing the death of Melvyn Stodley Davies, aged three. An expensive brief argued that young Melvyn deserved all he got because he did wantonly and recklessly run out on to the road, without due regard to the Highway Code, thereby making a right old mess of Mr Lanche's nice shiny car. The jury fell for it and Howard walked without a blemish.

He married Leonora Dyce in February, 1975. First daughter same year, which proves what a loving family man he was. Gap of three years; another daughter. Wife must have gone off it after that. Wife was daughter of glassworks owner and brought bags of booty to the union. They romanced each other at Keele student hops. Large hole in biog. over what happened next until he emerged as Labour hopeful for Slough West in 1978: their youngest-ever candidate. Bully for him. Came third. Not so bully for him. In '82 runner-up to loony Lib in Cornwall. Third time lucky in '86 Harding by-election. Maiden speech in praise of family values. Local profiles say he once held down a proper job, as a structural engineer. A right little globe-trotting one at that, engineering structures all over the shop – Libya, the Philippines, Malaysia, anywhere except bomb-site Britain. First pix all show him in construction hats of varying hues. It wasn't until '82 that he took his hat off and flashed his shag-pile hair. Interests: bird watching, walking and growing weeds. That's what he put in *Who's Who*, just to show what a barrel of laughs he was. Parly profiles paint him as a bit of a Euro basher. Occasionally climbs up on his high horse to chunter on about the plight of farmers, fishermen and single mums, though no one takes a blind bit of notice. So much for Howard Petworth Lanche.

I still had one hundred and eighty seconds to opening time so I looked at his pic file. He had chubby chops, a roundish face and a somewhat bouffant tangle of black-grey hair. A shade too narcissistic for a doting family man. He was the proud owner of a well-fed smile and he lacked the usual creepy blandness of a Labour backwoodsman. His wife, the unlovely Leonora, made up for it. You could have scared off hardened rapists with her mug shot. A big, sharpened nose, with marbles for eyes and a smile that never reached her incisors. She was built like a lamp post without the interesting bits. I felt an instant wave of sympathy for old Howie. Next his daughters. I saw what Oscar meant. Both were a mite debby, with hitched up snoots, but they sported full-blown mouths and eyes that knew what you were thinking. The elder one, Flora, was married to the sort of person she should be married to. Baby sister was presently studying marine biology at the University of San Diego, Calif. Some girls have more luck than is good for them. In fairness, she needed all the luck she could get, after the name they'd saddled her with. Eva Lanche. Try shouting that across the ski slopes at Klosters and see what happens.

Time up. I bundled the Lanche family back into its folders and hastened barwards.

Chapter Four

What with all the excitement I must have forgotten it was Sunday. That meant Hamptons, my usual after-hours refuelling station, was closed and shuttered. It also meant the Stone dive bar offered only a sprinkling of stoat-faced subs as drinking mates. I have my standards so I settled for a swiftie and headed out into the dark and wind-whipped night in search of a black cab. They were all tucked up in their little garages and I had to hang around for a chill ten minutes before a taxi rolled into view. It wasn't black: it was a shrieking pink. But I clambered aboard and off we bumbled towards Fulham with me feeling like Oscar Wilde on one of his wilder nights.

The story of Howard Lanche and his scarlet woman was a long way off my mind when we rolled up outside my gaff. Mostly I was debating what to do with the rest of the night, for the idea of prostrating myself before Sunday TV was a definite non-runner. Any other loose night of the year I'd just ring Rosie. Rosie is the dent in my pillow, the lip print on my gin bottle, the tofu in my fridge. I suppose you could call her my girlfriend. She's not a hack, but we shan't hold that against her. I could do with her company right now, but Rosie, the selfish trollop, was off enjoying herself in New York. That meant I'd just have to ring Olly and sweet-talk his missus into letting him out for a gargle. Maybe we could unchain Clive too.

My key was half a millimetre off the front door lock when I saw something that shouldn't be there. Beside the door there's a skimpy frosted glass panel which looks down the hallway, past the bedroom, bathroom, living room and so on in to the kitchen. And there was light in yonder kitchen.

I swung around to check it wasn't just a reflection of the street lamp. Nope. The street lamp flickers and flares. This one simply glowed. Then even as I watched it went out. Ah.

I sucked in air between my teeth. Not all that long ago I used to have a different flat to call home. And a most amiable place it was too, right up to the night some berk redecorated both it and me with petrol and struck a match. I survived, the flat didn't.

So now I am more than slightly wary of uninvited guests. The only other soul with keys to the place is Rosie, but as mentioned, she was presently off snorting Manhattans. I considered for a moment whether she might have given the spare keys to one of her dingbat chums, but even Rosie's not *that* crazy. Which meant I had a burglar as a guest.

The logical thing was to whip out my mobile and yell for the Old Bill. No, we'll pass on that one. By the time they'd get here, my intruder would be over the back fence and halfway to Peckham with my video under his arm.

Over the back fence. Now there's an idea. My 600 sq. yards of Fulham is the basement flat of what used to be a triple decker house. There's a foul cat-ridden passageway between it and next door. Now, if I squeezed down there without tripping over a wheelie bin, I could cop a peek over the fence and see what this desperado looked like. But I wasn't taking any chances. I filled my right fist with all my spare change and started skulking. I got a yard down the alleyway before I remembered my neighbours. They are *strange* people. They drink a lot of milk. Back I went to the front, and sure enough, there was a covey of empty milk bottles parked outside their door. I picked the meanest-looking one and off I went again.

So now I was looking at my back fence from a perspective I'd never looked at it before. It was just as boring as the other side. The fence is a couple of inches taller than me. I carefully lodged the milk bottle in one pocket, the coins in the other and hoisted myself up. There was sod all to see. Just a tiny patch of concrete paving and the darkened windows of the kitchen and the living room's patio doors. But hold a sec here. The living-room curtains were closed, and I hadn't closed them. Ohhh bugger . . .

I hung there three inches off the ground and figured the angles. The front door was unmarked, which meant the burglar had jemmied in the back. All I had to do was lurk outside the back door and wait for him. Then as soon as he stepped out, a quick one-two. Clunk with the coins and clink with the bottle. That should do for him.

Him? Just say there's two of him. Or even three? I did some more hanging and thinking. It is a little known fact that the area of the human brain which stimulates raw courage is also responsible for producing rank stupidity. Sometimes it gets them mixed up.

It suggested, 'There's only one way to find out: creep up and see.'

I couldn't fault the argument. I pulled myself up inch by inch until I was straddling the fence. Not the most comfortable seat in town. There was still no movement from the flat. I lowered myself down the other side. I landed a bit noisier than intended and that sparked another debate on strategy. If I peeled off my shoes I could pussyfoot right up to the patio doors and no one inside would hear a thing. But just say the bad guy/guys came strolling out when I was in mid-prowl? Doubtless I would want to kick him/ them in the nethers. The shoes stayed on.

I sneaked up towards the living room and nearly nose-dived over the stupid step. I bit my lip and told my big toe to stop whingeing. Beyond the patio doors there was only silence. I couldn't even make out whether there was a lamp on inside, largely because the previous owner had draped the doors with thick blue curtains nicked from an old-time music hall. So that left the back door. I floated like a wraith along the shadowed wall. Ever so gently I felt for the handle and turned it. Ha! Unlocked, just as I'd feared.

I paused hereabouts to listen to my heartbeat. It sounded tickety-boo. Yet it was still not too late to skedaddle the hell out of there. But hold it. Why should *I* flee? This was my own private territory, the place I laid me down to kip. If anyone ought to take to his toes it ought to be the scumbag toe-rag trespasser. For the first time I pondered what he might look like. Chances were he was just some runty little oik whom I could batter brainless while humming the theme tune from *Crimestoppers*. He might even be an old geezer with a dodgy leg and a passion for strong drink. And I should run away from the likes of this? Balls to that.

I puffed up my chest to its full thirty-eight and a bit. I unholstered the milk bottle and held it in the approved position. With the other hand I squeezed down on the door handle, softly, softly, sooooftly. The door inched open with only the squeakiest of squeaks. I sidled in. The main chunk of the kitchen was off to my right. Nothing there. I could see all the way up the hall to the front door. Still nothing. Maybe the lily-livered cur had already scarpered. And lucky for him too. The door to the living room was open. No lights, no movement from within.

I breathed out.

But I wasn't taking chances. For all I knew my thief in the night might well be the Phantom Sheet Snatcher of West Fulham. So I oozed up the hallway towards the young master's bedroom. This bit was tricky because my hall is tiled with a sort of blackish and yellowy white mosaic, therefore I had to ponce along like Rudolf Nureyev on Prozac. I was barely a foot short of my target when I saw the light. It spilled out from under my bedroom door. Then I heard the voices. Two men. Neither sounded under-sized or even a bit wobbly in the leg department.

Hell's blood!

I stopped stone dead. The milk bottle quivered in the silent air. I didn't even have to think about the options. The only way out of here was back.

But before I could even engage reverse the bedroom door opened wide. The milk bottle trembled for a nanosecond, then fell from my rubber fingers, smashing into a zillion diamonds across the mosaic. Likewise the lead crystal tumbler which the intruder was holding.

'AAArrrrghhh!' screeched Rosie and I in perfect harmony.

Later, oh *ages* later, we were still getting over our post-traumatic stress in the only way we know how. I was doing the pouring.

Rosie said it for the eighty-seventh time. 'It was meant to be a surprise.'

Yeh. So was Pearl Harbour.

I let it ride. We were on the living-room sofa with me sitting vaguely upright and Rosie slanted all over my lap, spilling blue-black curls. She looked different from the last time I saw her, three weeks back when I parked her on the Heathrow Express and she blurred me a kiss. But then Rosie always looks different from the last time. There are some constants though. She's always got long tumbling tresses, except when she ties them up in bunches or hangs them in corkscrew pigtails. She's got smoky-blue eyes, except for summer days when they're bright blue, or a cloudy grey when she's not at her sparkiest. Like now.

Rosie was still replaying the moment when she reeled out of the bedroom to find me waving a milk bottle. She chortled way down in her throat. 'You looked scared witless. You just froze there and dropped the bottle.'

She hadn't looked too clever either, *and* she'd splattered a crystal gin jigger all over the hall. But I'm

27

a forgiving sort. I'd already forgiven her for leaving the back door open after she'd sloshed tea leaves down the drain. I'd even forgiven her for switching on my bedside radio in the middle of a play, thereby making me think there was a couple of well-spoken blaggers cooped up in my bedroom.

Anyway I wanted to think of something more pleasant. I said, 'So how was New York?'

That set her going. I closed my eyes and let her ramble on. I don't remember a thing she said because I was just listening to her voice. Rosie's got the sort of voice which could make a recitation from the phone book sound hot stuff.

After a while she jumped up. 'Oh, I've got *another* surprise for you.'

Gulp.

She reached down by the sofa and came up with a bag emblazoned with a JFK duty free logo. I pulled out a slender bottle that proclaimed itself to be Balenciaga Pour Homme.

She said, 'Do you like it?'

'I don't know. I've never drunk it.'

But I gave her a nice big soppy one by way of thanks. When we got our breath back I said, 'You still haven't told me why you're here instead of three thousand miles away.'

I should have guessed. She'd blown all her money and had to fly home early. I made merry with the Gordons bottle again. 'What did you spend it on?'

Clothes, and more clothes. Many of them frillies.

Rosie said, 'I'm too tired now but I'll try them on for you in the morning.'

Now that was one surprise a man could truly enjoy.

28

Chapter Five

Back to the unresolved matter of Howard Lanche.

The doorstep kicked off on Monday evening. There was no point in starting earlier because Lanche was probably busy licking boots in the Commons. I stayed well clear of the office all day in the quaint hope the Editor might think I was spending my every waking hour out there in the frozen wilds, waiting for my man.

Rosie skipped off mid-afternoon to collect Blue, her putrid, scraggy, mangy moggy from the top security wing of the cattery. She'd also lined up a frenzied programme of lunches and drinkies with all her weird friends.

I left it until eight o'clock before I cabbed it up to Bayswater. I like it there. You can kid yourself that London is still a great international city amid the babel of its streets. Dark-eyed ladies sashay along in jellabas. Rastas rush by in bubbles of laughter, blokes in Wimpey jackets rub shoulders with slick little geezers in saviros. A saviro, I have recently discovered, is Japanese for a man's suit. It's a corruption of Savile Row. Now isn't that interesting?

Never mind. I got there ten minutes early so I'd have time to snoop around before assuming the position. Turnbull Mews is filed off Queensway, in behind towering stucco-encrusted mansions with big butch pillars. You walk along a street of magnolia porticoes and suddenly tucked away somewhere in the middle of them is a little red brick archway. Turnbull Mews. Or the entrance thereof. It isn't really a proper mews. There were never stables for frolicsome fillies here with room for the groom above. It was originally a dead-end street for jerry-built Edwardians who weren't into swinging cats. The houses were of the one-up, one-down variety. But the advent of Eighties' silly money and a cure for rising damp made this little plot a Klondyke for property pushers. One of these days it's going to pop up on the Monopoly board.

Turnbull Mews tries to live up to its name. It even has cobblestones. I tramped all the way down it, fetched up outside a lock-up garage, and tramped all the way back up again. En route I counted twenty doll's houses. Six of them had lights on, including number eight and number ten.

The mews played home to a bunch of wild bohemians. You could tell that by the sawn-off beer casks parked outside nearly every door, with crocuses or snowdrops wilting in the dark.

I lingered awhile outside number ten where two inches behind the double-glazed mullions a couple of chaps were having a pop at each other in highish voices. Probably something to do with the Liberty curtains. Not wishing to intrude on private grief, I drifted on to number eight. No voices here. Just humdrum music. The sort you begin to notice in movies when the girl starts getting her kit on again.

So number eight it was. I found myself a niche in

the facing brickwork with a squinting prospect of the street outside and settled down for the long night watch. Somewhere around the corner I could hear the cheery sound of drunks falling under passing cars. It's a tough life, this reporting business. I had to hang around as cold, as damp as Churchill's statue, listening to other people enjoying themselves.

Twenty minutes into my vigil Howard Lanche appeared. On foot. His face was caught in somebody's headlamps as he swung round the corner into the mews. He made an A to B line for number eight. He'd been there before. A stranger would have fallen on his face in the flower tub. He had his own key too. I cocked an eyeball down the hallway before the door shut me out. No sign of the invisible woman.

Lanche looked all set to stay put for a while. I shuddered back into my hollow like a corpse in a Spanish cemetery and tried to brighten up. I counted the good things about my situation. I was staying out of bad company and not blowing my money on drink. Then I counted the bad points. They came to the same thing. I had plenty of time to think. I had to do something to beat off the permafrost up Turnbull Mews. I was bored too. But most of all I was bothered. When the Editor wants somebody turned over, he just twangs his braces. Ten mins later you have two hacks and a couple of snappers camped out in the victim's front garden. Give us an hour or two and it's all in tomorrow's paper. Bish bash bosh.

But not this one. My brief was to do it gently. Why? And why did I not have a monkey at my shoulder to snap Lanche and his sweetheart? And why did the Editor say it was a highly sensitive story? Who was

the mole? Why did I have this dark suspicion the story
was destined for the spike?

These thoughts entertained me as the hours withered past. In her own flat down Battersea, Rosie was
already snoring away. Around me London got quieter
and quieter until it was down to a steady drone. Every
now and then you could hear the far-off banshee
of police sirens swooping in on some unfortunate
without a tax disc. I lit a cigarette.

And that was where Howard Lanche came out.

And that is where we came in.

Next day I saw her.

I'd got it all wrong. She wasn't blonde and she
wasn't the standard model of a femme fatale. She was
maybe five foot three, so about three inches below
the imagination. Her hair was short, ducked in at the
back and her eyes were blacker than currants in a
Christmas pudding.

On the off chance I'd zipped down to Bayswater to
see the mews in daylight. I was standing just outside
the archway when she popped her head out of number
eight and plonked down a milk bottle. I pulled back
out of sight. A minute later she came trundling by. I
gave chase.

She walked like one of those little boxy girls you
get waving banners and shouting the odds at protest
marches. She butted through the drizzle, head down,
chin in, face all squashed between the hood of her
parka and a five-inch layer of boiler lagging. God
knows what she wore when it was really cold.

She took short, busy steps so it was easy to keep

up with her. I eddied through the Bayswater flow, staying a good ten yards behind her bobbing head. It was lunchtime Tuesday.

All around us people were nipping into sandwich shops, tripping into pizza parlours, slipping into pubs. She marched on. I was beginning to question Howard Lanche's taste in totty when she suddenly skipped sideways into a handy pub. I bought an *Evening Standard*, counted my change and followed her inside.

It was a biggish bar with the neighbourhood riff-raff in one half, the suits and skirts in the other. I joined the riff-raff, ordered up a gin and tonic and vanished behind a pillar. There was a mile or so of mirror behind the bar so I didn't have to poke my head out to see what she was up to. She was in the flash bit. She hadn't got herself a drink yet, largely because she was still unwrapping herself. Off came the hood, the double duvet and all. Now I got my first look at her.

It was hard to describe her, in newspaper terms anyway. Tabloid hacks are supplied with three descriptions to embrace all womankind between fifteen and fifty-five – attractive brunette, blonde stunner and vivacious redhead. I suppose she was in the attractive brunette class. And for once that was close to the truth. She was tasty in a fragile sort of way. Underneath all that wrapping was a wisp of a girl. She was wearing one of those floppy Irish folk singer sweaters. Dirty white. Or ecru, as our fashion poppets say. She was within hailing distance of thirty but there was still something studentish about her. Maybe that was down to the outsize specs which had mysteriously appeared on her nose. She had a round face. Her eyes were the feature. Her dark hair was shorter than mine. She didn't look bad at all if you like them like that.

If she was expecting company she didn't show it. I watched her squeeze through the bar and flare her teeth at a passing barman. He grinned back because that's what he was paid for. She went into the rigmarole that all women do in pubs, treating the barman to a free demo of her thought process in action. All around her decent men were dying of thirst but she was oblivious of their pitiful cries. She pointed at a bottle. The barman said something. She shook her head no. She flashed her teeth some more to keep his attention. Eventually she settled for a Schweppes tonic. No gin. I heard the barman say, 'Ice and slice?'

That threw her. He explained the obvious. Thirty seconds rolled around before she said yes please to the ice but no thanks to the lemon. The rapidly ageing barman slapped it in front of her. He waited for the money. That was the first inkling she had that she might have to pay for the damned thing. Apologetic grimace. She dived to the floor and began rooting in her handbag. It was too painful to watch. I bought myself another gin. With ice and slice.

When I got back to my spot she was sitting down, just the other side of the pillar. So far she hadn't touched her drink. She examined her fellow customers with darting eyes. A giggle of girls at the table next door was whooping it up in the mistaken belief it was Friday afternoon. Her gaze swept over them, circled the lounge and came back to her glass. She took a sip. She was quite self-contained.

I was getting bored. I started reading the *Standard* and was halfway through a yarn about a burglar who ran a neighbourhood watch scheme, when I glanced across and saw a man approaching Miss X. She had her back to him. He touched her lightly on the left shoulder, she turned round to look behind her, by which time he was standing in front of her. Another swing of her head and she located the phantom shoulder tapper. She smiled, he smiled. He lifted one hand in brisk salutation. So whoever he was, he wasn't a boyfriend. He said, 'Hi, Sylvia.' Or it might have been Cynthia. I put him about five nine. Fair, crinkly hair. Thirty and a bit. A face in the crowd. Carefully casual in a blue mac, blue sweater, blue jeans. He had shaved that morning. Otherwise he would have had a blue chin to go with all the above.

He pointed at her glass; she waved a hand across it, indicating that one tonic was just about her limit. He edged over to the bar and bought himself something anyway. Now I could see his face better. It didn't tell me much, except that he had something on his mind. There was a tightness, an intensity about him. I realized that was the way she was too.

Holding a Coke in his leading hand, he threaded back to the table. He pulled up a stool and went into a huddle with her. He had his back to the bar and he was blocking off her face in the mirror. I slithered my way round the pillar. She was doing most of the talking, but her voice was too low to hear. Her chin jumped up and down as she spoke. He kept nodding, as if he had heard it all before. They were not having a barney, nor were they billing and cooing. They were discussing a problem, at least she was. After a while she shut up and started lapping her Schweppes. He sat in silence for a moment. Before he said anything, he took a long careful look around the bar. I had just time to turn my face away before he got round to me. I watched him in the bar mirror. He was giving me an ever-so thoughtful inspection. I pulled out the *Standard* and pretended to fill in the idiot crossword. One across: animal, six letters. I wrote Belker. One down, disease, six letters. I sought inspiration in the mirror. He was still looking at me. I wrote Belker again. I was beginning to enjoy this. I had another squint in the mirror. He touched her arm and nudged a head in my direction. She took a dekko, taking me in all the way down. She shook her specs at him. That meant I was okay. He forgot about me and the huddle commenced anew, this time with him getting the speaking part.

So whatever they were rabbiting about, it was not for others' ears. Lots of people sit in bars every lunch-time telling their innermost secrets. The difference is they don't expect other people to be the slightest bit interested. This bloke did. Even odder, he suspected there might be an eavesdropper in the vicinity with the express intention of earwigging him. So did she. And they expected the snooper to be a man, hence the sudden interest in my lissom figure.

I called up another Gordons, a large one this time, for I had much to contemplate. All right, she's having a fling with Howard Lanche, I told myself. And naturally she wants to keep that one under the duvet. But when two people are having a bit of extra-marital, they tend to play it secretly. That's half the fun. If they're worried about it getting out, they look worried. They don't get a third party in to do the worrying for them, and for my money, the crinkly-haired type looked a lot more worried than her.

I speculated on what they might be gassing about. Somehow I didn't think he was selling her life insurance, or that she was offering him a topless massage.

I lit a cigarette. Another point. Their concern was *not* that the Old Bill might be listening in. I take an especial pride in looking as unlike a police officer as possible. People trust you better that way. So they didn't eye up my Burberry and think, 'Uh oh, Plod's on our trail.' Nor was it likely they might mistake me for one of those muck-raking tabloid hacks you read so much about in the *Guardian*. They were worried, no, scared that some other low life was spying on them. Yet they had chosen to meet in a public place. Another conclusion: they were frightened of their supposed shadow.

That's as far as I'd got with it when he jumped up, waved goodbye and slotted out the door. No kisses. No smiles of endearment. I was caught flat. I deliberated over what to do next. I could keep an eye on her some other time. Yup, he's the one to watch. I melted back into the public bar and fought my way to an opposite door. That put me round the corner from his exit. I crossed the street, took cover behind the window display in a knicker shop and had a peek out. He looked somehow different when viewed through the flimsier bits of a pair of flaming scarlet bikini briefs. Behind me I could hear the shop assistants thinking, *'Pervert!'*

My target was standing on the far side of the street in the frozen stance of someone seeking a taxi. And a taxi arrived. Off it went with him bouncing around in the back. I shot out and flapped a frantic arm in the air. But the entire length of Queensway was singularly devoid of taxis, except for his rapidly disappearing cab. I said some rude things which I must have picked up from News Desk. There was nothing more for it now than to return to the boozer and see what Lanche's attractive brunette was up to.

I didn't rush it. I detoured back round the corner so that I came in by the public bar entrance. I cleaved a passage through to my pillar and cocked an eye in the mirror. Rats! There was now a middle-aged party in the seat where she used to be. I'd lost her. Even worse, the barman had chucked away my gin.

I went off in some dudgeon and bought myself an iced-blue shirt with a soft collar and double-button cuffs. That helped restore my customary sunshine. Somewhere along the line I rang the Editor. I got his secretary, Petra. She's blonde and not particularly famed for her keyboard skills, but she has her points.

'Who's calling?' she said, as if she didn't know.

I said, 'Smithson and Smithson, libel lawyers to the rich and famous, and also the Queen.'

'One moment, please, Mister Smithson.'

A new voice, or a new sound anyway, 'Whumphh?'

Oh, terrific. Belker. But he listened without interrupting whilst I favoured him to a five-minute broadcast of the story so far, laying particular emphasis on my hours in the icy blast. When I had done he was silent. I said, 'Hello?'

He said, 'Good work. Good. Keep it up.'

He wasn't getting off that easy. I said, 'You want me to keep on doorstepping the girl?'

'That's what I said.'

He likes to throw his beef about, does Belker.

I said, 'For how long?'

'How long?'

I inhaled. 'Yes. How long? When do I wrap it up?'

A blast of bluster from his end. 'When you've got something. That's when. Until then you keep up the surveillance.'

I said, 'It's not going to work.'

Belker thought that wasn't up to me to decide. He said so. As an afterthought he asked, 'Why's it not going to work?'

I said, 'The story's no good without pix. If we have a snap of Lanche leaving her drum with his trousers round his ankles we've got the story. Otherwise he'll say we made the whole thing up.'

Belker stonewalled. 'We'll talk about pix tomorrow. Give it another shot on your own tonight. And don't mention a word of the story to anyone.'

I switched off the mobile. I felt rebellious. If Rosie were around I'd have blurted out the whole thing to her. Not that she'd listen. The nearest soul was a skinny little geezer in a saviro and he looked like he had better things to do. There was no one to hear my tale of woe. I went to a bar instead.

Chapter Six

There is a saint, or at least a fallen angel, who looks after the unloved hack. He moves in a mysterious way, placing large heaps of luck in our paths so that we trip over them. This is how we really get stories.

I had forgotten all about the angel until just gone two o'clock that Tuesday afternoon when I set off in search of a sandwich to mop up the tonic. There was a Prêt à Manger joint a short stagger away. Next door to it was a trattoria dolled up in lilac and gold like a Neapolitan bordello.

As is the way with us London boulevardiers, I had a gawp through the tinted windows to see what the inmates were noshing. There wasn't much on view. Just one couple by a corner table. I couldn't see her face, but I saw his. I saw it and I walked right on past it. I walked for at least a step and a half before I said out loud, 'Lanche!' I put my other foot down and thought about having a think. Then I said to hell with it. I did a one heel turn and marched past the window again. He was still there. He was still Lanche.

I pushed open the door and without waiting for a waiter plonked myself down at a table. I flung my Burberry in an adjoining chair. By now I knew Lanche's companion was Miss X. They were maybe

three yards away. There was no one else in the restaurant. Their table was in an alcove off to my right
behind a hunk of trellis. She had her back to me. I
was positioned sideways on so the most Lanche could
see of me was my profile. Lanche was geared up like
the country squire. Green and yellow tweeds, waistcoat of same, burgundy tie with a tiny motif. It clashed.
Miss X was as last seen. I lit a cigarette and evinced a
sharp interest in a passer-by on my extreme left. I
followed the stroller all the way across to the right
where my peripheral vision checked in and started
sending back data on Lanche. He was at least a stone
overweight. He looked like a wealthy farmer. A
worried wealthy farmer. The girl was talking. Too low
to hear. Then Lanche said, 'I want to see her as soon—'

The girl's voice took flight. 'You can't. It's too risky.
She's—'

'—Good afternoon, sir.' The worst waiter in the
whole wide world was at my elbow. He forced a lavender menu on me. He had a name embroidered in
gold on his lapel. It said Giuseppe. I smiled a wide
and honest smile. I said, 'Ah, Giuseppe. I'm expecting
a friend. May I have a glass of house red while I wait.'

'My name is Albert, sir.'

I said, 'That is a nice name too. So just a glass of
wine until my friend comes.'

He said, 'This is Giuseppe's jacket.'

Over to the right Lanche and his cutie were
yakking away but I couldn't hear them. I said, 'Ace
jacket. Now, wheel out the wine, please.'

Albert had a dark and dour countenance. He had
Crucifixion eyes. He said, 'You wish to order now?'

I took a long breath. I said. 'I wish to order the wine now. The meal later. Okay?'

'You must have a meal first.'

I said, 'Fine. I'll start with an aperitif. A glass of wine.'

Albert said, 'Would you like to smoke?'

I was smoking. I said yes, I would like to smoke. Albert said, 'Then you must sit in the smoking section.' He pointed to a distant corner.

Over to my right the conversation was getting sparky. I heard Lanche say, 'But I *must* see her . . .' His girlfriend chipped back with, 'I'll give you two good reasons why you can't . . .'

I wanted to hear both of them. I said, 'Fetch me your finest fettucine con pesto, presto, Albert. And the wine.'

Albert had a small but very red boil on his chin. He said, 'You must smoke there.' He pointed at the outer darkness again.

'*Please*, Howard . . .'

I said, 'I don't want to smoke.'

'But she *needs* me . . .' That one from Lanche.

Albert said, 'You must put out your cigarette in the ashtray.'

There were no ashtrays. Albert's magnetic finger swung round to the smoking section again.

Lanche said, 'You're not listening—'

I said, 'All right, I'll stub out my cigarette there, but I'll eat here. It's my favourite table. Now, may I *please* have the wine.'

Lanche's girlfriend squeaked, 'You only *think* she needs you . . .'

Albert said, 'Fettucine was business lunch special.'

So?

So now I had to order it à la carte and it would take longer. I said, 'I've changed my mind. Toss me up an insalata de mare. And make it a whole bottle of Barolo.'

The woman with Lanche said, 'It's my idea. I haven't even told Eric—'

Albert said, 'Do you like music?'

I said yes. Albert said that was good, he would switch on the music for me. I said no. He raised his martyred eyes to heaven, shrugged, and went away. I tuned back into the neighbouring conversation. There wasn't one. Lanche was limbering up his lips. She had her head bowed. I made a pretty yacht with my napkin and waited. Lanche put out a big manly hand and touched hers. It was either a plea or a consoling gesture. It's hard to tell with these things. She stayed silent. He ducked his head towards her and spoke so softly he might have been mouthing the words. She straightened up. She said, 'It's no good – it's the only way—'

Albert said, 'Your salad.' He had stopped calling me sir.

I said, 'Where's the wine?'

He said, 'Moment please.' He skitted off sideways brandishing a beam at Lanche and Friend. He said, 'Everything to your satisfaction, signore, signorina?'

It was. Albert breezed past ignoring me.

Lanche's girlfriend said, 'Just three or four more days, then it's over.'

He said, 'I can't. I just can't let you do this.'

He had a voice with a westerly breeze blowing through it. Her words were too small, too tight, for you to fix an accent on. They went all quiet on each other. I stared at the passers-by staring at me. She sighed down her nose. She said, 'If you go there, you'll wreck everything.'

He said, 'I have—'

She said, '—'

Backstage Albert turned on the muzak. After that I heard nothing. There wasn't much more to hear. A couple of minutes later Lanche called for the bill and paid up. I poked my head into the menu as they passed. Outside the door they broke up. She paddled off up Queensway, he turned left.

I pushed a rubber squid around the plate. Albert arrived with the Barolo and a corkscrew. I told him to go away. He said, 'You want to smoke, then you don't want to smoke, you want to drink, now you don't want to drink.'

I said, 'I want to pay. No, I don't want to pay. But I suppose I'd better.'

He said not another word. I signed the Amex bill. No tip. The geek scratched his boil and handed me my copy with his boily mitt. I helped myself back into my Burberry. I turned as I got to the door. I said, 'The jacket looks better on Giuseppe.'

I had a mug of tea in a stand-up place down by the tube. It was a quarter after three. This was getting to be a very busy Tuesday. I played jigsaws with the snaps of their conversation. Lanche was anxious to see some woman. She didn't want him to. Who does a mistress not want her lover to see? His wife. That's who. At first Miss X had begged him. It didn't work.

She tried reason – 'You only *think* she needs you . . .'
That was a bummer too. So Sylvia or Cynthia or whatever that bloke called her in the bar moved on to
threats, 'If you see her, you'll wreck everything.' I
suppose that meant she'd give him the heave ho. But
it was an oddly unemotional threat. Nobody said
darling. No one brushed away a tear. They parted
without a kiss. But that might be because they split
outside the restaurant, in public view. Illicit lovers
don't usually canoodle in a crowded street. There was
another conversational snippet which didn't belong.
Lanche had said, 'I just can't let you do this.' Whatever
that meant. I moaned to myself. I'm the man who has
to know all the answers. I hate it when I can't see the
story. It makes me feel stupid. And there was no one
around to tell me I wasn't.

I cabbed it back to my flat to where the ansaphone
was blinking merrily away. Chatterbox Rosie. Letting
me know she was still locked in breathless gossip with
the girls, and, if I didn't mind, could I leave it until
tomorrow night before we got to grips again? No.
Cancel that. Tomorrow she'd something else on, so
make it the night after. Okay? Suited me fine. I'd a
doorstep all lined up.

I left it for a couple of hours before I legged it
across to Turnbull Mews for another fun-filled evening.
This time around I was more circumspect. At lunch-
time Sylvia/Cynthia had drunk in every detail of my
appearance. She might even have copped me in the
restaurant. If she found me loitering in the vicinity
again, bells would ring, alarums would sound. And
that would be End of Story. But as soon as she was
back in the arms of her huggy bear she'd forget all

about me and I could run stone-naked up and down the mews without her rolling an eyeball. Until then a dash of caution was in order. So, when I got to Pembury Villas, the street leading on to the mews, I skulked in the gloom on the far side of the road. There was still a fair bit of traffic batting up and down and there were thoughtfully parked cars to give me cover. I crossed the road, speaking like a mad thing into my mobile. I had it in my right hand so it hid my face. To the casual onlooker I was just another berk who'd got a poser phone for Christmas. There weren't any onlookers anyway, so it was all for nothing.

I sauntered into the mews still rabbiting. Her lights were on, the curtains drawn, the door closed. All was well. I started tacking towards my cosy corner. I was no more than nine feet away when my heart did a backwards double flip with a triple axel.

Somebody was already in my niche.

I changed direction faster than a drunk on a unicycle. Just the skin of a second later he saw me. I pretended I hadn't clocked him. I just kept on walking down the centre of the mews jawing away into the mobile. Only now I was talking out loud. And in an accent from a Mel Brooks movie.

I said, 'But listent, Villi, listent. I get it for you tomorrow. A promise. I tell you, I'm goink home. I am there already.'

The man in my niche wasn't a drama critic. He didn't applaud. I marched on down the cobbles, thinking at a hundred miles an hour. The shadowy stranger was watching *my* doorstep. Why? Who? The obvious answer was another hack, but the sliver of a glimpse I had didn't give me any clues.

I fetched up at the end of the mews outside a house which was in deepest darkness. I kept jabbering away at the phone while I prodded my pockets for keys. My gestures were all a bit theatrical so that the mystery man could follow them. I dug out the keys, paused, switched hands with the phone and made as if to open the door. At the last moment I recoiled in mock outrage, snarled in mittel European down the phone and turned, heading back down the mews. I was walking more hurriedly and muttering angrily to myself. I neared the stranger but I didn't even spare him a flicker. Just as I drew level I dropped the keys. It was only then I saw him.

'Vot!' I exclaimed in pantomime astonishment.

He stood without moving, without talking.

I gathered up the keys and studied him. He was touching six feet, burly with it, white, fair-haired and encased in a black or navy Barbour. I had never seen him before.

I said belligerently, 'Who are you, heh?'

He said, 'Who are you?'

I wanted to say, 'Ve vill ask the questions', but he didn't look as if he had a great sense of humour. I poked my finger in my chest and said, 'Me? I am Mister Tchermak. I sell the carpets.'

There was no answer to that. He just looked at me.

I said, 'I ham in charge of the Neighbourhood Vaaatch.'

He said, 'The what?'

'The Neighbourhood Vaaatch. Ve vaaatch out for our neighbours. For the burglars.'

He nodded but kept silent.

I said, 'There is too much crime here. All the time.

Ve have to keep open our eyes for the strangers. Who are you?' I narrowed my eyes.

He had both hands stuck in his pockets. He took one out and turned it palm uppermost to show he was not carrying a sawn-off shooter. He said, 'I am waiting for a friend.'

My gimlet eyes were slits of suspicion. 'Vaiting for a friend? I don't see any friend.'

The man in black, or navy, said, 'He's, uh, visiting someone there.' He pointed a solid finger in the rough direction of Lanche's love nest.

I said, 'Ah. Number ten. Mister Zizzych.'

He forgot himself. 'No. Next door. Miss Evans.'

Evans. Now that was useful.

I smiled warmly. 'Hoh, yes. Cynthia.'

'Zenia,' he corrected.

'Dot's vot I said.' Pub accoustics are shot to hell these days.

My new chum reverted to his strong silent act. I said, 'Beautiful girl, Mizz Evans. She also is a Neighbourhood Vaaatcher.'

He was non-committal about both her beauty and her crimebusting. But the thin set off his mouth said, 'Clear off.'

We both looked at her window. We both saw her shadow float across the curtains. I turned back on him. I said, 'Such a cold night for you to vait.' I shivered to show how cold it was.

He said, 'It's okay.'

I shrugged an eyebrow. 'Maybe you don't have to vait for so long. I vish you good evenink.'

He tilted his head to say, 'And the same to you, Bozo.'

I tripped out through the mews archway and never looked back. Which was just as well, for my face was a picture in puzzled concentration.

He wasn't a hack, even though the Barbour is standard clobber for a whole legion of tabloid doorsteppers, particularly the Royal rat pack.

He wasn't a copper either. If he had been, he'd have smacked me on the nose and charged me with assault. Another item made it rock certain he wasn't the Law: When was the last time you heard a London bobby speaking with an American accent?

I drifted back into the shadows of Pembury Villas and talked strategy with myself. My righteous, conscientious brain cells argued that we should stick it out all the cold night long, for such was the Editor's wish. My rogue cells said bollocks to that, and seeing they outnumber the good cells by a zillion to one, they won hands down. They said, 'Let's go find someone to play with.' The good cells tabled a last minute amendment. Let's see where Lanche is now, they argued.

I rang the Commons and got patched through to Jim Graham on our Parly team. I said, 'I'm buying. You drinking?'

Tears of rage and frustration. Jim said, 'I'm stuck here for a crappy Tyneside development zone debate. Total waste of time. It doesn't mean a thing to any reader south of Birmingham and the northern edition's already gone, so the Geordies won't be able to read it.'

I purred sympathy. I said, 'I take it the House is gummed to the rafters with our hard-working representatives?'

More tears. I took that as a no.

I said, 'Anything else on later?'

'Sod all. This is the only thing on the order paper, so they'll drone on for hours about Euro subsidies and capital development grants.'

I shuddered and promised I'd have a drink for him, for I'm noble that way.

It had been a useful conversation. Lanche was absent from the House. He might be in the mews with Zenia Evans, but I guessed not. I'd already rooted out all his private numbers from our Parly Editor's secret file. I called his Dolphin Square flat. It took five rings before he answered. Only it wasn't him. Just a mechanical woman saying, 'The person you are calling knows you're waiting; please hold.'

Maybe he was already on the phone to her. Whoever it was, he got rid of them quickly. Then, 'Yes?'

I switched on a vaguely northern accent, 'Mister Mboya, we have your call to Lagos on the line now. Go ahead caller.'

Lanche said, 'What? I think—'

I broke in, 'This is the fixed time call you placed to Lagos, Mister Mboya.'

He said, 'You have the wrong number.'

I said oops, silly me, or somesuch. He put the phone down on me.

So Lanche was at home. The good cells said, 'He might still visit Zenia Evans.' The bad cells stuck their tongues out and made rude gestures, and off we all trekked in search of a taxi. Twenty minutes later I was in Hamptons, a bottle of warm claret and a fresh pack of Bensons to hand.

Hamptons is a very awful wine bar staffed by out-rageously familiar young ladies who dispense vinegar in fancy bottles. It is the natural haunt of hacks and their sad consorts. It's not picky about its clientele so you also find the dregs of the High Court pickling their livers there. Not the actual villains, just their briefs and briefettes. We don't mind them. It just means we get to mix with a better class of criminal.

I was in my customary corner, listening with big tender eyes to Suzy, a *Sun* features page fluffy, who had a sorry tale to tell. She'd just been briefed to go find a herbalist and write a two-parter on the herbs that spice up your sex life. The title was: A Brief History of Thyme. You often get pin-brained jobs like these. Some dolt in the Editor's bunker dreams up a clever clogs headline, as above, and some poor hack is wheeled in to write a story to fit. Suzy wailed, 'What on earth am I going to write?' I helped her out. I said, 'You can quote me. My name is Basil. My wife is Rosemary. Personally, we've always found that sage is great for stuffing.'

That cheered Suzy up. She gave me a dimpled smile and tugged my tie playfully. That cheered *me* up. Alas, that's where it stopped. A bony hand fell on my shoulder and a dread voice crackled, 'How's about ye, boy?'

It was Mac, who was half the reason I was in Hamptons tonight. Mac is a serving officer in the Met. An inspector. Big deal indeed. But his company is sought by every crime reporter in the capital because he tells us things. In return, we give him money and everybody's happy. Next time you read a story about a soap star caught kerb-crawling at King's Cross, or about a boxer in a bar brawl, you'll know whom to blame. Mac runs a network of Old Bill informers who spend their days digging up stories for us. Now you also know why they don't catch criminals any more. Mac used to be a copper in the Royal Ulster Constabulary, hence the funny accent. He hails from Larne, County Antrim where, he assures me, people talk like that all the time.

I greeted him warmly and poured him a glass. I said, 'What's happening in the twilight world of PC Plod?'

Not a lot. A fish 'n' chippy murder down in Streatham and they were looking for the husband. Somebody was injecting rat poison into supermarket butter and demanding ten grand to go shop somewhere else. Two neo-Nazis lifted for a fire-bombing. I started nodding off. Suzy had already melted away.

Mac said, 'And what shenanigans are you up to, hey?' He always asks two questions at once.

I remembered why I wanted to see him. I said, 'I need a search on a girl. All I've got is her name and address. Can you feed it in the computer and see what comes up?'

Mac said, 'You think she's got a spot of previous, do ye?'

I said I didn't know if she was Lucrezia Borgia's nasty sister or my fairy godmother. Mac said, 'This wine's rotten altogether. Why do you want to know about her?'

I told him it was none of his business. He told me that was okay. I couldn't afford him anyway.

'How much?'

'Two fifty.'

I said, 'It was only two hundred quid last month.'

Mac said, 'Aye, I know. But they've suspended a sergeant they caught accessing the computer. It's getting dodgier all the time.'

I said he'd get the two fifty. He bought a bottle of alleged champagne. I gave him Zenia Evans's name and address and he repeated it a few times. Mac never writes anything down.

After that we got pleasantly plastered until it was time to chuck us out. Mac wanted to roll on to Indian Joe's, a club with the same high standards of service as Hamptons, but drink at twice the price. Somewhere in the course of the evening Mac had collared Suzy and I could see how things were shaping up. Never mind, I had Rosie back in Battersea.

I gave her a breezy call and suggested I roll around to tuck her into bed. Too late. She was already tucked, thank you. And anyway, she said, I was probably half-guttered after drinking in Hamptons all night. Considering she'd been doing the same, only in somewhere more salubrious, this was a shade harsh. I said, 'Does that mean you don't want me there to watch o'er you through the long night reaches?'

That's precisely what it meant. If Rosie had a better nature I'd have appealed to it. But what's the use? She said, 'Don't worry. There's always Thursday night. What night is it now?'

'Still Tuesday.'

'All right. Come round early and I'll cook you up something special. Okay?'

Grumble grumble. Yeh. I suppose so. I locked my libido back in its cage and ambled off home. There was nothing on late-night TV except a round-up of

Saturday's First Division soccer. I flopped down on the sofa and watched anyway. Somewhere between Bolton's home defeat and Bradford's goalless draw, the eyelids flickered and went out. I lay there snoring gently all the way through to ten past two in the morning. That's when the phone rang.

'Is that the residence of Mister Max Chard, ace crime reporter, hey?'

'No Mac. This is the home of his identical twin sister.'

I held the phone away because he was cackling again.

He said, 'Hey, remember you were asking me about that wee girl, Zenia Evans?'

'Strangely enough, I do.'

He said, 'Aye, well you're not the only one who's interested.'

'What?'

Mac said, 'She's missing.'

'What's she missing?'

He's easy to amuse. I let him have his cackle, then he said, 'You know what I mean. She's disappeared. They're looking for her.'

That's all he had. I called up Scotland Yard's press tape. She was the last item. In tones of utter boredom some now sleeping press officer read out, 'There is concern over the whereabouts of a Canadian visitor following her failure to keep an appointment this evening. She is named as Miss Zenia Anne Evans of Edmonton, Alberta, aged in her late twenties. A friend reported her disappearance after she did not meet him as arranged. Miss Evans, a charity worker, has been staying in the Bayswater area. When last seen she was wearing a grey anorak and dark blue jeans. She is described as five foot two inches tall, of slight build, and has short, dark hair. Anyone who has seen her in the past twenty-four hours is requested to contact police at Bayswater.'

That meant me. I lit a cigarette and blew long streams of smoke at the ceiling. But I didn't contact anybody.

Chapter Seven

I pestered the Editor for half Wednesday morning before he condescended to see me. He'd roped in Belker in case I started getting stroppy. They were drinking freshly ground coffee out of bone china cups and scoffing shortbread biscuits. They didn't offer me any.

The Editor licked away a crumb. 'What's your problem?'

He has bad breath. He always smells of Polo mints. I said, 'Maybe we should have the lawyer in here.'

That shook them. The Editor said, 'The lawyer?'

I said, 'If the Old Bill find out we're withholding information, we'll need a lawyer to keep us out of Ford Open Prison.'

They didn't exactly clutch each other for support but their jaws stopped mid-munch. Belker recovered first. He said in a faraway voice, 'What information?'

I lit a cigarette and straightened both cuffs. I said, 'The name of Howard Lanche's crumpet is Zenia Anne Evans. Yesterday afternoon I followed her. She had lunch with Howard Lanche in a trattoria in Bayswater. He had the vongole. Last night I doorstepped the mews again. Another man was also watching her place. She was at home. Lanche wasn't there. Later still she was reported missing to the police. The Yard is appealing for anyone who saw her yesterday to come forward. That means us.'

Note the subtle use of us. The Editor swivelled away and stared out of his picture window. Way off to the far left was St Paul's, and behind that, the Old Bailey with blind Justice on its roof. The Editor turned swiftly back. Belker spoke slowly and carefully as if he were picking the words out of a box of hand grenades. He said, 'Does anyone *know* you saw her?'

I said, 'The bloke in the mews. He thinks I'm a neighbour.'

Belker said, 'That's all right then.' The Editor nodded.

I said, 'No. It's not. I have a detailed description of the man who was watching her. She's gone AWOL. For all I know, he's got her locked up somewhere. Or he's topped her. The Old Bill say they are "seriously concerned". We are withholding information.'

There I go with that 'us' and 'we' stuff again.

A moody silence fell upon the congregation. Their coffee was getting cold. I said brightly, 'I'd better go and call the Yard.'

The Editor yipped, 'Not the police!'

I said, 'You're the boss. But if it ever comes out, you might have to explain why you're sitting on the story.'

Suddenly it was no longer 'us.' Just 'you'.

I tipped a centimetre of ash in the waste bin. I said, 'You could tell the police what we have and run the story: *MP's Lovebird in Mystery Flight.'*

The Editor didn't like the taste of them apples either. Belker said, 'Let's not get hasty, Max. The Editor and I had better think this one out. Hold off in the meantime.'

I said distinctly, 'You're saying I mustn't tell the police?'

Belker, dear, sweet, fat-headed Belker, went into meltdown. 'Not a word of this gets out until we have it sorted. Forget everything until we tell you.'

I said, 'I'm not happy about it.'

They heaved me out. I strolled back to my desk whistling something breezy. If I was unhappy I wasn't showing it. Nor was I showing the pocket tape with which I had just recorded the Editor and Belker conspiring to obstruct the Law. You've got to cover your back in this business.

While I waited for Beavis and Butthead to make their minds up I phoned Mac and got him to do some quiet delving. I told him to call me on the mobile when he got anything for I was off to the bar. All the other crime hacks were gainfully employed at Lewes Crown Court on the case of the crooked hitman so there wasn't much in the way of solid drinking chums in the Stone. Except for Frankie. Uh-oh.

His full title is Frankie Frost and he likes to pretend he's our top news photographer. The truth is he's a monkey with a rare enthusiasm for kicking down doors, chasing cars, invading privacy and all that. If he could only take pictures he'd be brilliant. When he's not terrifying the citizenry, Frankie gets fractious and turns to drink. When he's really glum he hits the spirits. It is then smart to drink in another bar, maybe even in another town.

Today his bony fingers were wrapped around a whisky glass and he had his nose sunk deep in it. All the warning signs were there, right down to the three-yard exclusion zone all around him. But today I wasn't feeling smart. I pulled up a stool alongside and pointed at his drink. 'More of the same?'

A greedy flicker lit his boogly eyes. 'Yeh,' he lied. 'It's Glenmorangie.'

No it wasn't. Monkeys are too mean to buy themselves anything better than cooking whisky. No matter.

I howled out for a large one for him, and just to keep him company I had a matching measure of Gordons. He made a vague stab at polite conversation. 'What you got going, Max?'

I said nothing worth mentioning and he said there was a lot of it about. We fell into our glasses. After a couple of rounds courtesy of me, he loosened up and began to regale me with the atrocities which have made him an outcast among the paparazzi.

The latest in the legend concerned Friday's funeral of paracetemol-popping actress Ferna Chellery. Ferna was in the super stunner category. Big eyes, big boobs, and all the rest. But here's the funny thing: our Ferna was not quite the riproaring man-eater as billed in her publicity. Off camera she liked to pick and mix her partners. Or as Frankie delicately put it, 'She caught both buses.' Though you've never read that over your cornflakes.

Anyway, Frankie & Co. all trooped along expecting a good day out, for luvvie funerals are always great fun. Thesps take themselves *sooo* seriously. At funerals they're irresistible. It's a delight to watch them sobbing their little hearts out while fighting like ferrets for the best camera position. You see better acting at these dos than you ever get at the Royal Shakespeare. The day kicked off well when a Beeb sound man insisted on standing in front of the wilder monkeys while Ferna's pretend boyfriend, a bit suss himself, delivered a mascara-smudging eulogy. Sadly half of it went unheard because the monkeys kept up a loud chorus of their single favourite word until the sound man got out of their way. That's why the Beeb never screened the boyfriend's poignant tribute. Back in the studios, when they came to edit it, the tape ran like this, 'We all remember Ferna as a truly great BLEEP. She made us BLEEP and she made us BLEEP. Most of all she gave BLEEP to those of us who had the fortune to BLEEP her.' You can't have that sort of thing going out on the six o'clock news.

We return to the funeral and the heart-rending moment when her supposed sweetheart kissed a rose and dropped it on the coffin. At least that was the script. What really happened was a freelance snapper banged Ferna's doddery old dad aside, sending him reeling into the parson who nearly joined Ferna in the hole. An alleged comedian with his own TV show and a plastic septum grabbed the star mourner and clasped him to his breast, thereby burying the bereaved boy-friend's nobly tragic mug in his pink jacket. The boyfriend flapped his arms in a desperate bid to get back in the picture, whereupon the rose shot out of his hand and ended up on the neglected grave of the dearly departed Annie Swann (1852–1896). The best snap of the day was the comedian's tear-stained face grinning into camera. The tears, Frankie explained, sprung from the fact that the upstaged boyfriend was busy kneeing the comedian in the goolies. That was the big pic in all the tabloids the next day. All except ours. We had a much moodier shot altogether, one snapped five minutes after the rest of the monkey pack had trooped off, leaving Frankie to pull one of his loopy stunts. His smudge showed a mysterious woman in black, a veil masking her features as she lovingly laid a wreath on the grave. There was also a close-up of the card she'd tied to the flowers. It read, 'Our passion burns bright. Good night, my beloved.' Aha! So Ferna's secret lover had broken cover? Not quite. The woman in black was one of Frankie's several girlfriends. So it was just as well you couldn't see her face. The message was written by a Picture Desk secretary with an O level. And the flowers? Oh, Frankie had just found them lying around the cemetery. But he billed the office twenty quid for them.

After the fun and frolics of Ferna's last matinee, our conversation languished a shade. Frankie suggested we venture on to the snooker club. I was more than half tempted but at that moment Mac rang back.

He said, 'I haven't much for you.'

'It was ever thus.'

He said, 'Do you want it or not?'

I said what the hell, let's hear it anyway. There was Zenia Evans's name, and her address, both of which I'd given him. There was also the fascinating titbit that she arrived in Britain two months ago, and the downright sensational news that she failed to keep a seven o'clock date at the Royal Lancaster.

I said, 'With whom?'

Mac said, 'What?'

I said, 'Who with?'

He said, 'Some fella called Eric Shernholm.' He spelt it out for me.

'Who's he when he's not getting jilted?'

Mac said, 'Another foreign body. A Yank. Age thirty-two, an occupational psychologist – whatever that is. Old college friend of the girl's. He reported her missing.'

I said, 'When?'

'Last night.'

I said, 'I know that. When last night?'

'Tenish. He phoned her house. No joy there.'

I said, 'And where does he live?'

Mac said, 'I told you.'

'You didn't.'

He said, 'Do the words Royal Lancaster ring a bell? Why all the interest anyway? We've just got her down as a routine missing girlfriend. They do that some-times just to piss you off.'

I said, 'Maybe your girlfriends do. Mine don't.'

Mac said, 'Aye? And where's Rosie been the last fortnight?'

He rang off before I could crush him with my blistering repartee. I looked around. Frankie Frost and his wallet had reeled off to the snooker club. There was just me and a meniscus of gin. I licked it up and steamed back to the office. There was a note on my desk, 'PSE SEE ME. TB.' Belker, proving that rumours of his illiteracy were ill-founded. I springheeled it down the corridor of doom and drummed out a lively blat-blat-blat on his door, pushing it open on the second blat. He was in close proximity to Jools, his inflatable secretary. She looked guilty, he looked peeved. I waved his note at him.

Belker said, 'Ah yes. I was looking for you earlier.'

I lied just to keep in practice. 'I was in the canteen grabbing a sandwich.'

Belker piled into his swivel chair. Jools knew where she wasn't wanted and squeezed past me. This was not as simple as it sounds. I flashed her a lascivious smile to let her know it had been great for me anyway. She banged the door on her way out.

Belker said, 'The Howard Lanche story: we hold fire a little longer.'

I didn't say anything. Belker sucked his teeth. He said, 'There is no evidence a crime has been committed against the girl. If you were to talk to the police they'd want to know why you were watching her. You would be forced to betray our source.'

The old journalistic integrity stunt. I said, 'I don't know who our source is, so I can't identify him. Or her.'

Belker said, 'The police would soon make the connection.'

Balls. If I couldn't work out who Deep Throat was, what chance had Plod? I just said, 'So I wasn't in the mews. I didn't see the bloke watching her. I didn't see her shadow flicker on the blind?'

Belker's grin met up somewhere round the back of his head. 'That's it.'

My bleep went off. I flicked a glance at the message: 'ZENIA EVANS OK – MAC.' I didn't let Belker know. I said, 'What do I do now – doorstep the mews again?'

His top lip rolled up to reveal a fence of yellow teeth. 'Don't be bloody stupid. We wait until she shows up before we do anything. Got that?'

I went off to my desk muttering to myself. Along the way I blew 20p on a plastic cup of tea the colour of burnt umber, or maybe it was yellow ochre. I gave Mac a call.

He said, 'Any other mysteries you want solved?'

'Not today, Sherlock. Where was the absentee hiding herself?'

Mac said, 'In France. She's still there.'

I said, 'How did you find her?'

That was a stupid question. They didn't find her. She had phoned home an hour or so ago to let folks know where she was. Our Zenia had apparently felt an overwhelming desire to hop on a Eurostar and go see the Eiffel Tower. All on her very own.

I said, 'Who says so?'

Mac said, 'She says so.'

I tried again. 'Who says she says so?'

Mac said, 'Eric Shernholm. The fella who reported her missing.'

I put the phone down and stirred the tea with my Bic. Why should Zenia Evans suddenly dash off to France without telling anyone? Why should she phone and tell them *after* she got there? Another mystery. The whole thing was shot through with them, and like I say, I don't like mysteries. If I kept on playing by Belker's rules, I'd end up even deeper in the dark. It was time to change the rules. Better still, change the game. I sat there pondering for at least fifteen minutes before I came up with anything. I went and got myself a plain white envelope. I folded two blank sheets of A4 paper, stuck them inside and gummed down the flap. In capital letters I addressed the envelope to Eric Shernholm, Esq., c/o The Royal Lancaster Hotel. I marked it private and confidential. As far as News Desk was concerned, I was still on an Editor's Must, so they didn't say boo when I slipped on my coat and dodged out of the office.

It was coming up rush hour but I ensnared a taxi in two minutes flat and directed it Bayswaterwards. The Royal Lancaster loomed up out of the grey all bright and welcoming. The girl at reception was even more so. She said, 'How might I help you sir?'

I thought of several things. I said, 'I have a letter for Mister Eric Shernholm. He's staying here.'

She flicked through her computer screen. 'Ah yes, Mister Shernholm.'

I gave her the envelope. 'Just dump it in his box. He'll collect it later.'

'Certainly sir.'

She smiled and turned away. I pulled out my cigarettes and lit one, all the while watching her. She moved along the bank of pigeonholes. Pop. In it went. The number beneath it was 422. By the time she turned round again I was halfway to the bar. I treated myself to a ten-minute break and a gin. That gave the receptionist time to forget me. I eased out of the bar behind an African tribal chief and forty yards of cotton. The lifts were over to my left. I got one all to myself and hit the fourth-floor button. Up there the corridor was deserted. The burgundy carpet soaked up the sound of my Loakes as I padded unseen to room 422. I gave the door one of those light taps they teach the girls at chambermaids' school. Silence. I counted up to five. The door opened six inches. It revealed the crinkly haired man I'd seen in the pub with Zenia Evans.

'You!' he said.

I said, 'I was going to say that.'

He had his back to the light and the corridor was on the sombre side so it was hard to see his expression. But he was not chuffed to see me.

I said, 'May I come in?'

He said, 'What do you want?'

'To come in.'

Shernholm said, 'Why?'

I said, 'I could turn on my heel and walk away and you would never know why. You could die without knowing. Isn't that a sad thought?'

He said, 'You're the one.'

You could take that any old way. I lifted an eyebrow.

He said, 'It musta been you. You were in the bar, watching us.' New York accent.

He looked over my shoulder to see how many of me there were. Only one. He said, 'I suppose you want to talk terms.'

I let him suppose away. He pulled back the door three more inches and I went in. It was a twin-bedded room with a couple of armchairs and a writing desk, TV and a minibar. I settled in a chair and lit up.

He said, 'Do you mind not smoking?'

'Yes.'

There must be some one bloke who designs hotel bedrooms so that they all look the same. My eyes battened on a pocket organizer parked on the bedside table. He said, 'There's nothing here for you.'

But he stowed the organizer away in a drawer. There was nothing else to look at so I looked at him. He hadn't seen sunshine for a while. His face was pale, his eyes blue. Even his hair looked like somebody had washed the colour out.

He said, 'How long have you been on to her?' There was a thin thread of bitterness in his voice.

I hiked a thumb at the minibar. 'Let's talk it out over a drink.'

He was strangely surprised. 'You drink?'

'It has been known.'

On the writing table there was the usual bumf – room service menus, tour brochures, hotel stationery. The top sheet had a single line of writing scrawled on it. It's a fact of life, people always have to deface hotel notepaper.

I said, 'How about the drink?'

He muttered something but he uncorked the bar and fetched a Booths miniature and tonic as directed. I had to remind him that a glass usually completes the set. He ambled off to the bathroom, pausing only to collect his organizer from the drawer. Suspicious cove, our Shernholm.

As soon as he was out of vision I shot up and had a snoop at the notepaper. He had scribbled: Lindy Trevett – 51 Alreson Avenue, Tottenhum. Don't blame me: that's the way he spelt it.

I was back in my chair before he returned with a cellophaned glass. He sat down opposite me and unwrapped it. Yesterday in the bar he was tense. Now he was as tight as a banjo.

He said, 'I didn't expect you to be English, but it makes sense.'

Not to me. I said. 'You told the police Zenia had disappeared.'

'Affirmative. You know this.'

I said, 'Then you said she'd phoned you from Paris.'

'So?'

'So you didn't get any incoming calls from Paris.'
That was a guess.

He said. 'Say again?'

I said it again. He got up and paced to the door
and back again, then back to the door and so on. He
was on his fourth lap when he fired off a dirty look at
me. 'You want Abigail.'

Abigail? Who the hell was Abigail?

I said. 'You're wearing out my eyeballs. Sit down.'

He was a well brought-up boy, for he sat himself
down. I said, 'My name is Max Chard and I am a
reporter, writing a story about your vanishing Zenia.'

People often get upset when I tell them what I do.
Eric was taken that way. 'You're a journalist?'

'More or less.'

Much opening and closing of the Shernholm
mouth. I helped myself to another gin. He got his
voice back in gear. He said, 'You can't write a word.'

He wasn't being critical.

'Because?'

'Because they've snatched Zenia. They've warned
me not to call the police.'

'Who they?'

He turned his head away. He said after a moment,
'Her ex-husband.'

'Does he call himself anything?'

'Um, Roy.'

I flicked ash off my Bensons. 'And why has Um
Roy snatched her?'

He pointed at himself. 'Because she ran off with
me.'

He was a rotten liar. I said, 'Kidnapping one's runaway missus is hardly the way to win her undying affection.'

Eric shrugged. 'This guy is a flake.'

I said, 'And who is Abigail?'

'Abigail?'

I reminded him, 'You said – and I quote – "You want Abigail".'

'Oh yeah, Abigail.'

'That Abigail.'

Shernholm got up and went walkies again. I gave him all the time he needed. After a while he said, 'Abigail is her daughter.'

It was not bad. I said, 'So Roy has kidnapped Zenia to make her hand over Abigail.'

He nodded. 'Yeah. He'll do anything to get Abigail.'

I am a naturally polite man so I didn't say bollocks. I just smiled at him in a certain way.

He said, 'It's true. He's obsessed.'

I had a faraway look in my eyes. I said, 'The way I see it is you lied to the police about Zenia. She's *not* in Paris. She has vanished off the face of this earth. The last man seen with her was one Eric Shernholm. Are you following this, Eric? Now if I were a copper, my first instinct would be to suspect you.'

He was hunched forward, watching me. 'You won't report this?'

I said, 'No. You have an honest face.'

A twitch of relief there. Almost a smile. He eased back.

I said, 'Where is Abigail?'

The smile went out the window. 'She's safe.'

I said, 'Maybe you don't know the procedure here: when someone gets kidnapped, their nearest and dearest goes to the Old Bill, the cops, and tells them. The police call in the editors and they agree to a news blackout. Give the Law a couple of days and they're bound to trip over Zenia. It's a small country, Britain is. The cops nick Roy, Zenia is reunited with her beloved Eric, Abigail gets her mom back, the sun shines again. That's how it goes here. Except for that bit about the sun.'

Shernholm shook his head. 'I can't go to your police. It's too dangerous.'

I shrugged as if it didn't matter. I squashed out my cigarette and said into the glass, 'Any other players in the game – apart from Zenia, Abigail, Roy and you?'

Shernholm said, 'No one.'

I stood up. If I had had a thumbscrew I might have got more out of him, but I doubted it. I gave him my card and wrote down my mobile number too. I said, 'If you want to tell me the truth, ring me anytime.'

He said, 'But you won't run the story?'

'Not yet.'

He opened the door and gave me an edgy farewell grin. 'Thanks,' he said.

'You're welcome,' I said.

Chapter Eight

My brain retired to its study, closing the door behind it. I tiptoed past because Old Brain doesn't like to be disturbed when it's working. Rosie was still out there tipping back the vino with her mates and I had a wide open Wednesday night ahead. I needed a diversion. So I called Tommy, my opposite number at the *Express*. He suggested a meet in a shebeen down by the Elephant and Castle. And why not?

You could tell it was an illegal drinking den by the number of coppers swigging away inside. There were some boisterous girls in the company and a pair of them attached themselves to us or vice versa. The hours whizzed past most pleasurably until it was clicking on towards midnight, by which time I was sort of pinned in a corner by this girl called Tina. Her skirt might have been six inches shorter than modesty demanded and she appeared to be wearing a backless sweater the wrong way around. It didn't mean she was a bad girl. We were hobnobbing along famously until my mobile interrupted. Rosie. 'You're in Hamptons again.'

I could have told the truth, but that mightn't have been so smart. I just said, 'How'd you guess?'

She said, 'Just rang to make sure you're being good.'

I looked at my watch. 'I could be in Battersea in fifteen minutes.'

Well that was just too bad because she was off to bed and had hung a great big DO NOT DISTURB sign on the front door. But she signed off with a noisy kiss.

I folded the mobile and turned back towards Tina. She had a strange and distant look in her eyes. 'Who was that – your wife?'

Maybe I was suffering from a surfeit of tonic because I didn't even think what I was saying. 'Rosie? No, she's my girlfriend.'

Honestly, my brain shouldn't let me out on my own. At any rate Tina suddenly lost interest in me and when last seen was purring in the ear of a local villain. I faded off home.

I was back in the flat and between the sheets when Brain came out of its study. It was wide awake and pulsing. It invited me to consider the item of Eric Shernholm. I tried to sleep. Brain wittered on. I gave in. I sat up, turned on the lamp, lit a Bensons and considered Eric.

The man was a bad liar. And strangely wired up for someone with a military background. Only blokes with a uniform in the closet say things like 'Affirmative' and 'Say Again.' I guessed he was navy from the way he had the hotel bedroom all shipshape. But he didn't drink.

He was *not* the missing Zenia's little passion blossom as claimed. The way they greeted each other in the pub said they weren't even close friends. More like working colleagues. And if he was the lover, what did that make Howard Lanche?

Then there was the subject of Abigail, alleged child

of Zenia. That didn't hold up either. Tug-of-love hubbies don't go around snatching their ex-wives.

And why did Eric lie about Lanche? He was adamant there were no English players in the cast. And who slept in the other twin bed in his room?

Despite myself, I believed his yarn that Zenia had been abducted. His jumpiness when I banged on his hotel door was real: something nasty had happened to her, and it wasn't him what done it. So where did that leave me? And had Howard Lanche snatched her? I rolled my eyes. My brain said, 'Sorry for bothering you' and sidled out. I slept.

Thursday was a bummer of a day. I got to the office to find I'd a whole bunch of new neighbours. Noisy ones at that. They were all wannabe hackettes with names like Cassandra and Tasmin who work on our Saturday Ambit throwaway supplement, or Armpit, as we prefer to think of it. Cassie and Taz and all the rest of the girls spend their working week calling up half-witted celebs and inviting them to rabbit on for 500 words, mainly about their sexual peccadilloes. No known human being ever reads this bilge, apart from the Editor and the girlies. The Editor thinks they're fab, with-it, trendy. The Editor is a child of the Sixties.

Go back two years and the Ambit section was tucked away in a distant corner of the office, some- where south of Letters' Page and the Readers' Ombudsman. But the nymphettes are younger and prettier than us and they make big blue eyes at the Editor. So bit by bit the harpies have encroached into the News Room. There are now more of them than there are honest-to-God foot-in-the-door hacks. By sheer coincidence every single one of them is a daughter/niece/lovechild of a former deputy editor or somesuch.

On this Thursday I blew into the hack ghetto to find it shaved down by all of four desks. I was met by a cluster of Armpit babes sticking a cardboard cut-out of Brad Pitt in the centre of their conquered territory. It was a bit like that snap of the US marines propping up the stars and stripes on Iwo Jima, only the marines didn't make as much fuss about it.

We hacks sunk back behind our consoles and gloomed. At length Jasmin and Tasmin and so on had phoned their boyfriends, drunk their coffee and filed their teeth. They were ready for work. I was doing nothing so I just listened.

Three feet away an Ambit waif picked up the phone and dialled a number. I think she thought the man on the receiving end could see her, for she tucked a curl between her teeth and pushed her boobs out.

'Is that Denis Kerrot?' she fluted. '*Hello*, Denis! This is Topaz Scaleni of Saturday Ambit!'

She talked the way girlish women write letters – sticking in exclamation marks and quote marks willy nilly. I don't know what Denis Kerrot said. He probably went, 'Yuh?', for Denis is an alleged footballer.

'We're doing a "sex" survey!' she shrilled. 'We're calling "top" personalities – like you – to tell us about their most embarrassing sexual encounter. Tee hee!'

Somewhere in a flash gaff out Chigwell way, Denis Kerrot scratched his belly and reflected to himself, 'It's a funny old game.' But I imagine he just gobbed on the carpet.

Topaz, swooping into asthmatic huskiness, said, 'We've been asking all the "stars" about the moment that "caused them to blush"!'

I could have told her that. It was last Saturday in the Chelsea match when he fluked the skankiest goal of the season. But Topaz had other things on her little tiny.

She continued breathlessly, 'Some "famous people" have really HILARIOUS memories of a first date. What about you, Denis? Do you have . . .'

Out in Chigwell Kerrot said something.

'*Really?!!!*' Topaz thrilled. 'Oh, you *MUST* tell me *ALL* about *THAT*!'

Denis, the Hammers' hatchet man, unburdened his evil little heart.

'*In a CAR?!!*' sang Topaz, happy in her work.

A bit more from him, a giggle from her, then, 'And her *MOTHER* saw you?!!'

I bet her mother didn't see him missing the penalty against Spurs. Topaz weighed in again, '*You didn't!!*'

Evidently he did, for her laugh broke a passing sub-editor's specs. Topaz said, 'Her *mum* was in the car too?!!'

You know that restaurant scene from *When Harry Met Sally*, where Meg Ryan is faking a mega good time? Well it reminded me of that. Only I wasn't sure Topaz was faking.

She put down the phone, cheeks flushed, pupils dilated. Deep in her violet eyes shone the sparkle of what passes these days for a story. Come Saturday, the great unwary British reader would be treated to the

squalid tale of how Denis Kerrot once bonked some old
scrubber and her daughter in the back of a Vauxhall
Cavalier. Topaz started pitty-patting away on her keyboard. I eyed her without charity. For Topaz is the
hack of our futures. One of these days you'll wake up
and she and Cassandra and others of the kid sisterhood
will be the disseminators of news. If we'd had them
around in Hitler's day, no doubt they'd have been
ringing up Eva Braun to ask, 'And what did *you* do
when you saw he only had ONE?!!'

If this sounds churlish, blame Rosie. I'd missed her
more than was good for me.

Somewhere in the course of the day the Editor, or
more likely Belker, told News Desk I was their own
pet lamb again. That meant my work on Lanche and
his flyaway turtle dove was at best shelved. I ended
up rewriting an agency story on a farmer who was
charged with murdering ten thousand fish. Well, that
wasn't the exact charge. He was done for poisoning a
trout farm because he suspected (wrongly) that the
fish tycoon was boffing his old woman. When you saw
the pix of her that seemed highly unlikely indeed. But
I cobbled together a story thus:

*Farmer Fred Giles suspected finny business between
his sexy wife and a wealthy trout breeder.*

All right, I know the bloke didn't breed wealthy
trout, but when you're pinned down to a fifteen word
intro, top whack, you've got to cut corners. I let the
copy stretch a bit, inventing a quote from his missus
– 'It was codswallop' – because we needed the length
for a page lead. I wanted to write in a crack from the

ex-fish owner, saying, 'She was an old trout', but you have to draw the line somewhere.

I zipped the stuff through to News Desk and they shunted it on down the line to Back Bench who prodded a sub awake. I stopped by his desk a few minutes later. He'd been scrawling out possible heads for the story. So far he'd got HOOK, LINE AND STINKER, followed by ONE MAN'S MATE AND ANOTHER MAN'S POISSON. Too long, too cryptic, too smart. Our readers wouldn't know a poisson if they found one in their chips. I knew what would happen in the end. The sub would nick my intro and slap a four-column header on it: FARMER FRED'S FINNY BUSINESS, and change the intro to *Jealous farmer Fred Giles suspected something fishy between his curvy wife and a handsome trout breeder.* Personally I preferred it when the trout were wealthy.

I ambled back to my desk to make my customary late afternoon phone trawl of the other crime hacks to see what they were writing. Nobody had anything worth lifting, though the *Telegraph* was running a page lead on a teenage girl found butchered at South Mimms. Her skull had been caved in with a crude hatchet, her corpse was naked, save for a brace of bangles, she was the victim of a ritual slaughter, and she'd had oatmeal for breakfast. She was also ten thousand years old. Terrific story if you were chief crime reporter on the *Cro Magnon Herald*. I passed on it.

I'd nothing else to do so I made a desultory start on another week's exes until I thought I could head for the Stone dive bar without anyone raising a fuss. Purvis, the duty night lawyer was there already and doing inordinate damage to the Glenfiddich. Maybe he had a cold. Purvis is great company, despite his sordid calling. He is wonderfully indiscreet about judges and fellow deviants. He's also a discerning soccer fan. He thinks Arsenal are rubbish. But I wouldn't hire him as a brief. We passed a round or two in amiable chit-chat until he tottered off to the office to spike all the interesting stories.

That left me alone with my Gordons. For the first time all day I thought about Howard Lanche MP, and Zenia Evans, abductee. There was nothing fresh to add to my thoughts of the night before. I went and knocked on Brain's study door. But Brain hid under the desk and pretended he wasn't in. So I thought about something else.

Chapter Nine

That Thursday night Rosie and I missed each other again because there was a farewell thrash for our newly fired City Editor. It was a well-attended do because he'd been sacked from several papers before and all the other City people came to drink his drink and ask how they too could become serial redundo collectors. He just smiled and said, 'Incompetence.' They didn't believe him. I did.

The jollity started off somewhere sensible but as the night wore on we felt the umbilical cord reeling us back to Fleet Street. We duly reeled. This once great avenue of egomania is now but another street. Even its legendary pubs, the Bell, the Tip, the Punch, are sad and spiritless without us. Or so we prefer to believe. As we tacked round the corner past where the Albion once stood I rediscovered the doorway where my hangover used to lie in ambush. This was the spot which every morning on my way to work I would approach unawares. I might even be whistling. But the instant I reached that doorway my hangover would leap out and wrap itself around me in a half-nelson, draining the pink from my cheeks and the sparkle from my eyes. Of course that was all years ago. Some-where along the line since then some sod has given the hangover my home address. Now when I open my eyes in the morning, there he is perched on the corner of my bed, a thin smile playing about his thinner lips.

Despite the warmth of our carousing company I shivered. But once we got ourselves squeezed up tight around the Bell's horseshoe bar, I forgot all about it. The conversation was good and the celebrated ex-City Editor was still buying.

Meanwhile far across the black Thames, Rosie Bannister was getting in her beauty sleep and doubtless dreaming of her beloved Max.

Meanwhile down in Dorset, Zenia Evans was thinking God knows what as she looked out on a cliff path with the sea surging two hundred feet below.

But I knew nothing of this until much later.

Friday I took the day off. And Saturday, and Sunday. In the course of the weekend Rosie and I got together properly and did some modest hell raising. I also watched some rotten rugby on the box, I bought a moleskin jacket the colour of lichen-covered concrete and Rosie dragged me off to a party that wasn't worth going to, I got my hair cut, it rained a lot. Samuel Pepys I ain't.

On Sunday while she lay on her belly thumbing through the colour supplements, I broke the habit of a lifetime and read the political pages of all the heavies. Politics is one of those things I keep well away from, like mineral water and the colour tan. But just this once I stuck my tongue between my teeth and started reading. I never knew there were that many boring words in the entire world. But I ploughed bravely on. My purpose was to see what Howard Lanche was up to in his other role as an MP. Quite a lot. The Sunday

Torygraph named him among a dirty dozen back-
benchers who were planning to vote against the
Government in a Euro barney.

It took some sorting out. The basic story was this:
our Continental cousins had voted themselves a larger
whack of British fishing waters. But they generously
agreed that our own seafarers should be allowed to
catch one underage whitebait apiece. Something like
that. The PM said, 'Oh, all right then.' But a bunch of
addled Tories had got it into their heads that this was
a Very Bad Thing, mainly because their constituents
had told them so. Then various rebel Labourites,
who had a few supporters in sou' westers, joined in
the fun and now they were telling the French, Spanish
and the rest to go sling their hook.

The big moment would come in next Friday's
vote on the Common Agricultural Policy. The way I
decoded the story, it seems that every year Parliament
has to rubber-stamp the policy. And every year all that
happens is some suit on the Government front bench
gets on his hind legs and says, 'I propose we reaffirm
our commitment.' After which everybody else goes,
'Rhubarb, rhubarb, rhubarb', and the vote goes through
without tears. But now that the Labour mutineers –
and the Tories, and all sorts of other miscreants –
were on the warpath, the entire Common Agricultural
Policy was heading for the knacker's yard. I don't know
what that adds up to but the *Telegraph* felt so steamed
up about the story it splashed on it. The PM was
'privately seething', the Labour Whips' office was 'in
uproar', senior figures were 'feeling betrayed'. The
rebels were led by an east coast left winger with a
reputation for being against whatever the party was

for. Lanche, as far as I could make out, was a bit player in the drama. The *Telegraph* wasn't even sure he would be joining the plotters, but it looked that way. The political editor hinted Lanche might chuck in the towel if the Eurocrats got their way.

I read the story through twice to see if I had missed anything. No. That's about it. I tossed the paper aside because it was nearly eight and Rosie was getting peckish.

So much for Sunday.

On every newspaper's News Desk there is a man they call the copytaster. He is called that because he doesn't write copy, and, if he's any good, he has no sense of taste.

It is his job to sift through the hundreds of stories that bleep up on his screen every day. He picks out the likely lads and copies them into the News Editor's file. The copytaster consigns the non-starters to the Spike.

In olden times there used to be an actual big brass spike in the middle of the desk. You could always tell a copytaster, especially one who liked his drink, because he had holes all over his hand. Then came new technology.

Now we have a button on the extreme top right of our keyboards. It's still labelled SPIKE and it is bright red, so that you when you're frazzled you don't mistake it for the SEND button, which is ash grey. Back to the present.

At 9.13 on a chill Monday morning, the copytaster

read a three para story from Dorset International Media (actually one old geezer with a laptop). It read:

The body of a young woman was found beneath cliffs at Raglan Cove, near Harding, Dorset early today.

Police say they believe she fell almost 100 feet to her death while taking a stroll along the coastal path. She is thought to have arrived in the town on Tuesday night.

Her identity has been withheld until next of kin have been informed. ENDSIT.

The copytaster spiked it. And who would blame him? A great newspaper such as ours is not interested in footloose women toppling to their doom.

At 11.22 a.m. another south coast stringer filed a fuller version of events. He put a bit of topspin on the story because he needed the money.

Police were last night probing the mystery death of a beautiful young woman at a picturesque beauty spot.

Most beauty spots tend to be picturesque, but we'll ignore that and read on:

Her partially-clothed body was found on a beach near where the hit BBC sitcom Last Resort *is filmed.*

Nice touch that, sticking in a bit of telly glitz. It sort of brings it all home to our couch potato readers. Anyway, to continue:

The attractive brunette plunged to her death from a 200-foot cliff at Harding, Dorset only five days after she arrived.

But last night detectives admitted they were baffled by the tragedy at Raglan Cove.

A senior officer said: 'The cliff path is very popular with walkers but no one reported seeing her during the day. We believe she fell to her death in the dark.

'But we are mystified why she was so scantily dressed because it was a bitterly cold night.'

Police added that they are still unsure how the victim fell. But they have not ruled out foul play. A post-mortem is to be held today. ENDSIT.

Our copytaster read it while simultaneously answering a phone and attempting to paw the News Desk secretary. He spiked the story. Again, I wouldn't blame him. It smacked of a workaday suicide and suicide stories are real downers, unless the suicidee is somebody interesting.

The tale of the nosediving artiste went quiet for a few hours. Then at 3.43 p.m. our West Country staffer filed copy. His went:

The beach where sexy Fionnuala O'Neill romps in the BBC hit sitcom Last Resort *was last night tainted with tragedy after the horrific death of a beautiful mystery woman.*

There's an intro that needs to be put on a diet. Still, our staffer had the right idea. This time the copytaster read it all the way through. He read:

Her half-naked body was found early yesterday (Monday) at the base of a 300-ft cliff – within sight of the location for the fictional holiday resort.

Police say the woman may have slipped on the treacherous cliff path. But they are not ruling out that she might have been pushed over the edge.

A detective probing the case said: 'There are several bizarre features.

'The woman was wearing only flimsy clothing, yet it was a freezing cold night.

'No one has reported her missing. It is a mystery

where she came from, who she was and why she was there. All we know is she turned up on Tuesday night.'

The victim was described as in her early thirties, around five feet four inches tall and with dark hair.

The Last Resort horror stunned the nearby Dorset village of Harding.

Last night (Monday) one resident said: 'Everyone is shocked. The whole country associates Raglan Cove with the fun and laughter of the TV series.

'But now there's a shadow on the sands.'

Thousands of day trippers visit the picturesque Downs, attracted by the stunning locations in the BBC programme. A new series is to be shot there later this year.

Last night (Monday) one of the theories circulating was that the woman might have been a lovelorn admirer of heart-throb actor Jon Glass who plays hotel owner Jed in the zany comedy.

There have been persistent rumours of an off-screen romance between him and Fionnuala O'Neill who plays Holly, his wacky receptionist.

The copytaster stopped reading and piped, 'Got a nice little one here, Angie.'

Angela Whipple, our fragrant News Editor, read it over his shoulder and said, 'I like it. That's the Page Three lead. Get the library to dig out pix on Fionnuala O'Neill and Jon Glass.'

Let us be honest here. No one in the paper was the slightest bit interested in the sudden crash landing of a mystery beauty, but for the fact she gave us the excuse to plaster Fionnuala O'Neill's knockers all over page three, thus bringing sunshine to the nation. Grauniad readers might snivel and sneer that we care more about showbiz frivolity than real-life death. This is true.

But all I can say is, bless Fionnuala's little cotton socks, and more to the point, bless her whacking great boobs. If it weren't for them, the story of the Raglan Cove corpse would never have made the paper.

And I would never have discovered Howard Lanche's secret.

I was oblivious to all the foregoing – the stuff about the copytaster and so on – until about 4.30 p.m. that same Monday. In the interim I was otherwise engaged in churning out reams of copy on the Met's latest crime figures. They showed that serious crime was 20 per cent down, minor crime 20 per cent up. If that makes you sleep any easier in your bed, forget it. All it meant was the Yard had cooked the books by reclassifying a whole stack of serious crimes as not very serious really.

When I shovelled my stuff out of the way I was feeling nosy so I switched my computer on to News-file. This holds all the copy our staff reporters have filed during the day. I always enjoy scrolling through it because you get to read your peers' copy before the subs put in the verbs and root out the pidgin English. Way down the list I came across our West Country district man's effort. I read it and silently applauded his artfulness in turning a one-para accident into a page top. Then I read it again. Hmmm, I said to myself, Harding: that's where Howard Lanche holes up. Odd, that.

I lit a Bensons and focussed in on the mystery

plunger's description. Just say . . . just say you knock a few years off her age and a couple of inches off her height. Who would that remind you of? The missing Zenia, that's who.

I exited from News-file and clicked onto Spike-file where I ran a word search on Harding, Dorset. That's how I found the two earlier pieces spiked by the copy-taster. They didn't tell me anything more, but they didn't tell me anything less either.

On impulse I picked up the phone and gave Hughie Gall, our West Country man, a bell. He is a mean and fiercely territorial hack. He wanted to know why I wanted to know about his story.

I said, 'I've been saddled with a boring disappearing mum yarn.'

Hughie said, 'So?'

In other words, keep off my grass or I'll rip your lungs out.

I said, 'It's a long shot, but my missing woman might be your stiff on the cliff.'

Hughie didn't say anything. I yawned and continued, 'My woman is from Lewisham. She's thirty-three, and she's called Rebecca West. Have the police stuck a name on your corpse yet?'

He uncoiled a fraction. 'They've got a name but they're not putting it out until they talk to the family.'

We wished each other cordial and deeply insincere farewells. I fell to brooding. I don't know anybody in the Dorset Old Bill so I wouldn't get any whispers from there. Of course I could have always asked Hughie to try out the name Zenia Evans on his local neighbourhood Plod, but I didn't want him anywhere near my story.

I puffed away on the Bensons until I cooked up an idea. I ruffled through the phone book and pulled out the number for the Canadian High Commission. When I got through I asked for the press attaché.

A man eating his way through an apple came on the phone. I introduced myself as John McCarthy of the *London Daily News*. Yes, I know the LDN folded years ago, but press attachés are notoriously ill-informed.

'Hi, John. What can I do for you?' said a brown baritone voice.

I said, 'We've got a story running that a girl, possibly a Canadian citizen, has died in a fall in Dorset. Do you have anything on that? I mean, have you been asked to inform the next of kin?'

He said, 'Just give me a second, I'll check with our consular people.'

He took two minutes. He said, 'You know, John, we cannot give out information.'

I said, 'I appreciate that. This is why I am calling you. We have a name and I don't want to run it in the paper until her family have been told.'

He said warily, 'What name have you got?'

'Zenia Evans.'

He went silent.

I said, 'Would you like me to spell it?'

He said, 'No, John. I heard you. Zenia Evans. You say you are not going to publish the name?'

I said smartly, 'Not unless next of kin have been informed. It is part of our Reader's Charter.'

He said, 'Next of kin have not been informed.'

I pressed, 'But it *is* Zenia Evans?'

He said, 'On record, I cannot confirm or deny. Off record, providing you do not use it . . .'

I said, 'It is Zenia Evans?'

He said, 'You did not hear that from me.'

Chapter Ten

I didn't say 'Wow!' until I was downstairs, round the corner and in the Stone. Even then I said it only to myself. I was drinking with a couple of monkeys, letting them gibber on about f stops and filters while I tried to think. My first instinct had been to rush in to the Editor and screech, 'Hold the front page!', but nobody talks like that in newspapers. A saner voice told me to be strong and silent which is what I was doing in the bar. Suddenly I noticed that the snappers had also fallen silent. They'd run out of fuel. I topped them up and off they went again.

So, I mused, what's to be done? It was easier to work out what I shouldn't do. Top of the taboo list was to go squawking to the Old Bill. If I did that they'd haul out their long-handled batons and set about me until I confessed all. Well, they mightn't exactly bounce my head off their boots but they'd give me a grim time of it. They'd also feel the Editor's collar and anyone else they had half a mind to. After that I'd stand as much chance of staying on the paper as Rose West has of becoming a registered child minder. I gulped on my Gordons.

Nor could I disguise my voice and give the Dorset woodentops an anonymous tip. That way they'd call a press conference and tell all the other hacks, and it was still my story. I considered ringing up Howard Lanche but I wasn't even supposed to know of his liaison with the ex-Evans character. That left me with what? That left me with Eric Shernholm, the inmate of Room 422 at the Royal Lancaster. He was hardly the most informative soul God ever put breath into, but at least he was a connection. Also, he was desperately anxious to keep the police out of his affairs. That made us kindred spirits. The more I thought about the idea the more attractive it looked. I turned my back on the monkeys, pulled out the mobile, and called the Royal Lancaster.

A man's voice answered the phone in Room 422. 'Yes?'

I said, 'Eric. It's Max Chard.'

He went stiff-jawed on me. 'Yeah?'

I said, 'I need to see you right now. I have important news for you.'

'What news?'

I said, 'Not on the phone. I can be at the Lancaster in twenty minutes. Call it half an hour. Okay?'

Eric didn't sound overjoyed at the prospect but he said okay and put the phone down. I should have known there and then that I'd blown it but I was too tickled with my own cleverness to catch on. If Eric was truly ready to meet me he would first have issued a string of conditions. Like (a) come alone, (b) no questions and (c) no.

But foolish youth that I am, I lingered over my gin before ambushing a taxi. When I got to the Royal Lancaster the receptionist cooed in sympathy, 'Mister Shernholm? I'm afraid he's just checked out.'

No, he didn't leave a forwarding address or any message for me.

I would have gone to the bar and consoled myself with something but I couldn't afford the prices. Instead I steamed out of the hotel, stole a taxi from under the doorman's nose and told it to deposit me at Turnbull Mews. It was all I could think of.

When I got there number eight was in darkness but I rattled the letterbox and pinged the bell just in case. Nothing. I turned away muttering foul oaths about Eric Shernholm. I wandered back onto the main street and thought: somewhere out there, maybe within a mile of this very spot, the bugger has found a new hideaway for himself. It was not an encouraging thought because central London has hotels the way the Sahara has sand dunes. And Eric Shernholm might not even be staying in a hotel. He could be dossing down with friends, for all I knew. And who were Eric's friends?

I got about fifty yards down the street before it hit me. Friends! Eric had scrawled a name and address on his hotel notepaper and I'd snatched a look at it when he was off fetching me a glass. I stood under a street lamp and riffed through my notebook until I found the relevant squiggle. Lindy Trevett. 51 Alreson Avenue, Tottenham.

What with the traffic, it took me half an hour and then some to reach the place. I told the cabbie to drop me off round the corner. Alreson Avenue was one of those grey humdrum streets off the High Road south of the Shopping City and branching in the vague direction of Wood Green.

On one corner there was a takeaway kebab joint,

on the other a place masquerading as an old Oirish post office inside which people were whooping and bellowing. It was an authentic repro Irish bar of the type we import lock, stock and Guinness barrel from Dublin. Though why the nation that invented pubs sees the need to buy them from somewhere else is beyond me. I passed it without a twinge.

Lindy Trevett, whoever she might be, was holed up in a mid-terrace house with barren windowboxes and a foot scraper parked by the door. She answered my knock fairly promptish and looked me all over before saying 'Yes?'

She was an ash-blonde halfway through her thirties, reasonably fanciable and I'd say she took a size ten frock, though right now she was wearing a big-collared coat over jeans and a pink denim shirt. The coat was open. She was either just heading out or coming in. I jumped in swiftish, saying I was Max Chard, which was true, and that I was a bosom buddy of Eric Shernholm, which was not. She seemed to believe me. She turned on her sweetest smile and said, 'Come in, Max.'

She led the way down a high and skinny hall. She paused to sling her coat across the bannisters. That gave me the opportunity to revise the matter of her frock size. The bottoms of size ten girls wiggle. Anything higher up the scale wriggles. And she was a wriggler if ever I saw one. But if she was more than a tad plumper than first imagined, she was as nothing compared to the treat awaiting us in the lounge. Sprawled centre stage on a matted rug was the fattest dog I've ever seen in my puff. He had his fuzzy brown head down in the pile and a leg stretched out of him at each corner with a colour co-ordinated tail stuck on the back. He didn't move. At first I thought he'd fallen off the ceiling.

Lindy said, 'Don't worry about Plug.'

I wasn't, as long as he didn't try to climb up on my lap. I took a seat and eyed Plug. He swivelled a pupil and gave a single thump of his tail. I smiled back.

Lindy said, 'He's really an old softy.'

I said, 'Do you mind if I smoke?' which was just meant to give me time so I could take in the general picture. She didn't mind. I rubbernecked around. If you left Plug out of the equation it was a neat and well-ordered room. Her taste in furnishings was maybe on the flowery side but women are often that way. Particularly women without men. The only photograph on show was of a Moses lookalike only this one's beard knew how to behave itself and he had square glasses. He was old enough to be her grandpop and he probably was.

Lindy sat herself down on a puffed up sofa covered in twirly swirly flower stems. She was at right angles to me. She said, 'How is Eric? I haven't seen him since Sunday.'

I said, 'I haven't seen him since last week.'

She said casually, 'With Abigail?'

There was just something in the way she said it. I snapped a glance at her but she was busy tracing a twirly stem all the way back to its root.

I said, 'He's moved from the hotel. He's in Uxbridge now.'

Lindy stared at the ceiling and mused aloud, 'Uxbridge? I wonder who he knows out there?'

I let her wonder away. I said, 'Eric isn't saying.'

She sighed and stroked her hair with fingers as small as a child's. No rings. She said, 'I don't suppose you can blame him.'

I said, 'Any news of Zenia yet?'

Lindy shook her head. Now she turned and looked directly at me. She had pale green eyes. She said, 'How did you get involved, Max?'

Oh dear, oh, dear. Here I go tap-dancing again. I said, 'I've had a little experience of this sort of thing . . .'

She had small even teeth. She said, 'Haven't we all. But forgive me – I'm forgetting my manners. Would you like a tea, coffee? Elderberry wine, perhaps? Non-alcoholic, of course.'

She laughed as if that was funny. I settled for coffee, she had a glass of elderberry wine. The mood was warm and friendly and I didn't trust it.

Lindy unfurled herself on the settee. There was a foxy little flirt in there fighting to get out. She said, and her voice dropped to a purr, 'I thought I knew everyone. But I don't recall Eric mentioning you.'

I said, 'No. He wouldn't.'

She wasn't giving up that easily. She said, 'And how did you meet him?'

If you don't like a particular question, answer a different one. Unless the Old Bill is doing the questioning.

I said, 'The first time I saw Zenia was when she was with us in the pub down Queensway on the day she vanished. What do *you* think happened?'

Lindy wasn't drinking her wine. She was up to

the same mischief as me. We were like a couple of pickpockets trying to nick each other's wallet.

She said, 'Are you Abigail's friend or Eric's?'

'Eric's.'

Over to the right there was a door. It began to open ever so slowly and just about as silently. It was spooky. Lindy was unaware of it. I eyed the door over the rim of my cup. Bit by tiny bit the front wheels of a wheel-chair rolled into view. I saw a pair of men's shoes, then a pair of men's twill trousers, and finally the man himself. It was the Moses character. He looked more alive in the photograph except for his weird bright blue eyes. He gazed at me. I gazed back. He was the downside of sixty. He had a big-boned head, squared off by the clipped down beard. He could have played the mad scientist in a Hammer movie. With his eyes still on me he said softly, 'Lindy?'

She turned and saw him. She shook her head. He nodded his. Without saying any more, he rolled back behind the door like a Galapagos tortoise pulling its head in.

Lindy uncoiled herself and closed the door on him. She did not mention him. It was as if he had never been there. She flopped back on the sofa again. She said, 'And what exactly do you do, Max?'

'Me?' I took in a long column of smoke and pulsed it out. I said, 'I'm a crime reporter and I'm writing the story of Zenia's kidnapping.'

Ooops. There went the elderberry juice, all down the front of her pink shirt.

'You're a—!'

Even Plug the canine land mass looked surprised.

I continued cheerfully. 'Yes. I'm a journo. And I'm reporting on Zenia, Abigail, Eric, you. The whole bit.'

Lindy had a naturally creamy complexion so I can't say if she went pale. But she was having trouble talking. I drained my cup and gave her an encouraging beam. She stood up and said in a very tight voice, 'I don't have anything to say to you. Please leave my house.'

It would have been more impressive if she wasn't dripping elderberry wine all over the dog. She pointed the way, 'Please leave now.'

Her eyes had gone hard and she was right on the edge of blowing her top. I tracked it back down the hall with her snorting down her nostrils three inches behind me. I wished she'd left the wine glass in the lounge. I got to the front door and turned to face her. She looked much uglier when she was angry. She had trouble with her voice. She said, 'You lied to me.'

The words were sharp and flinty.

I said, 'Yes. I made up that bit about Eric hiding in Uxbridge. But if you tell me what you know, I'll tell you what I've got.'

She forgot she was a sex kitten. She said, 'Get bloody lost.'

I was on the step now. I fastidiously wiped my shoes on the boot scraper. I said, 'If you want to know where Zenia is, just ring the coroner's clerk in Harding. That's a place in Dorset.'

She jerked back, 'What?'

I said, 'You'll work it out eventually.'

Lindy didn't say anything so I said, 'Zenia is a goner. Some nutter pushed her off a cliff. Or haven't they told you yet?'

I walked away before she could think of something to do with the wine glass.

I trolled off down the street feeling more than a mite narked at myself. That's twice tonight I'd screwed up. Lindy had told me nothing while I'd told her more than was smart. I knew now that I should have gone in softer, tickled her tummy and flashed my big blue eyes at her. That way she might have got careless and let something go. But no. I had to show off, just for effect. Just to watch her chin bounce off her knees. Pure bloody vanity. It'll be the ruin of me.

I was still simmering when the taxi pulled up outside Rosie's flat but I was also trying to jolly myself out of it. I said, 'Never mind. At least you know Lindy is up to her neck in it and she wants to find Abigail. But for reasons unknown Eric won't tell her where Abigail is.' I read that back to myself and it was still meaningless.

So I tried it out on Rosie. Or at least I tried it out on the back of her head because she'd just returned from the deli and was busy stuffing bean curd and *crème fraîche* and all sorts of junk food into her fridge.

I started with the Sunday morning briefing in the Editor's office, moving on to the tale of Howard Lanche. Rosie looked blank. Politics is not her chosen specialist subject. She thinks Thatcher still runs the shop.

I helped myself to a Gordons and explained carefully, 'Howard Lanche is a big cheese Labour backbencher. He wants divorce to be made a capital offence. He's got stacks in the bank. He's a doting husband and a father, or so he would have us believe. Before he took his seat in the House of Sleaze, he was a structural engineer. Before that he was a rotten driver who squelched a kid on a zebra crossing. But that was years ago.'

Rosie hauled out a wok and began stuffing it with strange and hideous things. She said over her shoulder, 'So what's the story?'

I said, 'The story is that Howard Lanche, devoted hubby et cetera, has been having naughties on the side.'

Rosie's eyes wished him a long and awful death. She said, 'Who is she?'

'A Canadian piece of mischief. Calls, or called herself Zenia Evans.'

Rosie demanded a full description. I gave her the full run-down, except for the bit that Zenia was fairly fanciable, for Rosie is funny that way.

She said, 'Is she attractive?' Meaning did *I* find her toothsome.

I rolled the gin around my tonsils and said absently, 'I suppose she is, if you go for that sort of wispy type.' Meaning I didn't.

I said, 'Anyways, we're straying off the path here. Zenia has a mate who calls himself Eric Shernholm.'

Rosie flicked her curls, 'Who's he?'

That was a hard one. Shernholm, I said after a moment, is a man in his thirties. American, possibly Canadian. He was Zenia's chum.

'Boyfriend.' Rosie corrected.

'Chum.' I corrected right back. 'I saw them together in a bar in Bayswater and they were just about good friends.'

Rosie doesn't believe a man and a woman can be

mere good friends. She banged the wok and flapped her lashes.

I said slowly, because I was also thinking it through, 'Eric's on the same side as her. Against Them. And don't ask me, because I don't know who Them are.'

I rethought that. 'Well, maybe I know who one of Them is.'

I told Rosie about the sinister bloke keeping vigil on Zenia's flat last Tuesday night.

She said, 'And you're trying to find him?'

I'd left a chunk out of the narrative. I said, 'No. The story's moved on: Zenia was pushed or fell off a cliff in Howard Lanche's neck of the woods on Sunday night. They found her body yesterday.'

Rosie whistled, which was not very ladylike of her but it showed her lips to max effect. She said, 'And you saw this bloke watching her place last Tuesday.'

I said, 'That's right. I was doing a spot of doorstepping to see if Howard Lanche showed up, but the mystery man was already waiting there . . . half a second, what did you just say?'

'What?'

I stood there with my mouth agape.

Rosie said, 'What is it?'

I said in total mystification, *'She wasn't there!'*

Rosie screwed up her eyes. 'Who wasn't where?'

I said, almost to myself, 'Zenia wasn't in her flat. She was already in Harding. All the agencies said she got there on Tuesday night.'

Rosie thought that was a hoot. 'So you were wasting your time watching an empty house.'

I shook my head vigorously. 'No. That's the point.

There *was* someone there. A woman. I saw her shadow on the blind.'

Rosie was tired of the puzzle. She said, 'It must have been someone else.'

A name floated out of the ether. I grabbed it. 'Aaah,' I said, 'it must have been Abigail.'

That started Rosie off again. Who was Abigail, and if so why. This time I laughed. The whole thing was hopeless.

I said, 'According to Eric Shernholm, Abigail is Zenia's daughter. But Eric tells fibs, so the one thing we know for sure is Abigail is not Zenia's daughter. Abigail, whoever she might be, is in hiding from Them, whoever they might be. Eric is protecting her. Zenia *was* protecting her.

'Eric and Zenia have a mutual friend, or somebody they know anyway. She's an Englishwoman called Lindy Trevett and she lives in Tottenham. She's got a dog as big as an elephant. Lindy's not a close friend because Eric is not telling her where he's got Abigail hidden. He doesn't trust Lindy but I don't know why not. Also, Lindy is strangely keen to find Abigail, only she pretends she isn't.'

Rosie said, 'What sort of drugs are you on?'

I said, 'The strangest thing of all is the story's an Editor's Must and I'm not even allowed to tell News Desk what I'm doing.'

Rosie had her back to me again. There was a vile stench drifting up from the wok. She said, 'Sounds like you've been at the magic mushrooms.'

'But,' I persisted, 'the Editor keeps pushing the story on to the back burner.'

She pulled out a big yellow plate and dolloped a

mountain of gunge on it. 'There,' she said. 'Eat up your greens.'

Deep in the warm folds of the night, with Rosie sleeping like a dormouse at my side, a still small voice asked unto me, 'Why are you playing detective, Max? After all, out there on the streets, there are legions of men in ill-fitting suits whom we pay to do the detecting for us.'

I told the voice, 'It's because something is going on and no one, from the Editor down, will tell me what it is. It's because I know I'm being used and I don't know why, or even how. It's because it's my story. Who would you bet on to get the story – me or PC Plod?'

The voice saw the wisdom in this and went away.

There was steel in my eyes, carbon fibre in my sinews when I strode into the office first thing on Tuesday. I marched right past News Desk without the customary grunt. I marched right past my own desk. The phone was ringing but I marched on, all the way down to the Editor's office. I gave the door a thump and marched in. Fortunately the Editor was there or I would have looked a right berk.

'Max!' he said with remarkable perception.

I said, 'I need to talk to you.'

The Editor frowned. He thinks *he's* the one who needs to talk to people.

I said, 'It's about Zenia Evans.'

The frown took on another line. He said, 'What about her?'

I said, 'Howard Lanche's girlfriend plopped off a

cliff in Dorset. In Lanche's constituency. The police say she might have been pushed.' I sounded like a robot.

The Editor creaked back in his chair. He said, 'Good God!'

I was warming up. I said, 'She was half naked. She fell a couple of hundred feet. She died as soon as she hit the beach. We've got the story on Three.'

The Editor said 'Good God!' again. He excavated a final edition from the pile and flicked to page three. He said, 'This one? The one about Fionnuala O'Neill?'

I said, 'That one.'

I sat down and lit a cigarette for the Editor is a slow reader.

He finished the story, took a last look down Fionnuala's cleavage and said, 'But it doesn't say who the dead girl is.'

I said, 'I got a tip from a Foreign Office contact last night. The police will put her name out today.'

The Editor's mouth did a goldfish impression for half a minute. He said, 'It might have been an accident.'

I said, 'It might not.'

He circled the bowl a few more times. He said, 'We'd better think about this.'

I looked out the window towards Fleet Street where there used to be real newspapers, real editors. I said, 'We've got a great story right now: Howard Lanche's Secret Lover in Mystery Death Dive. We can link him directly with her.'

'Yes, yes. I know.' The Editor fluttered his hands.

I said, 'I'll start knocking it out now.'

'No!' He was firm about that at least. He got up

and stood with his back to me chewing a biro. He must have eaten it halfway through before he came up with anything.

He said, 'It *is* a big story. I can understand your excitement. But we mustn't go off half-cocked. The best thing is for you to go down there. Yes, I want you to go this morning. Just look around and see what you can find out from the police. But *on no account* mention Lanche. I don't want you to write anything. Not yet anyway. Do a bit of digging and see if there's a connection.'

I said, 'There is a connection. Zenia Evans is his mistress. *Was* his mistress. Harding is where he lives.'

The frown was back. He said, 'I know that. That's not the point. Just find out what you can and be discreet about it.'

I said, 'What about Hughie Gall?'

'What about him?'

I put it in simple words, 'Hughie goes bonkers when anyone else turns up in his manor. He's got a machine gun post on the M4 to keep us out.'

The Editor said, 'You could always say you're on holiday.'

I showed my teeth. 'Hughie wouldn't believe me on principle.'

The Editor went tetchy. 'Oh, tell him something or other. But *don't* tell him the real reason you're there. And don't speak to anyone else in the office about it. Report personally to me. Or Tony Belker. Now, I want you to get this up and running right away.'

I said, 'Okay.' And I got up and walked.

Chapter Eleven

I pulled a rail warrant from our travel clerk. He asked, 'Second class?' and I gave him a look. He ticked the first class box. I left London on the 11.30 Intercity. We chugged out of Paddington slow enough for us to read the graffiti. First Class was a proper little hive of industry with pinstripes rattling off spreadsheets on their laptops. It was pleasant watching them work. I hailed the trolley man and got him to offload a heap of gin miniatures so that I might enjoy the spectacle the more.

The scene outside the windows was just as soothing. Sheep scudded away like clouds before a summer storm. Various birds flipped and flapped. Cows queued with outstretched tails to moon at us. Sunshine fired off flashguns from every passing pond and puddle. I could get to like the countryside as long as I don't have to go out in the stuff. Far above the black bone trees the sky was bright and blue and crackly round the edges. Three thousand feet up there a lazy jumbo swam by on its final approach to Heathrow.

Now that I was sitting comfortably I finally turned my attention to the matter of Hughie Gall. There are some who say he was once a warm and caring human being until his marriage went belly up. She left him for an older man. Personally I think Hughie has always been an unmitigated plonker. He harbours grievances, grudges, guns and snaggle-toothed dogs. He's the only man I know with bull bars on his office jam jar. I suspect he also has a stash of country and western records.

I suppose the sensible thing to do was to slip in there without telling him. But if by evil chance he found out I was there, then that wouldn't be very sensible. So I fell to concocting an excuse for trespassing on Hughie's little acre; one so complicated it gave me a headache to think of it. But that was as it should be. The more complex you make an explanation, the faster people lose interest in it. My story went like this: I'd been clobbered with a Benefits Agency investigation into Euro spongers who come here to soak up our dole money. My investigation was taking in Liverpool, Leeds and the south coast. In other words, I was riding roughshod over several district men's patches so there's nothing personal in it, Hughie. The line here, on the English Riviera, was that various Latino layabouts were working as skivvies in local hotels while bilking the state out of unemployment benefit. I talked it up in my head so that I almost started believing it.

Hughie didn't. I got into Bristol Temple Mead and I phoned him, 'What ho, Hughie. Fancy a pint?'

He examined my cheery invite from all angles and came to the slow conclusion that I must be somewhere in his territory.

He said, 'What are you doing here?'

I trilled an innocent laugh. 'Wasting my time. Join me in the station buffet and I'll tell you about it.'

He was there before I'd blown my first fiver on the one-armed bandit. Hughie Gall is huge, thick-necked and thin-skinned. An unhappy combination. He is often referred to as Herman, as in Herman Munster, but not in his hearing. His eyebrows form a straight picket line across his bouncer's mug. Beneath it, fierce brown eyes peer out at the world like a couple of badass mountain bears in adjoining caves. His jaw is square and heavily buttressed, giving the impression that he's on steroids. The rest of him is similarly chunky. He burst through the doors and pulped my hand. We performed the ritual of pretending we were glad to see each other while a barperson pulled two pints.

Now the niceties were out of the way, we tucked ourselves in a corner and got down to the biz. He stayed silent and suspicious as I rattled through my story. All the while his eyes were locked on mine. They told me I was a liar, an intruder in his Eden, a worm in his apple. I dived into my pint, signalling it was his turn to air his tonsils. Hughie was in no hurry. He sat there in a big brown suit drumming his fingers like a slow handclap on the table top. I had a couple of man-sized gulps inside me before he opened up.

Hughie said, 'Where are you going?'

I assumed an air of wearied indifference. 'Probably Torquay. But I wanted your advice.'

Hughie wanted to know why I wanted his advice which gave me the cue to turn on the smarm. Because he was the acknowledged expert on the world west of

Oxford. Because he was such a wise and perceptive type, and more, and much more.

He just said, 'Torquay?' He had stopped drumming but he was still of the opinion that I was a liar, an intruder in his Eden, etc.

I said, 'It's got more hotels than anywhere else. If there are illegal workers, that's the place to go. Unless you have a better idea.'

He had. He said, 'Try Brighton.'

Brighton is outside his patch. I smiled to let him know I knew what was on his mind. He smiled back, matey as a barracuda.

I said, 'Hughie, nothing would give me greater glee than to chase up this stupid story in Brighton or anywhere else outside your kingdom. But the Editor specified the West Country and even he knows that Brighton is not the West Country.'

Hughie stuck a thumb in his waistcoat. I didn't know they were still making waistcoats like that. We guzzled awhile. I drained my glass. He didn't feel like buying me a courtesy pint. He said finally, 'Give me a buzz when you've found a hotel so I know where you are.'

Cheeky bugger. I said, 'You've got my mobile.'

He insisted on sticking to me while I bought a ticket for Torquay. I clambered aboard the milk train heading thataways and waved him goodbye from behind grimed windows. He kept his thumbs tucked in his waistcoat.

Two stops down the line I hopped off and found a bar. I was anxious to get to Harding but I was even more anxious that Hughie lose my trail. I hung around until teatime and then I caught another slow train back to Bristol. There was an hour's wait for the Harding flyer. I hid out in the station buffet keeping my eyes peeled in case Hughie came back.

A fussy little diesel puffed me in to Harding sometime after eight. It was dark and cold. Now I was here I wasn't sure what to do next so I found myself a passable pub and had a gin and a think. My usual sources of info – the Old Bill – were blocked to me. If I contacted them, the chances were I'd get somebody who knew Hughie Gall, probably a fellow member of the snaggle-tooth dog breeders' association, and next thing Hughie would be in town cradling a twelve gauge. Nor could I get an update on the Zenia Evans story from a local stringer for the same reason. That left me with the hack's other traditional sources, taxi drivers and barmen. Or in this case barlady.

She was a middle-aged specimen in butterfly glasses and prissy apron. The way she lovingly polished the bartop and wiped up every errant spot of beer made me think she was the governor or the governor's missus. It appeared that the citizens of Harding observe a curfew on strong drink between the hours of eight and nine so that meant she and I were alone in the bar. As she flicked past with a saffron slop rag I gave her a wide open smile inviting conversation. She swept on.

I addressed her back, 'Cold out there.'

The back of her bonce nodded.

I rattled the ice cubes and listened to the silence. I said, 'It's quiet tonight.'

She said, still with her back to me, 'It always is on Wednesdays.'

Tonight was Tuesday, but it was her bar. I swigged

my gin again and said half to myself, 'Bet it's very different in season.'

That was supposed to kick-start her natural feminine yakkiness. It didn't. She put away the saffron cloth, picked up a puce one and started buffing up the pump handles.

I swallowed my gin noisily and put the glass down, taking care to park it dead centre on the thoughtfully provided beer mat. She took the hint.

'Another gin?'

I said that would do nicely, and while she was at it, to have a drink herself. She said, oh, just an orange juice. She charged me seventy pence for it, but she didn't open a bottle. Never mind, the imaginary orange juice got her vocal cords working.

She eyed me through her silly specs. There were shiny gold lozenges in each corner. She said, 'Your first time here?'

I said it certainly was, and, as a stranger in these parts, could do with some helpful hints. Like where was the best place to stay?

She was about to suggest a pokey room upstairs in her own hostelry then she had another look at me and decided that a man of such evident taste and discernment was used to something better than a candlewick bedspread and a communal bathroom. She suggested the Reen Court Hotel, adding the malicious rider that it was overpriced, impersonal and the food was too fancy for its own good. Her sharp eyes beguiled me towards a blackboard which billed her specials of the day as 'Lasagne, Baked Pot with Chilli, S'perds Pie'. I said I wasn't hungry anyway and the conversation withered again. She got on with buffing the optics.

I said I supposed that nothing much happened in Harding off-season and she said that's right. An idea suddenly occurred to her.

'Have you anything to do with the Road?'

I said, 'What road?' and she was off and running with the conversational ball. They were, she said, planning to build a whacking great four-lane dual carriageway by-pass. A Good Thing? No, an *awful* Thing, roughly on a par with Krakatoa and low-alcohol lagers. How so? Well, it would mean the end of life as Harding knows it. No more passing trade. Shops would put up shutters, cafés would go under, even some pubs, good grief, would ring out last orders. She broke off to serve some old codger in a donkey jacket and whiskers. He tottered off to a corner snug and she returned to the Road topic, remembering a few other spots facing doom and disaster, like the antique shops, the small hotels, and, though I didn't quite follow this, the ladies' hairdressing salon.

I got her to pour me another gin, oh, and an orange for yourself. While she dribbled liquor into my glass I asked her back, 'Who wants the new road?'

No one of note. Only the riff-raff out by Crandby and Lomer Cross who stood to make a bundle from it.

I said, 'And who is your MP supporting?'

The glasses swivelled over her shoulder and flared at me. 'Howard Lanche? He's been absolutely brilliant. He says it would turn Harding into a ghost town.'

I looked around the empty bar. I said, 'Yeh. That would never do.'

She nodded her head so fast her specs jumped half off her nose.

I said, 'Will this road go past his house?'

Apparently not. Maison Lanche was perched on the downs.

'The cliffs?' From me.

'The downs.' From her.

An idle thought popped into my head. 'Didn't someone just fall off the downs?'

'The cliff,' she said. Only about half a mile from this very spot, but the other side of town from Lanche's place. Curses. I sucked an ice cube and listened for more.

She said, 'It was some mystery girl, a tourist. You must have read about it for it was in all the papers.'

I said I didn't read newspapers because they were a pack of lies and she agreed with that. So what really happened? I asked.

It was her turn to look vague. The story was largely as writ. She added a few incidental details. The girl had arrived by train last Tuesday night. She went sky-diving on Sunday night. No one had seen her between Tuesday and Monday, when she turned up dead. She was carrying a small green rucksack which so far had not turned up. Nor had her left shoe.

I said, 'Maybe she was staying at a hotel up on the cliff.'

The landlady gave me a look of contempt. 'The downs. The only hotel out that way is the Reen Court but she didn't stay there. It's a real mystery.'

Yeh, you could call it that.

I plugged away with a couple more loose questions but she had nothing sensible to add. I tossed my glass back and headed out into the salty night. A taxi driven by a local who knew even less about the cliff plunger ferried me to Reen Court, a butter-coloured Edwardian mansion, now tastefully embellished with a TV satellite dish and a big red and white sign. It was set on a bump a quarter of a mile inland and commanded a wide sweep of the Channel curving away towards Cornwall.

I registered as one Eddie Stonelight of The Myrtles, West Squiggle. The receptionist, a trim young thing in scarlet and black, handed me a key weighing three stone and directed me to room one-oh-four.

There'd been only about five cars littering the gravel outside so I had my pick of rooms. Mine was on the first floor with balcony, sea view, small sitting room and a beckoning minibar. I shunned it and hung up my clothes in a wardrobe designed for Imelda Marcos. My watch and stomach agreed it was five to nine and time to eat.

I descended the crimson stairs to a dining room where the décor was of the forty shades of green school. The walls were mint, the frieze and pillars sage, the carpet jade, the napery eau-de-nil, and so on. The maître d', doubling as the wine waiter, lodged a couple of fat emerald folders in my hand and rolled off. I ignored my grumbling stomach and took my time about ordering. As a point of principle hacks always dine à la carte. I filed an order for Dover sole backed up with venison pie, a bottle of Mâcon Solutre for openers and a big butch burgundy for later.

I sipped white wine from a green glass and eyed up my half dozen fellow diners all of whom looked seasick in these surroundings. None of them struck me as the sort to heave Zenia Evans off a cliff, not even for a joke. I was tucking into the sole when my mobile broke the cathedral hush. I ignored half a dozen glares and chirrupped a hello down the line.

'Just where the hell have you got to this time?'

I said, 'Me? I'm here. Where you?'

She said, 'I'm home. Where's there?'

Twelve ears, fourteen if you add the waiter's, were tilted towards me.

I said, 'I'm down in the West Country for a couple of days.'

There followed the usual tirade of abuse, culminating in, 'You're supposed to be here. Why are you there?'

I squinted around. The earwiggers had stopped chomping so they could listen better. I said, 'I'm doing a survey on hotel rip-offs.'

Over in his corner the head waiter clutched his heart.

Rosie said, 'Eh?'

I said, 'Give me half an hour and I'll call you back.'

She said, 'Missing you.'

'Me too.'

Rosie said, 'No. You've got to say it out loud. Say you're missing your yummy little peaches and cream. Go on.'

I said, 'I'm missing my yummy little peaches and cream. And you too.'

She ripped off a dirty laugh and raspberried a kiss down the line. We all got back to our chomping.

I polished off the venison pie and drained the Burgundy. It tasted different from the stuff you get in Hamptons. Sometimes I have this suspicion that

Hamptons' drinks are sponsored by Alcoholics Anonymous.

I scampered up to my room, sprung a miniature from the minibar and rang Battersea. Rosie plucked up the phone and whooped, 'Hiya!'

I propped myself against the pillows and let her warble on about the dips and dunes of her day. I puffed two Bensons all the way through before she wound up the monologue. 'So,' she said, 'tell me what getting you're up to.'

About forty units a day, I suppose. I just rattled on a bit about news stories and assorted friends and enemies.

Rosie said, 'Are you still doing this Henry Lodge thing?'

'Howard Lanche. Yeh. But you don't want to hear about it.'

I was right there. She said, 'When are you coming back, then – tomorrow?'

If only. I broke it gently. 'It might take a bit longer.'

'How long?'

I said, 'Thursday, maybe Friday.' That was wiser than saying I hadn't the faintest.

She snorted. 'Why is it always you?'

Rosie thinks she's the only person allowed to pull my strings.

I said, 'This looks like a murder. I expect they would have sent the cookery editor or the political cartoonist, but they were both busy, so I got landed with it instead. And I'm stuck with it.'

There was silence at both ends. When she spoke again her voice was flatter. I could just see her smoky grey-blue eyes, only now there wasn't much blue in them. She said, 'I was really looking forward to seeing you again.'

'Likewise. Maybe you should have come back a week earlier.'

Rosie ignored that one. She said, 'I've got an idea.'

She said it in that giveaway voice which told me it was a rotten idea. I held my breath and waited for it.

'If you can't get back to London, why don't I go down there and join you?'

She must have been at the gin already.

I said, 'No. Absolutely and definitely no.'

'Why not?'

'Because . . .'

Because, Rosie, I am a hack, and I'm on a story, and right now it is my sole priority. I thought that but I didn't say it.

I said instead, 'I've got the last room in the hotel and I already have somebody sharing it with me.'

'Who?'

'Frankie Frost.'

'Oh, my God!'

Yes, I thought she might say that.

But she still hadn't given up. 'We could find another hotel and I could bring my work with me so I've got something to do when you're out on the story.'

Rosie is an artist. Not the lonely sea and sky variety. She designs pretty patterns for textiles. Her speciality is little bright-eyed lizards. They adorn half a dozen of my most favoured ties, plus other people's curtains and suchlike. Often she just tucks herself up in her plumpest armchair and trots out the designs in a sketchbook.

I pictured her curled up on the bed beside me,

doodling to her heart's content. It was a beguiling picture. But I held fast.

'No. There's a whole hack pack down here and when I'm not working I'm knocking it back with them.'

She said, 'And Frankie Frost.'

'Yep. He's here now. Want to talk to him?'

'You've got to be joking.'

There was a chunk of moody silence. This was one even Rosie couldn't win. So I skimmed away from the story and turned the topic back round to other things. She took some consoling, and, might I add, it was all one-way traffic. Finally we were mates again and after that we fell to talking to each other in tones which are nobody's business but our own.

I put the phone down and growled out a groan. I felt like Robinson Crusoe on Friday's night out with the boys. I wandered round the room, kicking this and that and thinking about Rosie. It didn't do any good. So I thought about something else instead: the sodding story. All right, I said to myself, let's get this thing sorted.

I floated down to the bar, stopping by at reception to borrow a map of Harding and its environs. It was a large scale Ordinance Survey job, for the hotel was much frequented by fresh air nuts who liked nothing better than a twelve-mile stroll before breakfast.

I retired to a corner of the Saverley Suite, otherwise the bar, to peruse my map and a large gin. Raglan Cove, the scene of the plummet, was readily identifiable. The neighbouring cliff peaked at eighty feet. There was a narrow corridor all along the edge of the downs which was owned by the National Trust. But about a hundred yards or so back there were houses.

I counted five of them, all of them biggish affairs. Half a mile from the cove there was a golf course, but I didn't imagine the late Zenia Evans had been out there practising her chip shots at deep dead of night. Therefore, chances were she was either going to or coming from one of the houses when she went flying. Unless, and this was a big unless, she'd gone out for a midnight stroll in her undies.

I folded the map and scaled the Scarlett O'Hara stairway to my room. It had been a long old day, and a day without point. I sighed a sigh ten years older than me as I poured the last gin miniature in the minibar. It formed barely a puddle in the bottom of my tooth glass. The pillow was propped up vertically against the bedhead. It was squashed in the middle where I'd rested against it listening to Rosie. I sat on the bed and squirmed my way back into it. I looked around this bland room. I was feeling sorely abused. Rosie, I suppose, was part of it, but not the main bit. What it all came down to was the job. We hacks are strange and mystical creatures. Every working day of our lives we have to re-establish our identities. And the only way you can do that is by getting your name splashed across a story. The bigger the by-line, the sharper your sense of identity. For that day anyway. Next day you've got to go out there and do it all over again.

But my name had not been up in lights for a whole week. And the way this story was trickling out it might be just as long again before I earned a by-line. Therefore my identity was getting a bit blurry round the edges.

This is serious stuff, deadly serious. If you don't

get your name pegged large on a story, you've lost something. And if it goes on long enough you cease to exist. I mean I've known hacks go without by-lines for months, and after a while they actually *disappear*.

Next thing is you're standing one night in Hamptons and somebody says, 'Whatever happened to Barney Bilderbonk?'

And no one knows. A collective shudder runs through the company. There is a second of grim and awful silence. And then somebody else says, 'Must be your round.'

We clamour for more drink and try to forget all about Barney Bilderbonk. His name is never mentioned again. But the fear is always there. Maybe someday the hack pack will pause in their gargling and someone will chip in, 'Anyone seen Max Chard recently?'

The glass was empty. I got up and brushed my teeth. I looked in the mirror and saw me glowering back at me. The strip light made a frizzing sound. I opened my lips and my teeth formed a wonky grin. I said 'bollocks' to them and switched off the light.

Chapter Twelve

Wednesday's breakfast at Reen Court came courtesy of the Voluntary Euthanasia Society – a heap of bacon, eggs, sausages and mushrooms fried in 120 proof cholesterol. The dining room, still green, was kitted out with technicolour paper napkins for the orally incontinent. I dabbed my lips delicately and went off walkies.

The sea rinsed its hair on the empty sands. Vast foamy surges bubbled over the shoreline and swept against the cliff. If all this is a mite poetic it's because I was breathing in neat ozone. Also I was eighty feet above sea level. I was on the cliff path. Last night, when I'd looked at the map, I'd formed the impression this was a proper walkway, where sheep might safely graze. In the flesh it was somewhat different. I've seen safer deathtraps. Every tussock of bleached grass was spring-loaded to turf the unwary overboard. If Britain had lemmings, this was the sort of place they'd come for their hols. I hoofed it up to the highest peak (175ft), feeling like Sherpa Tensing's great-grandad. I lit a Bensons and blew smoke into the westerly breeze. I looked around me. Way down the down was the spot where Zenia Evans had gone whoops, wheeee, whump!

My gaze traced the meandering cliff path down

through the bracken and gorse to Raglan Cove. There was the usual police clobber of poles and tapes and KEEP THE HELL AWAY signs to let you know this was where it happened. From where I was standing it looked the perfect place to toss someone off the edge of the world.

But there was something wrong here. It took me a minute or so to work it out. The cliff above the cove was admittedly one of the ups in the downs. But it was the lowest up for miles. I thought of Tony Belker and imagined the spot I would choose to heave him off. I was standing on it. One hundred and seventy-five feet down below me was a cut-throat rabble of rocks poking their noses in the air. I shivered and stepped back from the edge.

I tacked back down the path until I was at Raglan Cove. Or about as near to it as the police tapes allowed. I soaked in the scene. To be honest, it was a nice place to die. I peeked over the rim and saw a horseshoe of freshly washed sand. The high water mark came right up to the cliff face. There were only two small outcrops of rocks down there. I lit another cigarette and puzzled. *If* Zenia Evans was pushed over, the pusher was taking one hell of a chance. The cliff slope was littered with tuffets and brambles and sandy ledges. Any decent stuntman could roll down it without messing up his hair. *If* it were high tide, Zenia's plunge would have been cushioned by a yard or so of water. Unless she hit the rocks. But the pusher couldn't count on that. Or maybe he belted her with a lump of lead piping before giving her the heave ho. I'd have to find out what the post-mortem came up with. I was standing on the lip of the cliff. I raised my right heel and stamped. Six square inches of old England went tumbling down the slope. I groaned. My hopes of a meaty murder story also went over the edge. We were back with the case of the unwary walker. No story at all.

But I still didn't know why Zenia was up here, miles from anywhere, in the middle of the night. Nor why she was 'scantily dressed', as the stringer's story had it. I flicked my cigarette at a passing albatross or whatever.

So much for the path. Now what about the inland side of things. I set off on the roller coaster walkway heading east, away from Harding. I made heavy going of it for leather soles are not the sort of thing you should go trampling about cliffs in. Along the path I passed the occasional dog walker, most of them old geezers who skipped by me like mountain stags pursuing a fast buck. After an hour I crested another lump of sandstone and found, laid out like a picnic before me, the hamlet of Apson. That's what my map called it. Over to the right was a toytown harbour with piles of rust tied up alongside the dock. The town centre was dead ahead. I could see a single set of traffic lights winking halfway down the single street. Before them was a huddle of shops with a pub sign somewhere in there among them. I tripped downhill with renewed vigour.

Apson was the sort of place where everyone knew everyone else. Housewives gathered in clumps to admire the contents of each other's shopping bags. Thickset men in thickset sweaters waited for the pubs to open. Rats. I'd forgotten that civilized opening hours haven't reached this far south. I dawdled along the street looking in shop windows. I was peering through the mock Tudor mullions of J. Thrimble & Son, estate agents, when a photograph of a rackety old house caught my eye. The house, Victorian by the cut of it, had a spire sticking up at one side. Half an hour earlier I'd seen this selfsame spire when I surveyed the lie of the land around Raglan Cove. Pasted beneath the photograph was the standard estate agent's blarney.

'Red Gables,' Maidmont Road, Harding. Gentleman's residence set in 1.25 acres, uniquely situated with views of the coast and downs. Five recep. nine beds. two en suite. Gardens and outbuildings. Staff annexe. Garaging for four cars. In need of some renovation. Offers in the region of £350,000.

Suddenly I felt the pressing need to know more about Red Gables. I pushed the door and a rinky-dink bell rattled above my head. The office was a tight fit for its sole inmate, a well-fed sort dressed like a bookie and squashed behind a desk with his snout in a mug.

'Morning,' he saluted heartily. He didn't say whether he was J. Thrimble or Son. I turned on a silky smile and asked for the rundown on Red Gables. His busy little eyes summed me up. Yes, I looked as if I might have a third of a million to my name. He ruffed through a stack of folders, shooting out nosy questions. Was I down from London? How did I get to hear of him? Was I interested in property for development? Did I particularly want Harding? I told him this and that, which added up to nothing at all. He found the relevant folder and went into his bargain-of-the-century spiel. Magnificent character residence, ideal for conversion to private hotel or nursing home, subject to the necessary approval. I looked at the pictures. That line about 'in need of some renovation' was a touch optimistic. What Red Gables really needed was a dark night and five pounds of Semtex. But I stayed interested. I told him my big idea was to set up a residential arts school where fledgling daubers could stay and learn the finer brush strokes from my staff of ace artists. He said that was lovely. He blithely suggested they could redecorate the place in no time. I frowned and said they were sensitive artists, not house painters. Lovely, he said again.

I picked up an aerial snap of Red Gables and the coast road. I said, 'What are the neighbours like?'

I might have guessed it. They were lovely. Next door was Tom Davies, a Midlander who moved down here with his wife and daughter about ten years back. He ran a garage out by Lomer Cross, wherever that might be. On the other side was Alex Hartiwell, local and very friendly. But then a man in his position had to be friendly.

I said, 'What's his position then?'

J. Thrimble or Son laughed. 'Well he's a solicitor – represents all the important people in the area. But he's also the Labour election agent so you can see he has to keep in with the neighbours.'

Well, well, well. Howard Lanche's right-hand man lived only a girlish scream away from where Zenia plopped. I said without tone, 'Who else lives up there?'

Nell Warburton, an ancient native, with her bachelor grandson, Neville. Joe Capthorne, the butcher, the Jordan House. That was it.

I said, 'Mister Hartiwell. Has he a family?'

The agent waved his hands to reassure me. 'Oh no.

He lives alone. Very friendly chap. Always willing to show a newcomer the ropes.'

I pointed at the bumf in the folder. 'It says, "ideal for conversion, subject to approval".'

The agent waved his mug apologetically. He said, 'The council is very careful to preserve the amenity of the area.'

Never having seen an amenity I looked vague. He elaborated, 'Well, if you were planning to convert Red Gables into a, a what? A night club? Yes, they might regard that as detrimental to the locality.'

'Yes,' I pursued, fighting through the thicket of guff, 'but what about an arts college for residential courses?'

He puckered thick red lips. 'Providing it does not detract from the largely residential nature of the vicinity, and providing of course that it satisfies environmental and public safety criteria, I don't see any reason why they should not, ah, consent to your proposed development.'

I looked relieved. He added happily, 'I would not forsee any problems. After all, they gave permission for Jordan House.'

That was one of the bigger models on the cliff. I said, 'What's so special about it?'

He stirred his coffee with a chewed ballpoint. 'Jordan House? It's a convalescent centre for drug users. *Reformed* drug users, of course.'

I was intrigued. The thought of a bunch of crack addicts snorting the ozone tickled me. My raised eyebrows did the questioning.

He said, 'They are already cured when they come here. Oh yes, the Jordan House people gave the council very specific assurances on that. Besides, it's a church-run charity. We don't even see the, ah, visitors. So you need not worry about finding hypodermic needles on the beach, ha ha.'

He pronounced it hyperdermic. I beamed to show him that was a great relief. We chatted on some more. He wanted me to go out there and then and inspect the mouldering ruin of Red Gables. I said no, mainly because I was feeling thirsty right then and the clock in the corner had just bonged out eleven.

'Fine,' he said. 'How about tomorrow? Say around this time?'

I said terrific, I looked forward to it. He said lovely. I walked out and the bell tinkled bye-bye.

There was a whacking big refrigerated truck parked outside to my left. On the far side of the road was a pub with an open door. I aimed straight for it. I got one step past the truck when a silver Toyota skimmed past, missing me by the thickness of my Givenchy tie. The driver didn't even spare me a glance as he shot off down the street. I stood dead still, one foot in mid-air as I exhaled through dilated nostrils. Then slowly and with great care I crossed the road. I walked up to the bar. The barman said, 'Good morning, sir. Isn't it a beautiful day for the time of the—'

I was in no mood for idle chit-chat. I said, 'A gin and tonic please. A *large* gin.'

I took the glass in nerveless fingers and went light on the tonic. I swallowed half the drink in a single gulp. I lit a cigarette. My hand was not shaking but my brain was singularly stirred. All right, so it was a run-of-the-mill near miss. A genuine accident. Like a soap star scandal it just happens every day. It could have happened to anybody. That I could live with. But what made me shiver was I had recognised the driver who so very nearly killed me.

The last place I'd seen him was up Turnbull Mews. And he was watching Zenia Evans's flat. And that was the night she disappeared.

I lingered over the next drink, pondering deep and dark thoughts. Way up at the top of them was my innate caution of all things rural. We crime hacks have good reason to be suspicious of anywhere beyond the city walls. Innocent folk look at the countryside and see sleepy hamlets peopled with round pink smiley faces. But behind the smiles we see only wild-eyed axe murderers, psychos with shotguns and all the rest. And they get away with it for years before someone says, 'Arrr, why's old Seth always covered in blood?' If you don't believe me, just rifle through the files on the goriest murders and massacres of this or any generation: yep, 90 per cent of them happened way out there where the little lambs frisk and the birds warble sweetly all the day. I expect it's something they put in the air.

Anyways, I'd just been nearly squelched, whether by accident or design. And that settled it. I needed back-up. Besides this drinking alone business was no fun at all. So armed with a sudden resolve, I took myself off to a corner and rang the Editor.

Petra trilled, 'Sorry, Max. He's tied up at the moment.'

Nuts to that. I said, 'Untie him, then. This is important.'

I lit a Bensons and listened to her twitter away in the background.

'Yes?' The Great Man himself.

I said, 'I need a photographer.'

'What for?'

Well let's just have a wild stab at that one. 'To take photographs.'

Silence. Then, 'What photographs?'

I said, 'Sooner or later this story's going to break. The *Star*, the *Sun*, the *Mirror* will jump all over it. And we haven't even got a picture man in place.'

The Editor was stuck in his own little groove. 'What photographs?'

I said, 'Zenia Evans was killed just out the back of a house owned by Lanche's election agent. Lanche was there that night.'

'Good God!'

All right, maybe I was pitching it a bit high, but no matter.

The Editor snuffled air up and down his nose for a full minute. 'The police suspect Lanche?'

I said, 'They're doing door-to-door calls along the road. They've got in a forensic team for the footprints on the cliff path. So far there's nobody in the frame. But if they get to hear that Lanche was having it off with Zenia, they'll nick him.'

The Editor stopped snuffing. 'All right. You'd better have a photographer. But make sure he keeps a low profile.'

He was just about to shuffle me on to Picture Desk when he remembered something. 'Oh, in future speak only to me or Miranda.'

Miranda? The only one of those in our ant heap

is Miranda Briel, otherwise known as Crazy Horse. She's Assoc. Feat. Ed. which means she's entirely to blame for all the dross that nobody reads. It also means she's got sod all to do with us honest hacks. So why was I supposed to talk to her instead of Humpty Dumpty Belker? Maybe he'd died.

Nope. The sad news was he was still with us. But he'd waddled or been carted off to a back room to oversee M-PLUS1, our top-secret masterplan to drum up at least one new reader by the year 2001.

I said, 'Oh.'

The Editor wasn't listening. He just stabbed a button and had me switched through to Picture Desk. They took their time answering. I suppose they were squabbling over their banana rations again.

'I need a well-behaved monkey for an Editor's Must,' I said.

Whinge, whine. 'What's the story?'

I said, 'You'd better ask the Editor. But I need somebody low-profile.'

Picture Editors don't like hacks telling them how to run their show. 'You can have Frankie Frost.'

Frankie's about as low-profile as Canary Wharf but I suppose even Pic Eds need to have their little jokes.

I just said, 'Fine. But make sure he brings his cameras this time.'

I spoon-fed them directions and rang off feeling much happier with the world. I plopped my glass on the bar. The barman snatched it up and suggested, 'Another?'

I was sorely tempted but then I fired a quick glance at him. He had a round pink smiley face. I shook my

head no. He looked too much like a mass poisoner for
my liking.

Frankie scorched into town at teatime. You could hear
him coming two counties back. Just in case anyone
missed out on the grand entrance, he sprung a hand-
brake turn in the hotel car park. I waited for the gravel
to stop pinging off the windows before I ventured
forth.

The headlights of his office motor were still on.
They were sort of reddish. Frankie wound down the
window and waggled his snoot at me. 'Wotcha, Max.'

I didn't say anything. I was still examining his
headlamps. Frankie untangled himself from the seat
belt and came round to join me. There were bits of
grot and God-knows-what all over the left headlamp.

'What,' I said, 'is that?'

He was wearing a happy dippy smile. 'A rabbit. It
nearly got away and all.'

I drifted over to the other side. 'And this?'

'Another rabbit.'

This man poses the greatest danger to our bunny
friends since myxomatosis. There was a bigger splodge
across the radiator. I raised an eyebrow. 'Yet another
rabbit?'

Well, he didn't know, did he? Might have been a
fox, maybe even a badger. The loony grin was still
drooping off his jaw.

I said, 'You don't often see badgers wearing pink
gingham frocks.'

'Whaaa!'

He got down on his knees and started scrubbing

away at the gore and gristle. I lit a Bensons and waited. Three minutes later he jerked his head up. 'I don't see any pink gingham frock.'

'Me neither. I just happened to mention that you don't often find badgers wearing them.'

It took a while for this to seep all the way through from his ears to wherever Frankie keeps his brain.

'You sod, Max. You made me think I'd run over some little kid.'

And why not? He's clobbered just about everything else with a pulse.

I said, 'Check yourself in and meet me in the bar. I'll have a big long pint of cider waiting for you.'

'Cider?'

I said, 'Cider. That's what they drink down here. And you know what they say, when in Rome . . .'

He grizzled, 'Yeh. But the real reason you're buying me cider is because it's cheap.'

True. But I looked hurt anyway.

I was in the bar revelling in a Gordons when Frankie finally showed. He was breathing hard and there was a light flickering in his pop eyes, sure signs that he wanted to tell me something. Now this may sound strange, but it's utterly and absolutely true: when a hack and a snapper team up on a story, the last thing on their minds is the actual job. Heading the agenda is office politics, and Frankie was full of it.

'Have you heard about Belker? He's been knifed by Crazy Horse.' Frankie was lit through with glee, no doubt remembering all those times Belker had savaged his expenses.

In case I'd missed the point here, he added, 'He's

yesterday's man. The whisper is she's in line for his job.'

Rumour is terrific, but facts are what we're supposed to be about. I said, 'Who says?'

Well now it gets a bit murky. But the notoriously unreliable Dep. Pic. Ed. allegedly heard from his shifty boss that in morning news conference the Editor had whacked all Belker's ideas with a ball hammer. And whenever Miranda opened her tooth-infested mouth, the Editor had oohed and cooed. That was the rumour anyway.

I was adding up what this meant to me. The headline item was I no longer had to argue the toss with Butterball Belker. Sounded good. Better than good.

But now my immediate boss was the ghastly Miranda. Seriously bad news. My friends in the Features prison are woebegone souls. And understandably so. You can't smoke round there. Lunch is 55 mins max. Your exes are shaved to within an inch of their life. Then there are the temper tantrums and the public hangings. I sipped thoughtfully. For one ghastly moment I almost wished Belker was still running the circus. For a kick-off, Miranda's not much prettier. She's skin thin, but she's got these twin, yet quite separate, conical boobs. They point at you in a nasty accusing sort of way. Above them there's a scraped out neck and next floor up there's a face which belongs to some other species. Maybe a gerbil. It's puffed out in the cheeks and a couple of big teeth loom over the bottom lip. All this I could forgive, for women come in many and various designs. But there are two inexcusable points: Crazy Horse knows sod all about newspapers, even less about news stories. Secondly, and more worryingly, she'd be marking my expenses. I put my celebrations on hold.

I waited until Frankie had forked down his daily portion of steak and chips before I got round to telling him the story. I opened with the simple stuff. 'You know Howard Lanche?'

No.

Let's start again. I spelt it out as bald as I could. 'Lanche is the local MP. He's been boffing a girl called Zenia. Zenia's just fallen off a cliff out the back of this here hotel.'

'Dead?'

'Moderately so.'

Frankie said, 'So he's topped her.'

'That's a possible maybe.'

Frankie wiped his beaky nose on his napkin. 'Any pix of this bird?'

'Yeh. And they're all in the coroner's office.'

He turned gloomy. 'So what am I supposed to snap?'

That was his problem. Mine was explaining the rest of it. Like, who was the Man in Black? Where did Eric figure in the show? And Abigail? And Lindy Trevett? But I didn't want to short-circuit his little monkey brain, so I enticed him back to the bar where he chucked back cider by the yard and we talked gaily of Belker's imminent demise. It was a cheersome night altogether. We even toasted the Beast's passing. For such is the folly of youth.

But later, back in my room, I returned to the Lanche affair and began pulling it to bits. The big question was who was doing what to whom? The whys and hows would just have to take their place in the queue. I drew up a good guy/bad guy list. Top of the baddies was Lanche because (a) he was an MP, and (b), he was misbehaving like one. Under him came Lindy Trevett, largely on the grounds that I didn't like her and the feeling was mutual. Next, the Man in Black. I added the very vaguest of question marks to that one. So far the good guy list was a bit on the thin side. Well then, what about Eric Shernholm? His track record was less than inspiring. He'd lied to me and to the Old Bill. Furthermore, he'd done a runner when I'd gone to see him.

I lit a Bensons, poured a minibar gin and wedged myself into a squat blue armchair. By rights Eric should be way up there among the baddies . . . I was following this track when my phone burbled. Do you know, it's a funny thing about coincidences: they come when you're least expecting them. Or maybe that's pure coincidence.

A man with a wary voice said, 'Mister Chard?'

Nobody rings my mobile to call me Mister. I was twice as cautious. 'Yes?'

He pondered this a moment. He said, 'This is Eric Shernholm.'

I sat up. 'Eric! I was just thinking about you.'

He said, 'I, uh, guess I owe you an apology for, uh, avoiding you at the Royal Lancaster. You know, the night I checked out.'

'You also owe me a tenner in taxi fares.'

Eric didn't seem to think that was worthy of comment. He said, 'I had to move out. Things were getting too complicated. Did you know – Zenia's been killed?'

I said, 'I was on my way to tell *you* that when you cleared off.'

He breathed in and out a few times. He said, 'Are you still covering the assignment for your newspaper?'

'Still hot on the case. By the way, you said Zenia's been killed, not that she died. What makes you think someone killed her?'

He gave a tense little laugh. 'What do you think, huh?'

I flicked a pickle of ash off my knee. I said, 'I think it was an accident. I think she fell.'

He laughed again with even less humour. He said, 'Maybe. It was a strange place to fall.'

I said, 'I've seen the cliffpath. I've also seen logs that are harder to fall off.'

Eric said, 'I wasn't talking about the path. I was talking about *where* Zenia was killed. You know who's there at the moment?'

'Yeh, Joe Capthorne.'

He said, 'Say again?'

I repeated, 'Joe Capthorne. The local butcher. His house is nearest to Raglan Cove.'

Eric said, 'Never heard of him.'

'So who have you heard of who's here?'

He said, 'Our friend.'

I said, 'Never heard of him.'

This was getting silly. I lapped my gin and waited. He waited too. I said, 'Eric, who is this friend? Why are you phoning me?'

He went into pause mode. I smoked on. He said, 'Do you remember you gave me your word that you would not publish the story?'

I didn't, but I said I did.

He said, 'Maybe I've changed my mind.'

'Because Zenia's dead?'

He said quietly, 'Because I'm missing an Abigail.'

Eh? Now it was my turn for silent contemplation. I said, 'You've lost Abigail?'

He sounded embarrassed. 'She went to see someone this morning. Someone we thought we could trust. She hasn't come back yet.'

I said, 'Could this old friend be one Lindy Trevett of Alreson Avenue, Totten*hum*?'

He was silent, which meant yes, I said, 'Oh dear, Eric, you really have effed it up. Imagine sending a little bitty baby like Abigail up to Tottenham all on her own.'

He said tightly, 'Abigail isn't a child.'

'I *know* that. I knew it the minute you came up with that tug-of-love cock and bull yarn. What I don't know is, who Abigail is, or what she has to do with all of this. Care to enlighten me?'

He went back into his shell. 'Not yet. Maybe we'd better meet.'

I had to strain to hear him because he wasn't putting any inflection into his voice. I said, 'All right, but you'd better come here. I'm in Dorset. Now, who's this friend you say is here?'

He breathed through his teeth. 'You're in *Harding*?'

'Affirmative.'

He dithered. I squashed out the cigarette and gave him plenty of time to make his mind up. He said, 'If Abigail doesn't show, I'll be down. But not yet. I have to return to the States for a couple of days. Where are you staying?'

I didn't feel like telling him that. 'Call me when

you get back. And before you go, two things: who's the mystery friend and what's your number in case anything turns up at this end?'

More shuffling of feet. At last he gave me a 985 number. Ealing or thereabouts, I guessed.

Eric said, 'It's an ansaphone but you can always leave a message for me. I'll keep checking it. And I'll tell you about the friend when I . . . when I know it's okay.'

So the git didn't trust me enough to give me his American number, and all I had on the mystery friend was a promise of sorts. Still, it was something. After that we had nothing more to say to each other so we rang off. I lit a cigarette and puffed wonky smoke rings at the lampshade. My good guys list was still blank. There was stacks of room for Eric Shernholm's name. Just for the fun of it I rang the 985 number he'd given me. It rang and rang until I got bored. The roll call of good guys stayed blank.

Chapter Thirteen

Thursday was up and about its business long before Frankie and I broke cover. We made it just in time for the last slice of breakfast. He covered himself in toast crumbs and blobs of jam before he asked, 'What're we doing today?'

The main event, I told him, was to forage around a battered old wreck. Frankie looked interested. Most of his girlfriends fitted that description.

He said, 'Why?'

Why? Well, the house is next door to Lanche's election agent. It's um ... it's um the only thing I can think of. That seemed to satisfy him.

He asked, 'What are we going to do there?'

I said, 'We pretend we want to buy the place. I've told the estate agent my name is Ed and I want to set up a residential art college. Okay?'

Frankie said, 'And what am I supposed to be?'

That was a tough one. I looked at him in all his ghastliness. Frankie, I should have mentioned, is taller than two supermodels stacked on top of each other. He's also skinnier. After a while you get used to that. But the face and the clothes take a bit longer. He's got a long loopy mug, split right down the middle by a nose that doesn't believe in half measures. And the clothes? Well, you get the impression that somewhere out there is a very pissed off scarecrow.

So what could I make up as a fake cover for him? There wasn't one. I said, 'You're a monkey.'

He knows that but he got aggrieved anyway. 'Is that it?'

'Correction: you're my head of photographic studies.'

He was a happy monkey again. I looked at my watch. In the office right now the dregs of humanity were rehearsing for morning conference and polishing up their smiles. I had just time to call the Editor and give him a fill in, but not enough time for him to ask me stupid questions. He didn't even have time to listen. Instead Petra shunted me off down a siding. It ended in Miranda Briel. Before I'd even said hello she was firing away.

'I need a complete résumé of the story by the time I come out of conference.'

I said, '—'

'And I need it dictated directly to my secretary. Now, what's the line today?'

I said, 'It's still wide open on whether Zenia Evans fell or was pushed. But the police aren't working too hard on it.'

Miranda went, 'Hmm. Hmm. Hmm. I need to get up to speed on this right away, so I'll need full backgrounds on Lanche and his girlfriend.'

There were an awful lot of things that Miranda needed, chief of which was a boot up the bum. But I just said fine, she'd have it. For everyone in the office is careful not to cross the screaming harridan, mainly because there are strong suspicions that Crazy Horse and the Editor often get to grips with each other, horizontally speaking, after three or four bottles. Though if you saw the pair of them it's hard to say which one you'd feel the more sorry for.

Anyways, I got rid of Miranda and rounded up Frankie for the excursion to Red Gables. He wanted to drive there. I didn't want to passenger. So we schlepped down the coast road with a frisky southerly gale ripping divots off the backs of our heads. Meanwhile a neighbourly breeze from the Bay of Biscay hurled salt and seaweed and dead crabs straight at our teeth. Frankie yowled, 'Where is this bloody house?'

I didn't answer. I was too busy inspecting the neighbourhood. I was particularly on the lookout for a silver Toyota – such as the one that nearly did for me the day before. The first des. res. we came to was Jordan House. No Toyotas or anything else parked here. A sign informed: *Private Property. Visitors by arrangement only*. A strip of black tarmac curved away from the road to the front of the house which was largely hidden by clumpy evergreens but I did espy a closed circuit TV camera keeping a beady eye on the comings and goings. I was unsurprised. If I were playing host to a bunch of drug addicts, reformed or otherwise, I'd have electrified fences, bars on windows, rottweilers, the works.

We moved on. Next on the menu came Joe Capthorne's drum, a modern red brick bungalow of awesome ugliness. He had a flagpole minus flag in the middle of his lawn. There were also sad huddles of leafless bushes in neatly cut circles. Butcher Joe's house was much nearer the road and the picture windows gave us an insight into his heady home life.

A woman in her fifties, dressed in something from the Fifties, was toiling over a rubber plant in the lounge. The furniture was generously built and plastered with flowers. We shuddered and kept walking.

A four square house, as plain as a child's drawing, hove into view. This, by my reckoning, was where Tom Davies, his wife and daughter laid their heads. There was a lilac Ford Fiesta in the driveway which I guessed must be Mrs D's. The garden was plain and mostly trim, except for one corner where a rusting child's swing groaned in its chains. Around it were weeds and wild grass. It had been many a year since a child played here.

And then came Red Gables. By God, it was a monster. Sometimes it had three, sometimes two and a half storeys. There was stucco in some bits, bald brickwork in others. A big shaggy fir tree grew dark as midnight by the front door, casting black shadows across the windows. The spire affair was over to the right. It looked as if it had been nicked from a ruined church. A cracked drive wandered this way and that through brambles and shrubs of uncertain shape and size. It terminated in a patch of crazy paving where the accent was on crazy. The steps slanted to the left, the door lintel to the right. A circular window under the beetling eaves glared down on us as baleful as a Cyclops. Frankie sucked in his breath. 'How much do they want?'

'Three hundred and fifty thousand.'

'Pounds?'

No. Air miles.

Frankie was halfway up the drive. He looked like he sort of belonged there. I was lighting a cigarette when somebody coughed in my ear. I turned around expecting to see J. Thrimble or son. Nope. A different bod altogether. This one was in the last throes of his forties. He had a podgy mug with a porpoise smile slicked across the bottom half. The effect was somewhat sabotaged by the permanent shadow of the twice-a-day shaver. He beamed at me through black horn-rimmed glasses way too big for his face.

'Ah, you must be the people interested in Red Gables.'

News travels fast in these parts. I said, 'And you're from the estate agent's.'

'Good heavens, no.' His shoulders wobbled when he laughed. 'I'm, ah, what I suppose you could call your prospective neighbour.'

He produced a hand. 'Hartiwell. But just call me Alex.'

I looked at him with sudden interest. So this was Lanche's main man. The sun was bouncing off his specs so I couldn't see his eyes. Elsewhere there was a general roundness to him which made you think of a greedy guts seal. Except this seal was encased in a tweedy grey suit.

'Stonelight,' I said. 'Edwin Stonelight. Ed will do.'

'A pleasure to meet you, Ed. I hear you're interested in founding an arts workshop here.'

I said, 'It's a possibility. But I'm looking at a couple of sites.'

Just then Frankie came rearing up out of the shrubbery. Hartiwell stopped grinning.

'Frankie, my director of photographic studies,' I announced.

Our new neighbour made free with the hand again. 'Alex, Alex Hartiwell.'

'I'm Frankie.'

Yes, Frankie. We've already done that bit.

Hartiwell was still recovering from the shock but he soldiered gamely on. 'And I believe you're taking a look over the property this morning.'

These country types don't half gossip. I looked at my watch. 'Yeh. Any second now.'

At which point a whacking great four-wheel drive job nosed into the driveway with Thrimble at the wheel.

'Mitch,' greeted Hartiwell.

Mitch Thrimble was hardly the pushiest estate agent in the land. He just sat up there smirking, like he'd come fresh from the feed trough. He pressed a gizmo and the driver's window skimmed down.

'Good sailing weather, eh?'

That was directed at Alex Hartiwell. He shook his head sorrowfully. 'Too much on my plate, I'm afraid.'

Back to estate agent and part-time meteorologist Mitch Thrimble. 'Oh well. Time's a-wasting. Must get on.'

And just to prove what a man of action he was, Thrimble pushed the door open and abseiled down to our level. He had a red clipboard in his trailing hand. He frowned at it through squeezed up eyes. 'Mister Stonelight. Right?'

Wrong. But let's pretend otherwise.

He dug his spare hand into a pocket of his sheep-skin and came up with a great hoop of keys. There was a plastic yellow tag in the middle. The keys jangled like wind chimes.

'Now then,' he said. 'Let's get started, Mister Stonelight.'

But Alex Hartiwell had a better idea. 'Why don't I show Ed and, er, Frankie around? You're probably busy enough as it is.'

I liked the sound of that. It meant that on our trek through the place I just might squeeze Hartiwell into telling me more than he should about Howard Lanche. I aimed an encouraging smile Thrimble's way.

He was see-sawing over what to do. 'Well, I suppose there *are* a couple of things I should be . . .'

Hartiwell said, 'That's settled then. After all, I know the house as well as you do, if not better.'

Thrimble wavered. 'That's a fact, and no disputing.'

And with due ceremony he handed over the keys to Castle Dracula. We watched Thrimble haul himself all the way back up to his cockpit, mainly because the sight of his fat sheepskin upholstered backside was slightly less ghastly than the prospect of Red Gables. Off he roared, waving his mitt in the mirror.

Alex Hartiwell said, 'Now, gentlemen, shall we begin?'

That hoop had more keys than a piano, but straight off he picked the right one to open the front door. He saw that I saw.

'I imagine you're wondering how I knew which key? I've been in the house dozens of times, you see. I suppose I'm almost a caretaker.' Another merry wobble of the shoulders.

He led us at a cracking pace through a stone cold hallway which smelled of paint. We emerged in a clearing. Doors were dotted willy nilly all over the place. Wide stairs branched off to the left. And two storeys above us was a fanciful ceiling encrusted with fiddly bits.

Frankie unhinged his head to stare upwards. 'Gawd,' he said. For he is a religious man.

Hartiwell followed his gaze. 'I suppose you'd probably like to inspect the reception rooms first.'

He prodded open the nearest door. 'The, ah, drawing room.'

He paused to read off Mitch Thrimble's crib sheet. 'Measuring twenty-six by eighteen into the double bay, with original dado and . . .'

I stopped listening. I was smelling and tasting the place. It reeked of too much rain and too little air. But the main aroma was paint. The entire place had just been hit by a SWAT squad of decorators armed with fifty gallons of creamy emulsion. The drawing room was bare and barren. Not even curtains. Only the light bulbs remained in their sockets. Hartiwell rushed us on to the next door. Another big empty barn of a room awaited. At least whoever ended up buying the dump wouldn't need a feng shui expert to help rearrange the furniture.

My mobile suddenly cheeped, echoing like a demented blackbird in the emptiness. The display showed what I'd already guessed. The office wanted words with me. Tough. I pressed *call divert* and stuck the phone back in my pocket. Hartiwell upped his eyebrows at me. I said, 'Nothing important.'

'I receive calls like that all the time. But if you . . . ah . . . want to . . . break off . . .'

I didn't. So Hartiwell continued clippety-clop through the maze, all the while tossing out words like 'charm' and 'potential'. Frankie just shambled along in

145

our wake, knocking bits off things and scuffing the paintwork. Hartiwell led us on to the conservatory, a salutary lesson that one should not have a glass roof when there are seagulls in the vicinity. Beyond it lurked a kitchen with a big black iron cooker and a bigger blacker boiler. But it was lighter here at the back of the house. Someone had even cleaned the windows.

We passed on to a room with a couple of big high windows looking out onto half an acre of shaggy grass. It was performing Mexican waves in the breeze. What with all that grass and the occasional bony tree you couldn't see anything of the cliff path.

'The garden,' Hartiwell said without laughing. He turned away and began wittering on about the room. 'Scrubbed pine floorboards . . . built-in dresser . . . probably make a splendid dining room . . . now, I haven't got much time, so . . .' And away we went.

All the time I was mentally cobbling together a whole string of lies just in case he got around to asking any nosy questions. He didn't. He didn't even look at us all that often. Hartiwell was one of the most incurious people I've ever met. But I was running an eye over him. He had a round head with short grey-black hair clinging to the sides. Up on top there just a shiny dome. He talked with a built-in chuckle and his eyebrows did a lot of exercising. There was an odd softness about him. I got the feeling he was a bachelor in the gossip columnist sense of the word.

We left the scrubbed pine and creaked all the way up to the second-floor landing before Hartiwell ran out of wind. I supposed it was time I started working. I said, 'Who lived here before?'

'The previous occupants?' Puff, puff. 'They lived

146

here for about two years. Strange people. Didn't see much of them.'

'That's strange?'

'Yes. Indeed. There was an elderly chap, and then his son and daughter, or they might have been a married couple. And then there were always people coming or going. They never had much to do with anyone else.'

I said, 'A bit like Tom Davies.'

'What? Oh yes. Tom . . . he lives next door,' his voice trailed away.

I said, 'What did the people who were here do? What sort of work?'

He fiddled with the crossbar of his specs. 'They didn't encourage callers. Joe Capthorne always said they were dope smugglers. But Joe never thinks before he opens his mouth.'

I said, 'Why drug smugglers?'

Hartiwell wrinkled up his nose. 'Probably because of all the comings and goings, or perhaps because they didn't fit in with the community. But you mustn't pay any attention to what Joe says.'

I said, 'What does Joe say about Tom Davies?'

Hartiwell had turned round. When he turned back to face me the rubber smile was still in place. He said, 'Ah, Tom. Yes.'

I waited. He let the pause hang there for a clean five seconds. Then he said, 'Tom's the enemy, you know.'

No. I didn't. I just stood looking dumb and waiting for the rest.

'He's a *Tory*.'

Big deal. I thought they all were now.

I said, 'And what else?'

Mock outrage from our neighbourhood dolphin. 'Isn't that enough? It's enough for me, I'm afraid. But Tom's also an incomer, not a Harding man. Nothing wrong with that of course, but he seems to have a chip on his shoulder. Not an easy man to warm to.'

Frankie was bored with the conversation, and who would blame him. He wandered off, tossing me an inscrutable look which I interpreted as, 'I'm getting thirsty.'

Hartiwell was warming up for a fresh charge through the bedrooms when I slowed him down. 'Where have they gone?'

'Who?'

'The people who lived here.'

Hartiwell flapped a vague arm. 'Up north, I expect.'

Well they couldn't have gone down south without falling in the Channel so that made sense.

I said, 'Why are they selling the house?'

He was twitching to move on. 'I don't understand what you mean.'

I thought it was a simple enough question, even for an election agent. I said it again.

Hartiwell rolled merry eyes. 'Oh no. They're not the vendors. They just took out a lease on Red Gables. But they've done all this painting.'

I said, 'It's a pity they didn't take a paintbrush to the outside.'

He jerked his chin up and down. 'Yes. Yes *indeed*. That's partly why the vendor has put the house on the market. He lived here about twelve years ago and ever since then he has leased it out, to a variety of tenants. But one finds that sometimes the lessee does not live

148

up to the terms of the tenancy agreement. Sometimes they even neglect their financial commitments.'

'They did a moonlight flit,' I translated.

Hartiwell pushed out his bottom lip. He didn't want to talk about them.

I said, 'So who is the seller?'

'Didn't you know? I thought Mitch would have told you. It's our local MP – Howard Lanche.'

Lanche!

Well stone the crows and other fine phrases. So Howard Lanche owned a house on the cliff; a house with a bird's eye view of Zenia Evans's stepping stone to eternity. My eyes popped; my jaw dropped. Fortunately Hartiwell was rambling on about the architrave and didn't notice. I padded after him through three or four rooms without hearing a single word he said. All the time I was picturing Zenia Evans's last assignation with her lover under the bald glow of a light bulb in a room as romantic as a morgue. I was still musing thus when Frankie came up and poked me in the back.

'I've found the door that leads to the tower,' he announced. 'But it's locked.'

Hartiwell said, 'Not for long.'

He peeled off down a side corridor, so narrow we had to hoof it after him in single file. The procession was rudely interrupted when my bleep gave voice. Miranda Bloody Briel. Her message ran: *call me ASAP.* I could think of many worse things to call her, but she'd just have to wait. Onward down the corridor until we came to an abrupt halt at a plain wooden door. Somebody had splashed paint stripper over it but you could still see traces of mud-brown varnish. Out came Hartiwell's monster key-ring again. A key that belonged in a Frankenstein movie was produced and hey presto, the door opened. We took a quick step forward and an even quicker step back. In there was half the garbage of the western world. You couldn't make out the room's dimensions because of the packing cases, a scrap-metal bedstead and piles of yellowed newspapers stacked all over the place.

Frankie said, 'What a tip.'

Yeh. Just like the inside of his car.

Hartiwell said, 'The tenants appear to have used it as a lumber room unfortunately. It's all their old junk. But you could probably make it into a . . .'

The other two hung back. I went straight in. For this is where I differ from humankind. I love rubbish. Many a dustbin have I hoked through in my squalid trade, and many a page lead have I found therein. So I trawled the room with a connoisseur's eye. In the gloom of a forty-watt bulb it took a while to make out what was what. The room was hexagonal in shape and about sixteen feet across. I took a slow sweep from left to right. There was the torn carcass of what once might have been a kitchen dresser, then a yellowed enamel wash tub with a crank-up mangle atop, tea chests, a crate full of wine bottles (empty), a stack of magazines from the year dot, an olive drab sleeping bag, matted blankets splattered with white paint, a drunken standard lamp with its shade tilted rakishly, more tea chests, the skeletal bed and its steel-sprung base, a rusted tin bath, a cracked and spotty mirror, a box of junk labelled FRAGILE, a discarded Camping Gaz cylinder, an elderly gas cooker sporting more chips than it ever cooked, a leaning tower of papers, empty paint tins, a dead wireless, another tea chest.

Behind me Hartiwell said, 'But it *does* have the most wonderful view.'

Eh? I looked around. The place didn't even have a window.

He came to the rescue. 'The window is directly facing you.'

Maybe I don't eat enough carrots. Half a sec. There *was* something over there. A plain rectangle of slightly lighter gloom. I made myself as skinny as a snake and threaded through the canyons of junk. The window had a three-inch deep veneer of dust and gloop. I picked up an ancient newspaper and scrubbed a peep hole in the centre of the glass. It was still murky but at least I could make out daylight.

I peered down through the cobwebs and dead flies. The window looked out south across the downs. You could see the cliff path swooping and soaring towards Harding. Dogs flounced through the tall grass. Walkers crested the brows, their heads turned seawards.

You can only watch cliff-top strollers for a certain time before the pleasure palls. I gave it maybe ten seconds. I turned around and surveyed the room from this side. It was largely as viewed before only with the added bonus of having Hartiwell's round head poking up above the bedstead. I took a glance under the bed in case the previous inmates had left a pot of gold behind.

That was when I saw it.

I stopped breathing. Way in the background Frankie was bouncing his bonce off the rafters and Hartiwell was waffling on. I stood there as static as the standard lamp but a good deal more sober. I was now looking at the wash tub but without seeing it. I darted another peek under the bed.

It was still there. Half out in the open.

The only thought in my head was that I mustn't let Hartiwell see it. Or Frankie. He'd just go, 'Hey, what's that?'

I came round the bedstead so I was blocking the view. I pointed off to the side. 'You could start an antique shop with that dresser.'

Frankie said, 'Who'd be daft enough to buy that?'

Who cares. I just wanted to get out of there. I swivelled Frankie round and propelled him back across the room until we were well clear of the thing. I zinged one glance behind me. You couldn't see it from this angle. I began breathing normally. Hartiwell was saying, 'It would be a super room, if you cleaned it up.'

I liked it just the way it was. I made a big production out of looking at my watch. I said, 'We've got to step on it, Frankie. We have another couple of places to see.'

As I said it I pulled the door to the tower room shut. I rattled the key in the lock and handed it back to Hartiwell. He didn't notice anything wrong. Off we sped again, this time to excavate the bowels of Red Gables. I let them walk ahead until they were down the stairs and out of sight. I moved back smartly to the kitchen and made a minor alteration to the set-up.

By now Frankie's tongue was hanging out but every now and then he fired a look at me. He knew I was up to something. We eventually broke free of

Hartiwell, but only after we promised to drop in to his place for a coffee next time we were passing. Coffee? Does nobody drink anymore? But I said, yeh, absolutely. Halliwell jangled the keys at us in fond farewell.

Chapter Fourteen

As soon as we were out the driveway Frankie foxed up his eyes at me. 'All right, then, what's the game?'

I said, 'Let's get a drink first.'

He had no objections. We stampeded back to the Reen Court hardly talking. The bar was empty, but for a blonde in an over-stuffed green blouse grinning at us from behind the bar. She was big, in a round-the-world backpacker sort of way. Frankie treated her to his most hideous leer before sprawling himself across a window seat. I suggested cider but he'd gone clean off that. He demanded a large Glenfiddich, no less.

I spoiled myself with a generous Gordons and ordered a double Bells for him. He didn't notice the difference. He blotted up a fair whack of it before he got round to asking, 'What're you up to?'

I said, 'Remember the bed?'

'What bed?'

Back to the start. 'Okay, you know this woman Zenia Evans, the one who fell off her perch?'

I scanned his little monkey brow. No creases. He remembered.

I said, 'The Old Bill found what was left of her and one of her shoes. But they're still looking for her nice green rucksack.'

Significant pause here for dramatic effect. 'Now, just guess what was under that clapped out bed thing in the tower room.'

Frankie guessed. 'Her other shoe.'

You despair. You truly despair.

I said, 'The rucksack.'

His eyes went fuzzy as he soaked this in. I played with my Gordons, waiting for him to tell me what an ace reporter I was.

He said, 'How d'you know it's hers?'

'Because it's green and it's a rucksack.'

More monkey puzzling across the table. Then, 'Yeh. But—'

I shooshed him with a hard look. 'So tonight we go back there and nick it. And who knows what might be inside it?'

Frankie knew. His imagination was already up and flying. 'Pictures. Pix of this bird and the bloke.'

Yes, well, just about maybe. But certainly not the sort of snaps currently being screened in his fevered mind. I let him run with it anyway. 'Could be. She might even have left a suicide note.'

Frankie couldn't have cared if she'd left the secrets of the universe. His brain was still downloading the imaginary pix.

I lit a Bensons and said, 'So we do it tonight. Before dinner.'

'Naw. Better to do it later, when it's dark.'

No way. He'd be half-arsed by then.

I said, 'It's February in London. Even down here it's February. That means it gets dark early.'

'Uh.'

I said, 'So, as soon as that li'l evenin' sun goes

155

down, we lift the rucksack. I've left the back door open. And the door to the tower room.'

'Nice one, mate.'

But he was only saying that because his glass was empty. Tough. He'd just have to buy his own, for I had to go and sort out Miranda Briel. I left him looking for the key to his money belt.

In my room I smoked a pensive Bensons while I worked out what to tell her. There is an old and gold rule about dealing with editors and their deadbeat deputies: Never give them what they want; give them what they *think* they want.

All right. So Crazy Horse thought she wanted a shock horror scandal. And that's what she'd get, with gravy on top. I buzzed her extension, but she was out somewhere topping up her blood-alcohol level. Instead I got her secretary, the beauteous Dani. Dani has melting black eyes with a just-gone-midnight smile lurking in the corners. The hacks in our place are a motley lot, but we stand united on two points. (a) All News Desk people are utter plonkers. And (b), Dani could steal your breath away. Curiously she doesn't seem to know about the point (b) bit. And stranger still in our game, she's easily shocked. You only have to say bum anywhere within earshot and her eyelashes go all twittery.

Therefore I dictated the memo with due regard to her sweet innocence:

'*Sex pot politico Howard Lanche romped with his sultry mistress in a creepy cliff-top mansion.*'

Dani sucked in her breath and said nothing. But I could hear her lashes batting away like a butterfly on performance-enhancing drugs.

I'll spare you the rest of it because after that intro I got a bit carried away, with lines about wild nights of lust and sexy Zenia hopping off the cliff in a see-through negligee.

By the time I was done Dani was in the throes of post-traumatic stress. But I got her to link me through to Dinesh. He's our token ethnic hack. More to the point, Dinesh is my mate. He gives me the nod when Belker or News Desk are out for my bones.

Today he was bubbling over with hot-off-the-press gossip, all of it on the pasty-faced lard mountain otherwise known as Belker. Dinesh was laying six-to-four on that Belker was heading for the back door, just as soon as they could find a fork lift truck big enough to carry off his stinking carcass.

Joyous news indeed. But why was Belker getting the bullet?

Well, this is where it gets a shade muzzy. The background was that the Editor was running 7 per cent over budget and 3 per cent down on circulation. The previous Thursday he was due to break the sad tidings to the chairman, a man who weeps blood if he loses a favourite toothpick. Therefore the news that his very own toy tabloid was losing an entire forest of tooth-picks by the day was guaranteed to push him clear off the edge.

First, he'd rocket around the boardroom switching off all the lights. Next he'd boot the Editor up the jacksy. No, he'd get one of his creepy crawlies to do that, for boot polish costs good money these days.

All this the Editor knew. And just for once in his hapless life he tripped over an idea. He soft-soaped

Downing Street into setting up a one-to-one between him and the Prime Minister on the dreaded day.

So, when the chairman and his squishy-eyed side-kicks planted their bums around the boardroom table, they found themselves looking instead at Belker in his off-the-peg tent. Everything went as forseen, Dinesh reported. And Belker – oh, you just cannot imagine how much this gladdened the heart – had his rump kicked from here to there and everywhere in between.

But then it got even better. By now the chairman had taken his medication and was back in his seat. He dabbed the froth off his lips. 'Perhaps you would like to enlighten us, *Mister* Belker, on how we are to recoup this outrageous deficit?'

Oh yes. Belker was desperate to enlighten. And that's a first. So he rattled through a scuzzy programme of book buy-ups – *The Coke Walk* (ghosted ramblings of sex-crazed druggie model), *Hell for Leather* (more of the same by sex-crazed motorbike stunt nut), *Bold Front from the North* (yet more tosh from sex-crazed Scots TV weather girl). You get the pattern.

The chairman eased a fraction, most likely because Belker had mentioned leather. The chairman has a certain vested interest in that direction.

But just when things were calming down and all around the boardroom table the nodding donkeys were doodling on their big pads, the managing director kicked in. 'And what do we have on the schedule for news?'

This is beyond all human comprehension, but it's true: these top-floor cretins do not realize that hard news comes at us straight out of nowhere. They actually think we plan it all.

Belker rolled fast on the question. 'We have a three-pager next week on the star stalker, you know, the woman who—'

The MD hacked him down. 'What's in the pipeline on human interest stories?'

Belker opened and shut his fat mouth a couple of times to let them know he was thinking. And I bet I knew what was on his addled mind. Human interest stories. The entire point of *every* story in the paper is they're supposed to interest humans. If they don't, who else is going to read them?

But Belker couldn't tell that to the MD. So in sweaty desperation he began plucking open all the empty drawers in his head. Somewhere in there on a curled up musty yellow scrap of paper was Belker's one and only idea. Ever.

'Single mums,' he blurted.

He might have been speaking Tagalog for all down the length of the table no one flickered.

'Single mums?' said the chairman.

If Belker had the brains of a cornflake he might have noticed a sharpish lift to the chairman's tone. Happily he doesn't. And he didn't.

And so he blustered on. 'Yeh. Single mums. Not about them milking the benefit system and jumping the queue for council houses. That's been done to death. No, this is a *great* story about women whose biological clocks are running out and they're prepared to have a baby by *any* man, just so that they can—'

He stopped himself. Too late. Way too late. And that was the moment Belker knew he'd walked right off the end of the gangplank. For only about six months back the chairman's uglier daughter had given birth to a babe whose father had wisely marked X for no publicity.

There was a long stretched-out silence during which Belker felt his breakfast make a mad bolt for the emergency exit. His mouth was still opening and closing but he had given up thinking for life.

So far I'd let Dinesh tell it at his own pace. And most entertaining it was too. But I'm like any other hack: we love rumours but we need to know who's doing the rumouring.

I said, 'Who's the source?'

Carvell. He's the mega man in advertising. He's got a pushed-out face and a pushed-out chest. He also talks a lot. Which is how Belker's boardroom balls-up filtered down to our level.

I filled in the rest of it. The chairman told the Editor to shift Belker sideways, but not out, because that would mean having to pay him two years' redundo. They'd just make his life unbearable until he got the general idea and effed off.

In the meantime, the chairman invited the Editor to pick some other headbanger to sit in Belker's chair. The Editor said Crazy Horse, though he probably called her by her proper name.

And that brought us all up to date. I asked Dinesh, 'So how's she making out?'

'Doesn't even talk to us. But she's cracking down on the subs.'

About time too. 'How?'

Well, seems like Miranda had ordered them to ease up on the punny headlines. The sub-editors, a surly lot at the best of times, were in near mutiny, and just this once I was almost on their side. Any tabloid sub is only as good as the puns he can come up with. But that was their grief, not mine. I rang off light in heart.

It wasn't to last.

I winkled Frankie out of the bar and we headed for Harding. The main mission was to buy torches for the planned raid on Red Gables, after which we reckoned we ought to check out the pubs. What we hacks call research.

Harding in the flesh was a cosy little burg, mostly houses painted by Mothercare, all bunged together around a mesh of one-way streets. Its pavements were narrow, its citizens were not. This made walking about as safe as bungee-jumping without a rope. Every few yards we had to hurl ourselves into the teeth of the traffic to circumnavigate a stray Hardingite. One in three shop windows sprouted a sign for cream teas. In between there were places selling shells, stones, hamfisted paintings, antiques, sticks of rock and sunglasses. They weren't doing much trade in February. We soldiered on until we reached one of those big red-fronted places that stocks everything. Spades, cling-film, flea powder, fondue sets. Anything. You name it.

I named torches.

Nope. Everything except them ... but two doors along another shop had whole crates of them. While the shopkeeper was digging them out Frankie ripped off a wad of blank receipts. So now we had the torches. But no batteries. Back to the red-fronted place. Yep. They did batteries. But they didn't have any hooky receipts.

Frankie and I were getting twitchy. The whole

point of out-of-town stories is to rack up monster exes. And the only way you can do that is by collaring blank bills. Frankie looked at me and vice versa. There was only one thing for it: we hit the pubs.

We ploughed through three of them before we found this dumpy barmaid who in exchange for a leer from Frankie invited us to help ourselves to all the meal bills we wanted. We hunched happily over our pints. Not for long. Miranda Batface Briel saw to that with a series of snarly phone calls, the general tenor of which was: what the bloopity-bloop did my memo mean?

I did my best, purring sweet words down the mobile at her. And still she squawked. Then I got cheesed off. 'Miranda, this is a hard news story. But if you're not happy with me, why don't you send one of your little feature bunnies to cover it?'

You could hear her biting chunks out of the phone.

There followed a doom-laden silence. She came back on in steel-tipped tones. 'Don't you *dare* speak to me like that. Ever. This is not going to end here. You can be sure of *that.*'

And leaving the threat hanging like a storm cloud she slapped the phone down. I wasn't bothered. Just so long as I delivered on the Howard Lanche story, I was Miranda-proof. But first I had to deliver. I whistled up a few more pints because I had work to do.

On our ramblings through the town I'd stocked up with all the local papers. Now I opened the *Evening Mercury*, thinking that things had reached a pretty awful pass if I had to rely on newspapers for information. The *Mercury* carried a single column story on Zenia Evans.

The brother of a Canadian woman killed at the weekend in a mystery cliff fall is flying to Dorset to formally identify her body.

Police have named the victim as Zenia Evans, a 32-year-old social worker from Edmonton, Alberta.

Her body was found by a local man at Raglan Cove, Harding on Monday morning. It is believed she fell from a 100-foot cliff while taking a stroll. She was wearing only a light-coloured tee-shirt and a black slip.

Damn. No see-through nightie.

A post-mortem today revealed she had multiple injuries, believed to have been caused by the fall.

Police in Harding are treating the death as accidental. However they are anxious to hear from anyone who saw Miss Evans between her arrival in the town last Tuesday and her death.

Det. Sgt. Brian Ames said: 'We believe she was a tourist who may have rented a house locally.'

No mention of a small green rucksack. I flicked through the paper until I ran up against an 800-word wodge of stuff on Howard Lanche: *Maverick MP Set to Torpedo the Spanish Armada.* I took a long pull of my pint and began to read. It was written by one of those feature hacks with a sub's tragic addiction to puns:

Outspoken Harding MP Howard Lanche might be accused of trawling for votes in his campaign to scuttle his party's Euro fishing policy.

But he is quick to dispel this as a red herring. The Labour backbencher points out that his constituents face a net loss if our over-fished waters are further opened up to Spanish skippers.

Now the 48-year-old politician is tackling his own

party bosses and the Brussels bureaucrats in a bid to scupper the Common Agricultural Policy.

In an exclusive interview, Mr Lanche told me why he is defying the party machine to join Tory Euro-sceptics in a crucial Commons vote next week.

He said: 'I have been accused of letting down the Party. But the way I see it, the proposed changes would cause hardship to my constituents. They elected me and I must do my duty to them, regardless of party politics.'

Spoken like a Trojan. There were five columns of similar heroic waffle without anything worth mentioning. Nothing about Lanche's personal life. Nary a word about his late-night romps with Zenia Evans. Provincial newspapers just don't know how to play dirty.

I jettisoned the *Evening Mercury* overboard and embarked on the *Harding and Anson Tribune (inc. The Harding Weekly Telegraph)*. It was published too late for the post-mortem results so it carried only a rehash of the story on Zenia's last trip. A single paragraph stopped me in mid-gulp.

Mr Trefor Hughes who saw the dead woman arriving in Harding (now there's an interesting image) *said: 'I remember she had a green shoulder bag because she dropped it as she got off the train. She seemed to be in a real hurry.'*

I sipped my pint. Why does anybody hurry? Because they are late. You cannot be late for an empty house. But you can be late for someone. Therefore, Zenia was all a-flutter because she was keeping someone waiting. I pictured the railway station car park and Howard Lanche tucked up in his Range

Rover, tapping an irritable finger on the steering wheel. Yep. That was it. She was late for Lanche.

No, wait a minute. She couldn't have been late for Lanche. She arrived in Harding sometime after eight on Tuesday, just about the same time I phoned his Dolphin Square flat and heard him talk. That was no ansaphone.

So Zenia was late for somebody else. But who?

By my side Frankie moaned to let me know he was out of drink again. I pointed out the window. 'What do you see out there?'

He screwed up his eyes and all the rest of his face.

'Can't see a thing. It's dark.'

I said, 'Precisely.'

Duh.

I finished my glass. 'And now that darkness covers the land, what's our plan?'

'Oh yeh. The rucksack.'

We headed for the door with the barmaid yipping cheery-byes. We sailed out. Two seconds later I sailed back in again to pick up a pack of Bensons, leaving Frankie stamping his hooves outside.

I was not at my sharpest. I opened the door and strode boldly out. Next moment, WHAPP! – something whacked against my legs and knocked me into the gutter. I glowered round at my assailant.

She said, 'Oh dear. Are you all right?'

She was an utterly gorgeous Chinese girl in the second half of her twenties. She was standing at the push end of a wheelchair in which an elderly geezer dozed under a blanket, oblivious to the carnage.

'You just came out the door,' said the wheelchair pusher.

What did she expect – the window?

But she looked all set to burst into tears. And she *was* sensational. She blinked giraffe eyelashes my way. 'I'm sorry.'

My hormones got the better of me. 'No. It's my fault.'

Frankie backed me to the hilt. 'Yeh. He never looks where he's going.'

She was still a mite shaky.

'It's okay,' I lied. 'It didn't hurt.'

'But I almost knocked you down. Are you sure you're not . . .?'

'Never been surer.'

I could have stood there chatting to her all night but she remembered the old bloke up front. She touched his shoulder. 'Are *you* all right?'

The elderly party woke up. He was swathed about in blankets and stuff, right up to the nose. I don't think he even saw us. He mumbled four or five words at the girl. I made out only the last one: Abigail.

Now *there's* a name you don't bump into every day of the week.

I took her in lengthways, sideways, but this time it was professional. She was leaning over the old geezer and her black curtain of hair screened off both their faces so I couldn't see anything of him.

But *Abigail*?

How many of them do you know? I knew of only one: an Abigail who was mixed up in something funny with H. Lanche MP, and when she wasn't doing that, was strangely linked with Eric Shernholm, and stranger still, Zenia Evans, who was even more strangely dead.

This Abigail straightened. She was wrapped in a plain grey buttoned-up coat with a collar that made her head look too small. But it was a closely tailored coat, which let you know it wasn't just her face that was a bit special. Back to the face. No earrings. No visible signs of make-up. If it hadn't been for the old bloke, you would have put her down as a children's nanny. Only they don't usually set your pulse a-racing. She squeezed out a soft little smile. That was her way of saying goodbye.

She slotted the wheelchair into drive and aimed it across the street. It bumped down off the kerb, nearly smacking my shins again. The jolt as it hit the road made her passenger's blankets slip off his chin. A street lamp on the far side caught him full on. That was when I saw him. First the pair of big goggle-box specs and then the clipped down beard. I'd seen him only once before, and then just for a stray second. But it was the same bloke. No question.

I watched them trundle all the way to the corner and veer left. I was still standing in the gutter, heedless of the Nissan Micras thundering past me at five miles per hour.

Frankie said, 'Hey, some babe. Right?'

But I wasn't thinking about Abigail. I said, 'The bloke she was pushing; who does he remind you of?'

Um. Father Christmas.

Not even close.

I said, 'How about Moses?'

'Moses who?'

*

The big question was where did we go from here? The assault on Red Gables beckoned, but I was hungry to know more about Abigail. Especially what she had to do with the replica Moses who had made a brief roll-on appearance in the middle of my chat with Lindy Trevett.

Frankie said, 'We find a minicab joint. Huh?'

'Let's follow the Chinese bird.'

He was up for that. He didn't even ask why. But I reeled it out to him as we shadowed Abigail through the streets of Harding. I think he got about ten per cent of the yarn. It was easy peasy following the wheelchair even though I made sure we kept a clear twenty yards behind. The wheelchair bumbled along for a minute or two then stopped while the driver waited for a hole in the traffic. Bump. Down onto the road. Tilt. Up another kerb. And so on.

We dogged after it for the best part of half a mile, with me talking and Frankie asking stupid questions. Abigail stopped. I looked around and saw we'd reached the railway station. The wheelchair vanished into the gloom of the car park. I held back. If we followed them in there they were bound to spot us. The station front was too well lit. I towed Frankie across the road and into the lee of a blue van which carried the motif *J. Capthorne. Butcher & Poulterer*. We hung around peering into the black.

Frankie said, 'They've caught a train. Let's find a bar.'

'Only if you're buying.'

His mouth shut with a bang.

People came and went at the station. There were too many clumps and clatters from that direction for us to hear what, if anything, was going on in the car park.

Frankie began thinking like the tabloid snapper he's supposed to be. 'There must be a back way out of there.'

The same thing was worrying me. I said, 'We'll give it ten minutes.'

It was slightly longer than that before anything happened. In the furthest corner of the car park a pair of sidelights flicked on.

'Is that them?' Frankie in my ear.

It could have been the 5.15 from Paddington for all I knew but I said yes with a quiet certainty.

The sidelights were set well apart, so they weren't on a motorbike anyway. The lights showed no signs of moving.

I said, 'Keep your head back', for Frankie was sticking his noodle round J. Capthorne's windscreen.

We must have waited another ten minutes before the headlights came on and started moving towards us. It was too big for a car. Maybe it was one of those things that J. Thrimble got about in. I took a squint through the van's passenger window. The driver had his full beams on. I pulled back. We could hear the approaching whatever-it-was now. It had a big rumbly engine. I guessed it was another van only bigger than Capthorne's little blue job. It was directly behind our shelter. We crouched beneath window level and waited. A scooter buzzed by followed by a prehistoric lorry. A pause, and then the engine revved and our quarry pulled out of the car park. It swung left. Frankie was between it and me. As it lurched off I stood up to get a dekko at its contents. So did he. All

I saw was the back of his unwashed neck and the corner of something white.

'Get down!' I snarled.

'What for? They can't see us.'

'I can't see them either.'

The chunk of white visible over his head tacked left again and was gone. Frankie said, 'I saw it all right. I think there were three or four of them.'

'And?'

'There was at least one other woman. Older.'

'And?'

'It was a big white van and I think it had tinted windows.'

'And?'

'And? What else is there?'

I blew up. 'Was it a Ford? Was it a Ferrari? Was it a fire engine? Did it, by any wild stretch of the imagination, have a number plate? And did you, by any even wilder stretch, get its number?'

He said, 'No. But the Chinese bird was driving.'

Chapter Fifteen

And so to the house of ill-repair, also known as Red
Gables. We hunted down a minicabbie and got him to
drive us back to Reen Court, for Frankie wanted to tool
himself up with all his cameras. In the cab I took him
through it again. This time he remembered the van
was really a minibus. No markings. No helpful hints.
It was still white and he was still sure there were three
people behind its tinted glass. Might have been four. I
rolled my eyes and lit a Bensons.

The driver said, 'This is a non-smoking cab.'

'In which case this is a non-tipping passenger.'

He went into a huff and spoke no more, which is
how I like my cabbies.

Back at the hotel there were two messages
awaiting, both from Crazy Horse. She wanted me to
call. It was seven thirty, give or take a minute, which
meant she was now biting the necks off bottles in
some cruddy bar. She could keep until morning. I took
a shower to get my faculties chrome-polished again.
Frankie hammered on the door.

'Ready?'

I told him to go treat himself to a drink because I
was on the phone to the office. I was only half-lying.
I was on the phone all right, but at the other end

was Rosie. To my utter amazement she was actually interested in the Howard Lanche story. I suppose it's the way I tell them.

She said, 'You think Zenia was staying there, in the attic?'

'The tower room.'

Even from a hundred miles away I could picture Rosie curled up on the sofa, twisting tendrils of bluey-black hair into corkscrews. Maybe she was in her bathrobe . . . maybe she was . . . oh dear, oh dear. This imagination of mine was cruel beyond belief.

Rosie said, 'Why was she down there? You said he was still in London.'

A tricky one that. I said, 'Forget Lanche for a moment. Maybe Zenia came to see his wife. She's called Leonora by the way, and she's a real tough egg.'

'Why did she want to do that?'

How come you can never tell a woman a story without her firing off questions every time you hit a comma? I once asked her and she said, 'Do we?'

I said, 'All right. Just picture it like this: Zenia is having a real humdinger of an affair with Lanche. They can't keep their sticky little mitts off each other. Zenia wants to be his own little lychee fruit for ever and ever. But there's one problem . . .'

'Leonora,' guessed Rosie.

' . . . who doesn't even know her husband is putting it about. So Zenia turns up in Harding to break it gently to Leonora. God knows how Zenia pitched it, but they agree to meet in the old house.'

Rosie jumped in, 'And Leonora kills her.'

'Not exactly. But they have a barney. Leonora throws a wobbly, Zenia comes out with all the dirt. The

172

secret assignations, the candle-lit suppers, the nights of bestial passion . . .'

Rosie ripped out a dirty laugh.

' . . . bestial passion,' I repeated sternly. 'Whereupon Leonora turfs a tea chest at her and Zenia storms off along the cliff path, hotly pursued by Leonora. They tussle on the edge of the cliff. "He's mine, all mine," shrieks Zenia. Leonora says, "Go take a flying jump." And either she pitches her rival over the edge . . .'

'Or?'

'Or Zenia takes a step backwards and saves her the bother.'

Rosie said, 'You should write fiction.'

'I usually do.'

She said, 'What about Abigail? Just say *she* was the mistress?'

That's one I hadn't thought of. And one I didn't intend to think about now, for the minutes were clicking away and I still had a house to pillage. So I signed off with all the usual and went to round up Frankie.

We took the cliff path. Most of the time we weren't even on the path because it veered too close to the edge. The wind sang through our teeth. I didn't want to use the torches so we reeled about like a pair of first-time drinkers, tripping over our own feet. After five minutes we'd gone maybe a hundred yards. My right hand was cut by an amorous bramble. Frankie was swearing fit to bust. I said, 'Sod it. There's got to be a better way.'

Frankie howled, 'What?'

We turned back and did the sensible thing. We took

the main road. The pubs hadn't shut yet so there was only a sprinkling of traffic. We kept our collars up, chins on our chests. You'd never seen anything so suspicious. We passed Jordan House. A heavily sedated light spread a pool of yellow around its front door. Otherwise the place was comatose. Joe Capthorne's bungalow was similarly asleep, but next door Tom Davies's place was positively festive with a brightly-lit lounge and a glow from an upstairs bedroom. I elbowed Frankie. 'Look. Remember that?' For there in the driveway was parked Joe Capthorne's blue van, the very one we hid behind at the station. I wondered briefly what it was doing in Tom Davies's drive. Then Red Gables loomed up out of the night and I forgot all about it. We sneaked up the drunken drive between trees that soughed and sighed. If a headless horseman had reared up out of the shadows I wouldn't have been at all surprised. We skirted the wall of the house until we were round by the back door. The wind was less boisterous here and we were able to talk. Frankie said, 'You don't have to come in. I'll take snaps of everything.'

Since when did he start giving the orders? I said, 'Get your gear ready. We're not hanging around here all night.' That was just to put him back in his place.

The kitchen door was as I'd left it. I pushed down the latch and it fell open with not much more than a soft thunk. Frankie trod on my heels. I turned round and gave him a glare. It was too dark for him to see but he got the idea. I closed the door behind us and stood listening. They say old houses always make noises at night. Red Gables had the whole repertoire. Bumps, creaks, wind whispers. Frankie was all set to

press on. I held him back and tried to isolate the
noises. That one was the windows rattling in their
casements. That one was a dripping tap. And God only
knows what that screek was. It was only now I realized
my torch was not the most suitable tool for the operation. I flicked it on and rapidly flicked it off again. It
had a beam you could spot in Cornwall. Happily
Frankie, ever Mister Mean, had treated himself to a
torch about the size of a Bensons. I was forced to follow
him and his needle of light through the kitchen, past
the dining room, up two flights of stairs, along the
skinny corridor, down a half flight and onwards to
the tower room. Our passage was accompanied by
boinngs, cracks and curious rustlings. By the time we
got to the tower room his eyes were glowing in the
dark. He nobly stepped back to let me have the honour
of opening the door. It yielded with a long drawn-out
wail. It hadn't done that before. I took the torch from
him and switched it off. We stood in the doorway and
listened. All I could hear was Frankie's guts having a
slanging match. That, and the rest of the house kicking
up hell behind us. The tower room was strangely
silent. I held back until I could just about make out
where I thought the window was. I said, 'Stay here.'

I switched on the torch with my fingers clamped
over the lens so that only a shard of light spilled out.
It must have been a trick I picked up from the movies.
The beam showed me the general layout of things. I
kept the torch on for a longish second, memorizing
where everything was. I switched it off and followed
my mental map across the tower room. I got one step.
Bump. Another. Bang. And so I battered my way
through the obstacle course until I walked into the far

wall with a satisfying thud. I felt my way along it. The window was about seven feet off where it ought to be. But I got there. I took off my Aquascutum and felt for a curtain rail. There wasn't one. There was however a handy nail which stabbed my thumb to let me know it was there. I draped the coat over it. I felt all the way round until I was sure the whole window was now masked. Then a tentative flick of Frankie's torch. Things seemed okay but I treble-checked. Yep. That was it. I hauled out my own Batlight and turned the thing on. Frankie recoiled blinded.

Things looked different in the five-zillion candle-power beam. When I moved my hand, the bony shadow of the bedstead reared up on the wall and threatened to pounce on me, the piles of papers tottered and swayed. Frankie said, 'Stop effing about, Max.'

I got down to knee level and placed the torch flat on the floor. It rolled away, clattering against a paint tin. A disgusted tongue-clicking came from the doorway. I retrieved the torch and wedged it firmly in place so that it shone under the bed. There was the small green rucksack, right where it was before.

'Is it there?' asked Frankie, halfway down Tea Chest Canyon.

'Gone. There's just a couple of naked women.'

'Well fetch one out for me.'

I fetched. The first thing I noticed was that the rucksack made tracks in the dust and there had been dust under it. My Holmesian brain deduced this meant it must have been parked there recently. I now had it before me. It was not one of those wardrobe affairs which they park on the back of paratroops. It had the dimensions of a kid's schoolbag. On the top flap was a darker green rubberised oblong which said United Colours Of Benetton. There were no side pockets. Just the main bit and a zip-up front pouch. The rucksack was light and there was a lot of unused space in there. Frankie was bending over me, his knees banging the back of my head. I took a deep breath and pulled at the drawstring.

The first thing we saw was a wash bag with bold red and blue stripes. I handed that to Frankie while I probed deeper. Half a dozen Mars bars followed by a woolly red sweater. Then tights, no-nonsense knickers, a bra (black), a blue shirt with a pattern of green squiggles. A pack of Kleenex, half empty, a hairbrush with a couple of brown hairs snagged in its spikes, a battery alarm clock, thick socks. That was it. I zipped open the front pocket. I told myself, 'If Zenia had any damning letters, they must be here.' Myself said, 'Balls. They're probably all locked up in Turnbull Mews.'

I pulled out a slim black book. Scrawled across the cover in gold leaf was the single word: *Addresses*. I turned to the first page. A bunch of names but nothing that stood out. I flickered through the other pages. I saw Lanche's ex-directory number, and Eric Shernholm's. It was different from the one he'd given me. Frankie said, 'What you got, Max – snaps?'

I kissed the book and rolled my eyes at the rafters in gratitude. The book went into my inside pocket. There were several pieces of differently coloured paper, all with writing on them. They were not our dreamed-of passionate letters – they looked more like notes – but they went into my pocket too. The next item was not on my mental menu: a teething ring, ivory with a battered silver bauble on the end. I handed it to Frankie. His eyebrows semaphored that he had no idea either. But I didn't expect him to. And then there at the very bottom of the pouch I felt something hard. I knew what it was even before I drew it out. It lay there in the palm of my hand, the light sliding off its plastic casing.

'A tape,' said Frankie.

And it wasn't by the Spice Girls either. It was a plain Boots' ferric ninety-minute tape. Zenia, or some-one, had pencilled on the label: 'Howard'. I let out a whoop. Frankie jumped and an adjoining pile of *Car* magazines collapsed and died all over the floor.

He said, 'Is that all? Clear out of the way and I'll bang off a few shots of the rucksack.'

When he was done I moved slowly around the room checking for other signs of Zenia's squat. I found the camping kettle lodged in a three-quarters full packing case. With it were a mug, a tin of powdered milk and a handful of tea bags. No food. She was a tidy girl, our Zenia. She'd tucked all her discarded Mars bar wrappers in an old jam jar. The sleeping bag held a long faded rose tee-shirt which must have been her nightie. I rummaged around for a good ten minutes but came up with nothing else. Frankie in the doorway said, 'Let's go. I'm getting hungry.'

Yeh. And thirsty.

I switched off the torch, retrieved my coat and got out with only minor lacerations.

Frankie hotfooted it down the stairs five steps ahead of me. By the time we made it to the kitchen I was puffed out. I said, 'Slow down. Let's walk out of here like civilized people.'

He started jabbering the minute we got outside. The wind which had been biffy all night now threatened really to lose its temper. It ripped the words from his mouth so I didn't have to listen to him. I hushed him up anyway. He growled a bit but went quiet. I suppose we were seen the moment we reached the front of the house. But we weren't to know that. We meandered back down the drive. We were easy to spot now because we were silhouetted against the grey of the stucco. I turned to look back at Red Gables. Even in the dark it was an eyesore. Beside me Frankie said, 'We have to come back tomorrow in daylight so I can do snaps of the place.'

'Yeh. And I need to put back all the stuff I took.'

We turned away.

And there right dead in front of us a dark figure roared, 'Who the hell are you?'

Frankie yelped.

I was feeling much the same, except I was also thinking. The first thought that bubbled to the surface was: don't say anything.

Instead I opened my mouth and pretended to speak. The dark stranger said, 'Whaaaat?' He had to yell it because of the wind.

So I did the same thing again. It worked. The dark figure took a step closer to hear my words of wisdom. I got a better look at him. I'm reasonably tall but he had the edge on me. He also outpointed me heavily in the beef stakes. But I've got more hair. He had nothing up top except for some very long, very fine strands which originated somewhere behind his left ear and were slicked all over the bald bit. Or at least that's what they did in normal weather. Now thanks to the gale he looked like the Last of the Mohicans with his finger stuck in the live socket. It's amazing how a small detail like that can soothe the nerves.

I screamed back at him, 'What did you say?'

He pushed his face straight at me. 'I said what do you think you're doing, snooping round here?'

I gave that one a second to simmer. 'That,' I said, 'is none of your sodding business.'

He kept his face where it was. I couldn't make out any of it because of the shadows, but I reckoned it was not at its sunniest.

It was his turn to simmer. He said, 'I've got a good mind to call the police.'

Oh, what the hell. Let's go for it. I said, 'You may call the police, but somehow I doubt you've got a good mind.'

Another long drawn-out 'Whaaaat?' But he'd heard me all right. He was working out the odds. He could smack me a belt on the nose. No problem. But standing just a yard adrift of me was a nine-foot high monkey who looked capable of anything. How was the dark stranger to know that Frankie wins medals for cowardice? I pushed the advantage. I went further than that. I pushed the stranger in the chest.

'And who the hell are *you* anyway?' I challenged.

He swung his head at Frankie, back to me, back again to Frankie. He reversed a half step so that my hand wasn't poking him any more. I said, 'You want to talk to us, come here.'

And I turned about and headed for the shelter of Red Gables. Frankie clattered along in my wake, but the man with the questions was in no hurry. I got to the porch of the house, lit myself a Bensons and waited. He was wary as a cat but he came. And he was still a mite narked about something. I got it in first. 'I asked you who you were.'

I could see him better now that we were out of the shadows. Squarish face, heavy ridge of eyebrows, big mouth. He was giving me the full eyeball. If I was a burglar, I was the first one he'd ever seen kitted out in an Aquascutum. That didn't make him any the matier.

He said, 'I don't like people prowling round my property.'

Oooh, hark at her.

Time to change tunes. I said, 'Let's get this right. You're saying you're Howard Lanche and this is your property?'

No, he wasn't saying that. He wasn't saying anything. The ball was still with me. I said, 'So when you call the Law and I tell them you're pretending to be Howard Lanche, you'll look pretty stupid. Do you know the penalty for impersonating an elected member of Her Majesty's Government?'

Actually there isn't one. They just shove you in the loony bin.

He said, 'Howard Lanche.'

No question mark, but an awful lot of sub-surface aggro in there. And that told me all I needed.

I said, 'Okay, if you've forgotten your name, I'll remind you: it's Tom Davies, you live next door, you vote Conservative, and your missus drives a lilac Ford Fiesta. How am I doing?'

'I want to know why you're prowling around here in the middle of the night.'

I said, 'You'd better get your story straight. The way I see it *you're* trespassing on Howard Lanche's private property. That's what we'll both say – my mate and I.'

Frankie said, 'Yer.'

Tom Davies screwed up one edge of his mouth. 'So you're both friends of that bastard Lanche. Might have guessed it.'

I said, 'For what it's worth, I've never met him. But if I do, I'll be sure to pass on your regards.'

'You do that.'

I pulled on the Bensons and studied Davies. I've seen the type loads of times before. You find it in many a hard-nosed copper who knows he'll never make inspector. But there was something else. I said, 'Why all this grief about Lanche?'

'He won't tell you.'

'Then why don't you?'

A slow shake of the head. Davies was winding down. But he made sure he would remember our faces. I wouldn't forget his either. And just as he turned to lumber off, he threw out his thought for the day. 'You watch Lanche carefully or he'll stick a knife in your ribs.'

He disappeared into the wind and darkness. Frankie breathed out. 'He's lucky I didn't chin him.'

Chapter Sixteen

It was half past midnight and the Reen Court was still serving drink and we were still drinking it. There was the fag end of a golden wedding knees-up going on centre stage in the Saverley Suite and no one paid us any attention. We sat in the half moon window seat applying first aid to fragged-out nerves.

Frankie said, 'What was he doing there anyway?'

'I don't know. Tying back his gate to stop the storm nicking it? Admiring his daffodils? Digging shallow graves? Anyway, he lives next door; he's got a right to be there.'

Frankie said, 'Betcha he grasses us up to Lanche.'

'Fifty quid says he won't. They don't even speak to each other.'

Frankie hastily cancelled the bet. We both drank deeply. I don't ruffle easily, but Davies's guest appearance in the night's entertainment must have wiped a good five minutes off my life. And for what? Well, now I knew that Davies had a pretty major thing against Lanche. But that was all. It didn't strike me as a fair exchange.

So I began thinking of other mysteries. I started with A for Abigail. I'd pictured her in many shapes and sizes, from a little pink baby onwards. But I'd never thought of her as Chinese. Or Japanese. Or whatever. That bit didn't matter. The main thing was she was here. And in the company of Grandad Moses, last seen doing Galapagos tortoise impressions in Lindy Trevett's living room. And what was he doing here? Never mind him. Back to Abigail. She was really and truly the absolute business. No wonder Eric Shernholm wanted to keep her all to himself.

I moved on up the alphabet. What does B stand for? Bollocks. I couldn't think of a B word. Wait. How's about blackmail? Now there's a thought. Just say, let's just say Lanche is flying his kite with Zenia. But she's got her own agenda, and she starts putting the squeeze on him. After a while he gets fed up paying out, so he puts paid to her instead. No, he was in London. He gets somebody else to do that. Who? Alex Hartiwell, of course. He's Lanche's election agent. Hmm. That's a bit airy fairy. I'm not sure what the role of election agent entails, but I suspect it does *not* involve heaving your MP's lovebird off cliffs to see if she can fly. So let's leave that one and get back to Abigail.

Meanwhile, and you'll find this hard to believe, Frankie too was doing some thinking. He said, 'That Chinese babe, I couldn't half . . .'

I didn't want to hear. I said, 'Let's take a bottle up to my room and we'll have a look at the stuff from the rucksack.'

But all the way up Frankie insisted on spelling out his foul fantasies. By the time we got to my room I'd gone right off Abigail.

I emptied out my pockets and rooted through the spoils. I put the tape cassette to one side. It was too big for my pocket Olympus which meant I'd have to buy another recorder tomorrow. Okay. What else? Next came the teething ring.

'What's that?' asked Frankie.

I told him.

'Why did she have that with her?' Frankie again.

'Maybe she had toothache.'

'Oh.'

We examined it together. The ivory was yellowed. The ring had four bands of silver spaced around it so that it look like a scaled-down lifebelt. From one band there dangled a two-inch-high yacht. The yacht was bent and battered.

I said, 'It must be a boy's. A girl's would have a pony or a flower or something.'

'Where's the whisky bottle?'

I fiddled around with the teething ring for a minute but it didn't look like telling us anything more about itself so I looked at the rest of our trove. The address book was an old one. But the London numbers carried the new codes. Lanche had a string of listings – his flat, his house in Harding, his office in the Commons and his constituency association. There was a separate entry for Hartiwell with an asterisk against his name. Lindy Trevett was in there along with a host of people who didn't have any second names: Maretha, Paul, Richard, Carol-Anne, Megs, Naomi. That one was crossed out. Most had American or Canadian area codes. There was a fair sprinkling of 213 prefixes which I knew was Los Angeles because I've an old girlfriend with a 213 number.

I pulled out the sheaf of papers I'd found in the rucksack. The first one was a lulu. It was on bonded notepaper the colour of Parma violets. The writing was in black ink. It had all the curves and fancy bits that women stick in. The sheet was headed: *Five Steps To The U.* Frankie hooked his nose over my shoulder so that he could pretend to read it too. Beneath the heading were five single lines:

1. *Seek the powerful*
2. *Serve him*
3. *Sequester him*
4. *Seduce him*
5. *Secure him*

Frankie said, 'What does sequester mean?'

'It means lock away. It's what the Americans do to juries in big cases.'

'Why does she want to hide him away?'

I said, 'Maybe it means to isolate. You know, cut him off from his friends and loved ones.'

'Why'd she want to do that?'

I said, 'They all do.'

The next sheet was a letter written in a sloping angular hand. It was addressed to the Turnbull Mews house and dated 15 February.

Miss Evans, Howard has confessed to me that he is still seeing you, despite my objections. I demand you leave him alone. Yes, we have our problems, but I am quite sure that we will find a solution. Your involvement only adds to my unhappiness. That is something I will never forgive. L.

'Who's L?' from Frankie.

'Leonora. His missus. I don't think it's Lindy Trevett.'

'Who's she?'

I said, 'If you don't shut up I'm going to take that bottle away.'

On the next piece of paper there was a crude map drawn in a felt tip pen. I gazed at it for a moment before I saw it depicted Maidmont Road. The houses were all marked with a cross. The one for Red Gables was circled. The one next door had *Alex* scribbled alongside in bold masculine capitals.

I said, 'Looks like her first time here.'

The rest of the stuff was unremarkable. A train timetable for Harding, a postcard from Montreal with a commonplace greeting, a letter from somebody called Paul who had nothing interesting to add. I shuffled the pile away. Frankie was on the glum side. 'No sodding pictures.'

I said, 'But there's the tape.'

'Yeh. And a great snap that's going to make.'

I said, 'Give me the bottle.'

'I was only saying I don't have any pix.'

'Well clear off to your own room and you can rant as much as you like.'

He didn't wish me sweet dreams.

It took me a while to get to sleep. I thought about the Parma violet paper and its cold-blooded contents. The writing was patently Zenia's. It matched her address book scrawl. But it didn't match my own take on her. I lay there picturing Zenia Evans as first seen. I'm usually not far out on first impressions. She came over as an intense, serious woman with worries on her mind. Hardly the attributes of your average femme fatale. I remembered too her lunch date with Howard Lanche. He was set fast on seeing someone. The other person was a her. His wife? That sounded likely. And Zenia said he couldn't see her. That tied in with the

Sequester him line on the violet paper. But there wasn't any sign of seduction in her approach.

I thought about the letter from L. It suggested that Howard Lanche had bared all to his wife. Her reaction didn't figure. I conjured up our library snap of her. By my reckoning Leonora was more the type to cleave the head of her hubby's mistress rather than send her ambiguous notes. What did she mean, '*Your involvement only adds to my unhappiness*'? And there was that line about the Lanches' problems. So he was going off the rails. But would he confess as much to his wife? Not unless he wanted to wake up dead. Still, married people do strange things.

I reviewed all the stuff we had found. Then I started thinking about all the stuff we hadn't found. Any snapshots or incriminating letters were probably stashed away in Turnbull Mews. But there were certain items missing at this end. Where, for instance, was Zenia's coat? She didn't breeze into Harding wearing only 'a light coloured tee-shirt and a black slip'.

I closed my eyes and thought no more.

Friday morning we shot into Harding straight after breakfast, bought a cheapo tape recorder, blagged a blank bill, and shot right back to the hotel. We didn't even stop for a livener. The maid was in the room when we returned and we had to bite our nails until she'd plumped up the pillows. We chucked her out and slotted the tape from Red Gables into the player. I had my own pocket tape running so I could get a copy of things.

It opened with a harumph, a cough or two, and

then Howard Lanche got going. He didn't sound too sure of himself. The words he used were not in his usual lexicon, you felt. He said them as if he was tasting them for the first time. And this is what he said:

'I love you. I will love you always . . . you are in my thoughts and prayers every night and every day . . . and I know that you do not want me right now . . . but my darling, I want you so much . . . I cannot lose you . . . You may think I have not forgiven you for . . . but someday soon, I pray, you will see that there is nothing to forgive . . . You may not believe it now but just put your trust in our love. I want so very much to wrap you in my arms and tell you how much you mean . . . When I last saw you, you were angry with me. You think I want to take something from you. My darling, all I want to do is *give* you . . . give you the love you truly need. Tonight I sat in my flat and I cried for you. You do not want to hear this. It doesn't help you. When you hear this tape I think you will become angry again, you will think I am rejecting you. My dearest, I can never reject you. You will always be a part of me . . . But . . . you have heard too many lies . . . I wish there was some way I could show you the truth . . . I wish you would believe me. The only thing that keeps me going is the belief that . . . that you will come back to me . . . Good night, my darling. Goodnight . . . I love you.'

It tailed off with a little break in the voice.

I ran the tape all the way through and tried the other side. There was nothing else.

Frankie said, 'He's giving Zenia the elbow.'

'Sounds more like she's junked him.'

189

We played the tape again. From start to finish it ran one minute fifty-two seconds. Not the longest of long goodbyes but there was no mistaking the emotion. I lit a cigarette and scratched my head.

I thought out loud. 'This might be old stuff. When I saw them in the restaurant they were having a bit of a go at each other, but there was nothing heavy like this.'

Frankie had a brainwave. 'Maybe the tape was waiting for her when she got to the house.'

I raised a superior eyebrow. 'And she just happened to have a tape recorder concealed about her person. She played the tape, took it out, then ran to the cliff and slung herself *and* the recorder over. Yep, that makes *perfect* sense.'

Frankie said, 'Still better than anything you've come up with.'

My riposte was rudely interrupted by the bedside phone. Alex Hartiwell, inviting us for elevenses. Personally I can think of better ways to celebrate eleven a.m. but I said all right.

I had just got rid of him when my mobile chimed in. Dani. 'Max? I've got Miranda Briel for you.'

Curses. I'd forgotten all about her. She came on wearing Doc Martens. 'What are you doing?'

'And good morning to you. I'm chasing a woman called Abigail.'

That threw her. 'Abigail who?'

'She's a ravishing Chinese girl who's mixed up in the whole Lanche affair.'

Crazy Horse said, 'The story's dead. Drop it.'

I said what? so she said it again.

'Why?'

Because she told me to, that's why. It wasn't enough. I said, 'I've been doorstepping Lanche night and day. I've been chasing people all over the place. Now you tell me I'm wasting my time. How come?'

She took the soft option all news executives go for when their stupidity is hauled into the stark light of day. 'It's the Editor's decision. We've been sold a pup.'

Not for the first time, but I didn't say anything.

Miranda said, 'Apparently our source added two and two together to make five. There never was any affair between Lanche and that girl.'

I looked at the tape. I still didn't speak.

She said, 'Seems it was all to do with his Parliamentary business.'

I said politely, 'Oh really?'

'Mmh hmm. This woman is – was – involved in social work in Canada. Lanche was interested in ah, ah how child maintenance is collected in Canada. That's all. So I want you back today.'

I said, 'And she was down here to brief him?'

'Just get back here and forget Lanche. It was a bad tip-off. These things happen.'

Especially when you've got people like Crazy Horse running loose. I said, 'And what about her death?'

'How many times do I have to tell you? Get back here *now*. This is one you'll just have to chalk up to experience.'

I'll bloody well chalk it up to expenses. I said, 'Give me a day.'

'You've had plenty of time just swanning around and not doing any work. *I'm* reorganizing news-features, and I need extra effort from everyone. You included.'

I pitched one last time. 'Miranda, I've set up a meet today with Lanche and his wife. If I call it off, he's going to think there's something funny going on.'

Only the smallest of pauses. 'No.'

And that was that. She'd just pressed the Spike button on my story, and it rankled. Somewhere in all this tangle was a thumping great exclusive trying to fight its way out. But we were leaving it there for some other hack to trip over. And that hurt. This was *my* story.

So how could I con Miranda into seeing it my way? The problem was I had yet to learn how to handle her. Now if it had been Belker, I could have snowed him with lies and promises until he finally rolled over and said all right. Belker? Why did the fat oaf have to go and stick himself on the death list? But wait. Time after time I've seen news execs with their heads on the block, only to be reprieved as the axe was whizzing down. And the very next day they were back where they used to be. The same reprieve might, just might, come Belker's way.

Rule number four in the Max Chard book on how to survive in newspapers is Keep Out Of Office Politics. Sometimes I even make it rule number one. But I was fed up going by the rules, mine or anybody else's. So I picked up the phone and rang the beast.

'Yurrgh?'

He wasn't eating. That's just his usual cordial hello.

'Tony, this is Max Chard.'

A longer yurrgh, and one with an extra question mark.

I said, 'I've been called off the Howard Lanche story.'

'So?'

'Well this doesn't make sense. The story's shaping up to be a belter.'

He was very quiet, and that's a new one. I had to kick him into some sort of reaction. I said: 'I'm getting briefed by Miranda, and I'm not sure she . . .'

I left it to him to fill in the blanks. Long stodge of silence and then he said, 'Yeh.'

It was a 'yeh' that didn't mean a thing.

All right, here goes. I said, 'Crazy Horse is rubbishing your story.'

Another 'Yeh', only this time he sounded as if he was sitting up.

So far Belker hadn't slapped me down for calling her Crazy Horse, but he still wasn't biting.

I was moving too fast for him. I said, 'Tony, you sussed this was a big one right from the off. And I've got to hand it to you, it really is a honey. But Miranda keeps telling me I'm wasting my time following up your tip.'

That got him. He rose on the hook, rippling the surface with his flabbety paws.

'She said that?'

My eyes were as innocent as the first day of summer. 'Several times.'

He needed more line.

I said, 'Howard Lanche has agreed to meet me today – it's okay, he still doesn't know who I am. But Miranda says your story's utter balls and I've got to get back right away.'

He went quiet. I gave him yards of time. He came back dripping caution. 'You may not have heard, but the chairman has asked me to oversee a special project. That means I'm on a temporary break from news.'

Temporary? Ha! Temporary is an awful long time in newspapers.

'But,' he said, 'I might have a word with the Editor.'

I cut in sharpish. 'Just one thing, Tony. I'd be grateful if you kept this conversation confidential.'

'This is purely between us.'

I was wishing him an unusually matey goodbye, when he suddenly said, 'And Max? . . . Thanks.'

He even meant it.

Frankie had heard only my side of the action. And it scored a flat *nul points* from him. 'What you doing, licking up to bloody Belker?'

'Wait and all shall be revealed to you, my little chimpy friend.'

We waited longer than I expected. Then Crazy Horse came back on. She was a fraction less thuggish than before.

'Max. You haven't left yet.'

Nope.

She said, 'I've taken into consideration what you said about meeting Lanche today. I've suggested to the Editor you stay put for another day.'

And?

'And the Editor agrees with me. But after that, I want you straight back.'

That was all. But it was enough. I put away the phone and turned to Frankie. I said, 'Frankie, tell me a lie.'

'Why?'

'Because that's what everybody else is doing.'

*

We were late for our date with Alex Hartiwell. Frankie was hell-bent on driving us there. No way. I'd rather be twenty minutes late for Hartiwell than forty years early for eternity. So back down Maidmont Road, where today the weather was merely playful. We passed the Davies abode. Nothing stirred. On past Red Ruins, and there stood the Hartiwell drum. I stopped thinking and Frankie stopped gibbering. Here was a house. A real house. It was tall and handsome and it knew it. The style was pure stand-up-straight Georgian. It was painted a sea-fresh blue, with a shiny dark blue door. A big brass knocker winked in the sun. The windows were floor to ceiling and they looked out onto a clean-cut lawn. We were standing in the driveway with the house to our left. To the right, a solid wall of rhododendrons marched away to the back garden.

Frankie said, 'Wow!'

I merely admired.

He said, 'Bet it's got a swimming pool or a tennis court out the back.'

'More likely a gazebo and a belvedere.'

'Wot?'

'A shed and a pigeon loft.'

'Oh.'

The front door swung open and Hartiwell breezed out on to the step, smiling like he'd already scoffed all the biscuits. He gave us the big hello to let us know he'd forgiven us for keeping him waiting. He was decked out in a rugged navy sweater, with joviality busting out of it.

But the main question booting around in my head was would he be jovial enough to introduce me to Lanche this very day?

Frankie had his own daft questions. He poked a finger at the house. 'Is this yours?'

'The house? Yes, well, no. Family house, if the truth be told. I merely inherited it.'

He went into reverse so we could get into the hall where Frankie stood admiring himself in a mirror the size of Wales. It was a high and lofty hall, a sort of daffodil shade with doors closer to Kentucky bourbon. There were more doors off that hall than you'd find in a DIY sale. Hartiwell pushed open the first one on the right and ushered us in. This, he said, was the drawing room. We looked around an acre of Wedgwood blue and cream and said very nice. He went off to play with the percolator while we took stock. Hartiwell was fond of boats. You could tell that by the gallery of seascapes littering the walls. None of them was knocked up this century. On either side of the mantelpiece there were shelves, packed to the gunnels with fat blue books. They weren't from Book of the Month Club either. Most were thick as bricks with crimped up titles you had to squeeze your eyes to read. *In the Wake of the Clippers: a Master's Journal, Cecil Rhodes and His Role as the Architect of Modern-day Africa*, that sort of thing. Though way up on a top shelf was a thinner volume with a purplish spine and silvery lettering. I canted my head through ninety degrees to read the title: *How to Achieve the Ultimate*. The ultimate what it didn't say.

The furniture had the honeyed look of age. The whole room might have been furnished by the Beeb's period props department. That was what was wrong with it: it belonged to somebody long dead, not the present chubby incumbent. But he had stamped his mark on it with silver-framed photographs by the score. And the funny thing was he figured centre stage in every one of them. In about ninety per cent of the shots he was either on a boat or standing beside a dead fish. And I don't mean a wriggly little trout either. These were things you could measure by the furlong. Some had swords on the ends of their snoots, some had flippers big as sails, and all had teeth like chain-saws. Enough fish.

I looked instead at the general boating shots. Plenty of yachts, right up from the origami school of boatbuilding to a great hulking job which called itself the *Ultramarine*, out of Santa Ana. Hartiwell was sitting at the fat end, roped into a chair and grinning with all his teeth. In the biggest frame of all, was a snap of him and Howard Lanche. The picture was cropped so that Lanche was missing an arm. The men were wearing almost identical sweaters, the sort you wear to go sailing round the Isle of Wight. Lanche was holding a tankard aloft in salutation. Hartiwell was giving out his full 1,000 kilowatt beam into camera. That boat was called, so help me, the *Leonora Floreva*, out of Harding. So much for boats and fishes. What else? Not much. Hartiwell holding a lace-shrouded babe. He looked awkward but the baby even more so. Just one other pic, this time with a dark-haired woman who was no more than passable.

I cast around for anything else of interest. Nothing. I began opening cupboard doors. Piles of papers and little else worth recording. There wasn't even a half bottle of dry sherry.

I closed the last door just as Hartiwell blew in with the coffee. 'Have a seat: sit down,' he urged.

I eased into a two-seater sofa. Frankie sloped into the folds of its big brother. Hartiwell poured coffee, talking all the while. 'Ah, I see you were admiring my rogues' gallery. Sugar?' A nod of his head to the first snapshot. 'My niece, Annie. Milk? No cream, I'm afraid. The chap with me in the large photograph is Howard Lanche. You know, the owner of Red Gables. I'll just put these biscuits down here. Help yourselves while I get Simon off the phone.'

Simon? What Simon?

A couple of minutes later Hartiwell returned trailing a thin wispy geezer with pale hair and flitty eyes. I put him the same age as me, which is a good slice younger than Hartiwell. He was wearing a grey pinstripe with a blue and gold tie over a cream shirt. The knot was tight up against his collar. Maybe he was a civil servant.

Hartiwell patted him fondly on the shoulder. 'Simon is one of our rising stars in the party.'

Simon answered that with the vaguest hint of a smile.

I stood up. 'I'm Ed. I'm looking over Red Gables. And this is Frankie.'

I had to add that because Frankie had a mouthful of Jaffa Cakes and was beyond speech.

A slight nod from Simon. Then he turned away and said to Hartiwell, 'You must excuse me, Alex, but I must call . . .'

He didn't get round to saying just who he had to call, but Hartiwell said, 'Fine, fine. I'm sure we'll understand.'

Another nod from the bloke called Simon and off

he went. Hartiwell lowered himself into a chair, still talking. 'Yes, a very bright young man, Simon.'

I'd just have to take his word on that one.

He turned his goggle eyes on me. 'I can see you're not interested in politics, Ed.'

'Only sometimes.'

Hartiwell said, 'We have a little spot of local bother here at present. Transport and Environment wanted a new by-pass built, but unbeknownst to them, the local people were firmly against it. And as if that wasn't enough, there is now a plan to limit local fishermen's catches. So, as you can see, there's an area of disagreement between the local party and the Parliamentary party, which is why Simon is here.'

I caught only about half of that. 'Simon's an MP?'

'No, no. But he probably soon will be. He's a ministerial aide and is helping to advise on a middle ground.'

I said, 'It doesn't sound much of a rumpus.'

An indulgent chuckle from the armchair. 'Yes, that may be how it appears to those not caught up in it, but it makes my job difficult.'

I was supposed to ask how. I didn't. He told me anyway, 'Anyone outside the Party assumes everything is in the hands of their MP. But more often than not, the hard slog is done by local activists – the constituency secretary, the volunteers, the election agent. And if they do their job well, the MP takes the credit.'

I said, 'I get it. You sort out the messes for Howard Lanche and he gets the glory.'

The floppy tassles on his shoes bounced. 'Oh, Good God, no. Howard is not at all like that. I certainly didn't mean to give that impression.'

Yes you did.

He said, 'But let's talk about something more enjoyable.'

I let him pick the topic.

He glanced across at the colony of snapshots. 'Are *you* interested in fishing, Ed?'

Very. But not the sort of fishing he was talking about. He got up and started drooling over his collection. 'That one's a tuna I caught off the Yucatan. Fill quite a few cans, eh? And this is a swordfish of course. But my favourite is the big shark here. Nearly ripped me out of my harness. Caught him off California. He's a real monster.'

I said um-hum and so forth until it eventually dawned on Hartiwell that deep-sea fishing rates at least eleven out of ten on my boredom scale. He settled himself back in the chair and said, 'But I didn't invite you over this morning to bore you with politics, or indeed, fish.'

I said, 'You want to know if we're interested in Red Gables.'

No. Wrong again. Hartiwell said, 'It's simply that Howard is having open house this afternoon. He asked me if you'd like to come. There'll be lots of, ah . . '

Lot of what? Drink? Women? Dead bodies?

Hartiwell said, ' . . . local people, and if you have any particular questions for Howard, well, I'm sure he'd be only too pleased to tell you.'

Not the questions I had in mind. No matter. Mainly I was thanking the Fallen Angel of Hackery who had fixed up a meet with Lanche without me even having to ask. But I didn't leap out of my socks at the invite.

I said, 'Well . . . I *was* thinking of having a look for properties further down the coast . . !'

Hartiwell hunched forward. 'Why not just take the day off? It'll be a very informal get together. Just from three till seven. I'm sure you'll both enjoy yourselves. I promise you, no sales talk.'

I was still dragging my heels.

Hartiwell said, 'He's a wonderful host. Lots of food and drink and . . !'

Frankie stopped him right there. 'Sounds good. Where does he live?'

Hartiwell said, 'Oh good. I'm so glad you can make it. His house is The Maltings, out by West Kerrow. It's only a couple of miles away. Any taxi driver will know it. Or if you'd like a lift, I'd be happy to oblige. Now, more coffee?'

But I already had all I came for. Anyway, something in my head was screaming for a proper drink. So we got out as fast as we could and made it straight back to the Saverley Suite in eight minutes flat: a new record.

We drifted up at The Maltings a quarter after four. I was expecting a hulking barn of a place, with about a thousand little crooked windows staring out of the ivy. I got the big bit right, but nothing else. It was at most ten years old and you could have mistaken it for a Travel Lodge if it wasn't for all the fancy trimmings and the monster garden complete with statues, pond, and just about everything else. The view too was worth a few bob, for The Maltings was bedded down on a headland looking out on a wide blue sea dotted with fishing boats and the like. By the side of the house there was a whole heap of parked cars, mostly of the

sort you see advertised in the Sunday glossies. So
Lanche must have some ritzy chums.

I was wearing a near-black Paul Smith suit and a
thin grey crew neck sweater. I could have been anything from a rock impresario to a bloke who flogs
paintings down New Bond Street. I could not have
been a tabloid hack. Frankie was . . . oh, let's just leave
that. We put on our best Sunday smiles and bing-
bonged the bell. They were kicking up a fair racket
inside so we hung around shivering on the step for a
couple of minutes before anyone answered. The door
was opened by a woman with a dorsal fin sticking out
of her face. It could only be Leonora Lanche. She was
a tall woman. She looked down her hooter at us. 'Ah,
you must be the . . .' her face puckered in thought,
then, 'Ed. Ed and Frankie. *Do* come in and help yourselves to a drink.'

I took to her immediately. She also seemed to be
strangely keen on us. She pinned me by the elbow
and steered me around outlying thickets of drinkers
and scoffers. Frankie fell behind and when last seen
was heading for a table knee-deep in bottles. Leonora
Lanche sorted me a good-sized gin and tonic before
leading me off again. She fired out the occasional question along the lines of how did I like Harding. She
wasn't nosy. She didn't even mention my professed
interest in Red Gables. She had very sharp brown eyes
and after a while you forgot the snoot and focussed on
them. She gave a running commentary on the passing
scenery. Councillor So-and-So, Mrs Thingummy and
her son Thingy. Leonora's observations were shafted
with rays of mischief bordering on the edge of malice.
'Got to keep Tommy's glass filled: once it's empty, he

starts talking', 'Mind your suit – Miriam's best friends are *all* red setters', 'Meet William. He's a bent cop.'

She left me in the custody of William who was talking through a mouthful of ham sandwich. I nodded yes and no and looked around me. The living room was a split-level job with a massive square pillar in the centre holding up the ceiling. There was a fully-grown fireplace in the pillar with ledges for various artistic bits and pieces. I was standing on the upper level where the wood was ripe as golden Virginia. Downstairs amid the throng you could make out the occasional yard of French blue carpet.

William washed his sandwich down with half a tankard of beer. He said, 'What sort of line are you in?'

I said I was in education management which glazed his eyes and made him not want to ask anything more. I said, 'You're a police officer, eh? I gather you've had a tragedy down here recently.'

'The suicide?'

'I thought she fell.'

William waved his tankard in denial. 'Oh no. She jumped. She was seen.'

That was a new one. 'Who saw her?'

'The husband.'

It was a good gin but not that good. I said faintly, 'Whose husband?'

'Hers.'

'I didn't know she was married.'

William said, 'Two kids. Boy and a girl.'

Light glowed in the distance. I said, 'I think we're talking about different people. I was thinking of the Canadian girl who fell off the cliff.'

'Her? Oh, I thought you meant Chrissie Poulter. She jumped in front of the farm lorry.'

'Aaah.'

'Aaah.' William lapsed into companionable silence. I had to jog him awake. With a helping nudge or two he rattled through the Zenia Evans story so far. He was the detective inspector in the case. His betting was she'd topped herself but the pathologist was . . .

William suddenly went schtum. I reckoned he felt he'd said just a little too much. Maybe I should change the subject. No. This might be my only chance. I said, 'A couple of years back a friend of mine took his own life. It was clearly suicide. He'd even phoned his sister just before he did it. But I remember the pathologist caused the family a lot of grief because there were a couple of minor details that puzzled him.'

William nodded his head in sympathy but was silent.

I said, 'And it all added up to extra work for the police.'

'Yes. Pathologists forget that. What were the "minor details" in your friend's case?'

I said, 'Just some prescription drugs in his system. Nothing to do with the death. Is that what your pathologist is making a fuss about?'

William said. 'No. It's a bruise.'

I looked no more than politely interested. 'A bruise?'

'Yes. Nothing much. Just one that doesn't fit.'

I walked away from that one. I said, 'These scientists have to go through every little thing, don't they? Right down to what the girl had for dinner.'

He didn't take his cue. He just swigged at the beer.

I said, 'I remember reading about this girl at the time, and it looked like a suicide all right. Or I think that's what the police said. Why was that?'

Because Zenia had gone all the way to Harding without telling her friends, guessed William. Because she was out on the cliff in the middle of the night. Because she was only half-dressed. Because she didn't know a soul in the town. Because that's the sort of thing young women get up to if you don't watch them.

I said, 'Don't most suicides leave notes?'

William shook his head at my ignorance. 'That's just something that people say. Chrissie Poulter didn't leave a note, did she?'

'Any idea why she committed suicide?'

'I suppose it was the kids getting on her nerves or something.'

'I meant the Canadian girl.'

'Oh her? Might have been boyfriend trouble, bad debts, a hundred and one things. She might have been barmy.'

'Who might have been barmy?' asked a smooth voice in my ear. I recognized the owner without turning. Howard Lanche.

William said, 'We were talking about that Canadian girl who threw herself off the cliff.'

Now I turned so I was full face to Lanche. He was wearing a convivial smile. It didn't waver. He said, 'Great shame, a young girl like that.'

He said it as if he was talking about a bad offside decision. Not even that serious. It was as if Zenia Evans had never lived. Or died.

William had forgotten my name so I effected my own introduction as Ed Stonelight. Lanche's smile broadened a centimetre. 'Ah yes. I heard you were interested in Red Gables. It's my house, you know.'

I refrained from telling him it was a dump and waxed lyrical about its location, moving on to my grandiose scheme for an artists' colony. Lanche listened earnestly. He studied me and I studied him. I don't know what he saw but I saw a man who appeared thoroughly at ease. No sign of tears here. The last time I'd seen him he was arguing bitterly with Zenia Evans. Now I looked into his warm pink face and saw a different man. It was a good trick. Only a slight hooding of the eyes betrayed there might be someone else in there.

I ran out of inventiveness about my arts college and switched the spotlight on him. 'I believe you're keeping the Prime Minister awake at nights.'

He gave that one a light laugh. 'I don't really think so. Are you a student of politics, Ed?'

I said I wasn't because I felt like telling the truth for a change. But, I pressed, what was all this about a mutiny?

Lanche said, 'It is purely a slight divergence of opinion. I feel – several of us do – that our Community partners are perhaps overlooking our fishermen's traditional rights.'

I said, 'So that's why you're going to vote against the Party?'

A bigger laugh. 'You sound just like a journalist. There were certain misunderstandings. Small things. But they were magnified out of all proportion. There never was a rebellion or a mutiny. That was a pure invention by the media.'

I grimaced to show I shared his contempt for that

scumbag profession. I said, 'So you're going to vote with the Government?'

'Of course. I always was.'

I wanted to steer the conversation round to his wife and family but a tugboat of a woman buffeted through the crowd and dragged him away. He threw me a farewell apologetic smile. I went off in search of drink.

Over the next hour I met more worthies than you'd ever find in the *Telegraph* obit columns. This made snooping tricky. But I spotted Hartiwell and the man called Simon down by the drinks table. Hartiwell was rabbiting non-stop. I switched my interest to the several snaps of Lanche, his wife, his elder daughter, his younger daughter, his dog and various permutations thereof, usually with a boat in shot. I also saw a pic of him and Hartiwell sharing a joke. It was the same as the one that adorned Hartiwell's table. I kept an eye open for both Lanche and Leonora in case either of them burst into tears. They didn't.

I was talking to a rather tasty woman, who patently was not interested in talking to me, when I ran a routine check on Lanche's activities. He was standing by the centre pillar listening to a tall bloke who had his back to me. This time Lanche wasn't smiling. I emptied my gin and said I was going for a top-up. I took a roundabout route so I could get close. I rounded the corner of a stout guest and stopped with a sharp squeal of the brakes. I could see Lanche's friend in profile now. That was enough. Only six feet away stood the man in black, the mystery American who hid in the shadows the night Zenia Evans vanished. The man in the silver Toyota who nearly chopped my legs off. The man who knew me as Mr Tchermak, the mittel European carpet seller of Turnbull Mews.

I executed a swift reverse into the milling throng. I wanted to get out pronto, but I also wanted to watch the body language between Lanche and the tall man. I posted myself downwind of William the Plod and watched through my empty glass. Lanche was nodding his head in slow agreement. He kept doing it. It was like watching a psychotic bear. I guessed he had heard what the tall man was saying many, many times before. The tableau lasted maybe two more minutes then Lanche lifted his head and his smile was back in place. He had found the social mode button again. The tall man put out a hand and touched Lanche on the upper arm. It was a gesture of reassurance, a gesture of complicity. Alex Hartiwell and Simon, the bloke we'd met at his house, rolled up by Lanche's shoulder. The tall man said something to Lanche and he turned and was gone. He had not smiled once. Lanche watched him go. He turned back to Hartiwell and Simon and he looked the happiest man on earth.

I bet I didn't. I was thinking I'd better get out of there if I didn't want the stranger to bump into me and try to buy a rug. I buzzed off to the lavatory, got out the mobile and ordered a minicab as of now. Then I went Frankie-hunting. He was shooting the breeze with Leonora Lanche, or she was doing most of the shooting since he was engaged in an heroic struggle to empty every bottle in sight. Leonora welcomed me with open eyes. I gabbled out apologies, along the lines of important things to do and all that, but thanks for an ace party, see you again, blah, blah, blah. She acted sorry, even begged us to linger longer, but the minicab arrived and that got us off the hook. Her last words were, 'Lovely meeting you both.'

And not many people can say that without laughing.

We made it home to Reen Court and our seat by the window. I was sifting through the afternoon's haul, particularly that line about Zenia's mystery bruise.

Frankie said: 'Lanche makes you feel at home all right.'

'He's a politician.'

He said: 'His wife is a bit of a dog, but she likes you.'

'She likes everybody: she's the wife of a politician.'

Frankie said, 'Nah. She said, "Max is a very enterprising young man." '

'What?'

He repeated it.

I put my glass down. I said slowly: 'What *exactly* did she say?'

Frankie looked at me as if I was one of his dafter monkey mates. 'I just *told* you. "Max is a very enterprising young man." '

'That's it exactly?'

'Word for bloody word.'

I stared at Frankie. He said. 'Satisfied?'

I said: 'How does she know my name?'

His mouth fell open but nothing came out.

Chapter Seventeen

That Friday night while everybody else was out enjoying themselves we stuffed the green rucksack back in its place at Red Gables. This time without the imbecile Davies scaring the daylights out of us. Then back to dine in near silence. I was still chewing over the indigestible fact that Leonora Lanche knew my name. Which almost certainly meant that she also knew what I was up to. And Frankie too. And if she knew, so did her husband. So just how did they come by that info?

Frankie pushed away his plate and burped. 'Want to know something else?'

Why not?

He said, 'Alex Hartiwell was really brown-nosing that skinny guy we met at his house.'

I said, 'Is that a guess?'

'He never stopped whispering in his ear, and you should have seen the way Hartiwell was running around fetching him drinks and sandwiches and things.'

I said, 'I did.'

'Sure you did. Bet you didn't talk to the daughter though.'

This time my mouth fell open. 'What daughter?'

'Lanche's daughter. Great boobs, you could really—'

Fantasy Island could come later. First I needed the unvarnished facts.

I said, 'And her name was . . .?'

Urgh. Faces he's good at, names he forgets.

Lanche had two daughters. Flora and Eva. I tried out both on him. It didn't help. The best he could come up with was, 'The one that's a real belter.'

I gave up. 'And what did she have to say for herself?'

Frankie said, 'I landed myself right in it, 'cos I said to her that Hartiwell and that geezer might as well have been holding hands and she took it dead sour. She said the bloke – Simon, yeh, that's the name – is the brains in some sort of government think tank and he's the assistant to one of the big shots. But I can't remember *his* name.'

'Is that all you have to offer?'

Nope. He had even more useless information to impart. 'Remember that snap in Hartiwell's place this morning? You know, the one where he's standing beside Lanche on some boat?'

I said, 'Sure. And now you're going to tell me that Lanche has one exactly the same.'

His woodpecker eyes were bright with scorn. 'That's what you think. Hartiwell's copy is badly cropped so that you only see half of Lanche, but Lanche has the full shot, showing them both.'

And just what did that mean?

Frankie said, 'Think about it: it shows that Harti-well is big-headed. I mean he cuts half of his boss out of the pic just so that he looks more important.'

You often forget that Frankie is capable of thought.

So in those rare moments when he does come up with something, you take a good hard look at it. All right, this one worked. Maybe Hartiwell was an egomaniac, but that didn't mean anything. We've got a whole office full of them.

Anyway, the only question I wanted answered right then was how did Leonora know who we were. I murdered a bottle of Beaune while I popped it all in the blender. Frankie was shovelling drink back too, but I don't imagine there was much thinking going on. After a while I reckoned I might have it on how my cover got blown. I had to delve back the best part of a year before I came up with a matching scenario. And this is how it went:

Our special investigations unit had been working on a shock horror exposé of a Serb war criminal living in Purley. Two days before we were due to run the story the *Observer* splashed it. They even had the same sources. The Editor called me in and said, 'Somebody's leaked the story. Find out who.' I sought out our primary source, a money-grubbing neighbour. After a few drinks and a fifty quid note he came out with it.

He said, 'Your boss has a big mouth.'

'Eh?'

The tipster said, 'Last week he was at a party and he was boasting to an old mate about the great story he had up his sleeve.'

'How do you know this?'

'Because your Editor's pal works for the *Observer*. Next morning his pal came on and asked me all about it.'

I returned to the office.

'Well?' demanded the Editor. 'Did you find out who gave the story to the *Observer*?'

'You,' I said, and told him how.

Outraged shrieks, protests of innocence. I just smiled to let him know he wasn't kidding me. The Editor blustered, but our hunt for the mole was called off there and then.

I toyed with a kiwi fruit and tried out the big-mouth boss business on the present shambles. It fitted. I could just imagine the Editor showing off at a poncy Islington cocktail thrash, probably to some Labour spinner. 'Believe Howard Lanche has been blotting his copybook, whisper whisper. I've got my crime man Max Chard onto him.' Next morning, maybe that very night, Howard Lanche gets a call from mission control, tipping him off that I'm turning him over. They might even have sent him a snap of me. And that's how Leonora knew my name.

I sighed. It didn't matter who'd grassed. The upshot was still the same. Now Lanche knew who I was, there was no fun in the hunt. I didn't see any per-centage in the story any more. Lanche would play it safer than the Arsenal back four. Anyway, what was the story? That an MP had bonked a girl who later fell off a cliff? A girl with an unexplained bruise.

I hadn't really given the bruise the attention it deserved. Why was the pathologist fliffing and flaffing about it? Because it wasn't caused by the fall. Which meant it was caused by something else *before* she plopped overboard. So ... let's just say somebody brained Zenia with a blunt instrument. That made it murder. And that meant there was still a peach of a story waiting to be picked. But it was going to stay well out of my reach unless I stopped piddling about as Ed Stonelight and started acting like Max Chard.

I growled.

'Wot now?' from Frankie.

I said, 'Lanche is laughing at us. Can you believe that?'

He couldn't.

I said, 'So tomorrow we're going to forget everything the Editor ever spouted about low profile and discretion. Tomorrow we'll stitch Lanche up. And his wife.'

Frankie cranked himself upright. An evil smile fractured his face. 'Yeh. The whole works. Yeh. They won't be laughing when we've done with them.'

Come Saturday morn, and he was raring to go. He drove through Harding so fast I barely remember it. Only a single snapshot of a vicar in a toytown car giving us the finger just because Frankie ran him off the road. Half a mile on we pulled up in a screech two millimetres off Howard Lanche's fancy brickwork. We were both out of that car before it had stopped humming. Frankie already had a slew of cameras hanging off his neck. God, it was good to be working again.

This time I thumbed the bell without putting a smile on my face. I had to ping twice. Leonora, frocked up in black on black, opened the big door.

'Hello . . . ah . . !' she said. She held it for one tick too long, then, ' . . . Ed and Frankie.'

She did the whole routine with lips, eyes and all the rest, but it still wasn't a happy hello.

I said, 'You know my name. And it's not Ed.'

She had the height advantage, standing one step

up on me. She also had the territory. Not for long. I switched round to Frankie and said, 'Snap her.'

Cluck-*zzzzt*-cluck-*zzzzt*! He banged them off so fast she didn't even have time to slam the door. Now we had the edge. Leonora did her best. 'What, just what, is going on?'

I lit a Bensons and said, 'We've got a bum snap of you, because you're all in black and you're against a dark background. But your face is a picture, believe me. It still is.'

She got her various features back on message. She even chiselled out a tight little smile. 'I don't quite know what you're doing, but perhaps you'd better have a word with Howard. Come in. Please.'

She was pretty cool. And that's not how normal people react when I bang on their doors. Frankie was still zinging off smudges of Leonora, the house, the back of my head and anything else that took his fancy. I called him to heel and we followed her through the hall and into the lower deck of the living room. Howard Lanche was over by the central chimney affair, behind a table, which wasn't there yesterday. He had his head down over a pile of papers. Leonora sang out, 'Oh, Howard: we have . . . em . . . visitors.'

No response from the sitting member. She called 'Howard!' again, only this time without music. He glanced up, saw Frankie's cameras and did a double take. He was wearing reading glasses. He put them aside and shot a look at Leonora. She had her back to me so I don't know what sort of signal she flashed him. But he stayed in his chair a moment. When he stood up he was doing his best to act cordial. And innocent.

He said, 'Ah, gentlemen. If this is about Red Gables, it would really be better if you talked to Mitch Thrimble.' He jerked a thumb at the papers on the table. 'As you can see, I'm somewhat snowed under.'

I didn't answer. I went and sat down in a squat blue armchair by the window. That way I could see what both of them were up to. Leonora was po-faced. He was switching from her to me and back again.

I said, 'Yep. It's about Red Gables. And all the rest. Especially Zenia Evans.'

He tried to play bewildered. 'I don't follow you, Ed.'

I said, 'You know my name is Max Chard. You also know what I do. You even know why I'm here. So let's stop dancing.'

Lanche came round from behind his desk and paced out a semi-circle. He slowed to a halt about five yards away, but he had his head lowered. He was working out how to skew the story. Leonora got in first. 'Yes. We knew Zenia,' she said without tone.

This looked like it might take some time. I said, 'Maybe we should all sit down and sort the whole thing out.'

They did, but not until Leonora had gone and fetched an ashtray for me. I don't know what that says about her, but it was impressive in its own small way. While I was waiting for everybody to settle, I was also puzzling: why hadn't they simply told me to naff off? Maybe I'd find out.

I opened the case with the juicy stuff, tossing it directly at Lanche. 'Your girlfriend, Zenia Evans, was thumped on the back of the head and pushed off a cliff. Mostly when girlfriends get topped, it's the boyfriend who does the topping. Or if he's not the type, a jealous ex-boyfriend is happy to oblige. And just sometimes, if neither of *them* are into murder, it's the vengeful wife who goes a-killing.'

I flicked over to Leonora. 'So how about it, Leonora? Did you push Zenia into the ocean?'

She sat there, quite stiff, her hands lying flat on her knees. No expression one way or the other. She said, 'You are typical of the tabloid media. You level quite outrageous accusations without a single shred of truth to them. You cannot print a word about Zenia and us.'

She eased. People often make this mistake. They think they're smarter than us. I showed her my teeth in a smile. 'Here's what I *can* write. Howard Lanche had a long-running relationship unquote with Zenia Evans. He bought her lunch the very day she left for Harding, which, by strange coincidence, is where he lives. The police say publicly that she knew no one in Harding. Yet you, Leonora, have just told me, that you *both* knew her. And so far you haven't let the police in on the secret. Our paper could publish every word of that. Now, what would your average tabloid reader make of it all?'

I waited, but neither of them felt like making a guess. So I rolled on. 'And here's another item which our lawyers would happily let us print: when Zenia reached Harding, she hid herself away in Red Gables, which is owned by Howard Lanche.'

He shot up. 'How did you know where?'

'Because in my spare time I'm the property corres-pondent for the *Big Issue*. How do you think I know it – I'm a crime reporter. It's my job to find things out.'

Lanche breathed in and out heavily. He said, 'You are placing the wrong construction on the facts.'

'Me? I haven't stuck any construction on anything. I have reported various interesting things about Zenia Evans. If you think there's any nasty innuendo in there, you're going to have to hire yourself one hell of a libel lawyer to find it.'

Leonora said, 'I think I might like a drink. Anyone else?'

Just the other three of us. Lanche didn't speak, didn't move, didn't even look my way while she was off unbunging the bottles. Frankie meantimes floated around in the background, taking snaps of the Lanches' snaps. Leonora came back stiff-legged and dished the glasses up on a big yellow wooden tray. Whisky for three, gin for me. They were all hefty measures. Nobody said, 'Cheers.'

I lit up a Bensons and said in a by-the-way fashion, 'How come you wanted Zenia to stay in Red Gables instead of a decent hotel?'

He wasn't thinking very fast. 'It was her choice, though I tried to persuade her otherwise.'

Thank you, Howard.

Now I had a whacking great lever. I said, 'So let's just imagine I run the story: what do you think would happen next?'

Leonora stood by her man. 'He didn't kill anyone.'

God, these people think the law applies to somebody else. I said, 'The first thing that happens is you are both lifted on charges of criminal conspiracy.'

That made their glasses tremble.

I spelled it out. 'Criminal conspiracy to withhold material evidence in a murder investigation. Not tough enough for a life sentence, but it could earn you a couple of years in the slammer. Both of you.'

Nobody jumped at the murder line but Leonora sketched out the defence. 'Howard merely did not disclose that he knew Zenia. And that was purely because of his reputation as a—'

'—He also "merely" said nothing about where she was staying. He also "merely" said nothing about why Zenia was in Harding. Add up all those "merely" bits and it comes to prison. Whichever way you want to cut it.'

I sipped and smoked and let them stew in silence. Leonora naturally recovered first. 'Quite what do you want from us, Mister Chard?'

'I prefer Max. Tell me why Zenia was here.'

'No!' That was Lanche, and just this once he sounded tougher than his wife.

I said softly, 'You sent her to her death, yet you won't even say why.'

'I didn't know this would happen.'

I said, 'But Leonora did.'

She turned her face half away and spoke at the wall. 'You would not understand.'

The one thing I didn't understand was how they thought they could get away with it. I funnelled in on her. 'Putting it mildly, you didn't like Zenia. You even wrote, warning her to keep her hot little hands off your husband.'

Leonora was full-face on again and there was a change in her eyes. She was damn near smiling. She said, 'You insist on making the same mistake: Zenia was never his mistress.'

This was getting away from me and I couldn't work

out how. I mean, I was sitting with enough stuff to wreck her hubby's career and land them in chokey, and she was still not yelling for mercy. So what were they holding back on? But of course, what else?

I said, 'True, Zenia was not his real girlfriend. But she *was* shielding the real one. And her name is . . .'

I can be an awful old ham at times. They were both sitting forward, waiting. I milked it for five long seconds, then I dropped it in, ' . . . Abigail.'

Ha! I'd got them there. Lanche made a 'whoof!' sort of noise. Leonora squidged her lips like a steam press. I rattled the ice cube to let them know a gin would come in handy. There was a dead pause. Way off in the background I could hear the seagulls yarking at each other. Leonora got up without speaking and took the glass from me. Howard Lanche opened his mouth as if to say something, but she nailed him with a look.

So we kicked our heels through another batch of silence until she returned. There was a little speckled jug of water on the tray. Last time she'd mixed her Scotch fifty-fifty. Now it was almost neat. She said, 'I do not know anyone called Abigail; do you, Howard?'

'No.' He didn't look at her.

I said, 'That's odd. Zenia knew Abigail all right. And her chum, Eric Shernholm knew her very well. But I suppose you've never heard of him either?'

That's right.

Leonora was fastened on him. She said, 'Howard, can you honestly say you've never heard of a woman called Abigail. Honestly, truthfully.'

He looked straight back. 'The name means nothing to me. I swear it.'

Leonora remembered me. 'I believe Howard. And equally, I can swear on the bible that I do not know an Abigail.'

Swearing on bibles doesn't impress me much. I've spent too much time down the Old Bailey for that. I just said, 'In which case, this will not interest you even slightly: Abigail is in Harding.'

Lanche popped his eyes at me. But not a flicker from Leonora. She put her glass down and said, 'I quite fail to see what this has to do with *us*. Perhaps, Mister Chard, you might like to tell us a little of this "Abigail"?'

And why not? I trotted it out, keeping my eyes hard on him. 'She's say, twenty-five, or a year off either side. She is in the company of an old bloke who gets around in a wheelchair. She drives a big white minibus.'

Frankie thought it was time he chipped in. 'Yeh, and she's a real babe.'

Lanche was looking at me over the rim of the glass. He repeated, 'She drives a minibus.'

Something was wrong. I could feel it slipping through my fingers.

Leonora said, 'How absolutely fascinating, Mister Chard. And you have seen Abigail?'

There was a sharp edge of sarcasm in the way she said it. She truly didn't *care*. Yet I *knew* that Abigail was in the middle of all this stuff with her husband and Zenia Evans. So why wasn't she fazed? Even Lanche was looking less tense. Why? I hit on the answer right away. Abigail was his secret playmate and he'd clean forgotten to tell his wife. These things do happen, you know.

Lanche said, 'You still haven't told us anything about her.'

Frankie plugged the gap. 'She's a knock-out Chinese bird with big b—'

I shut him up. 'Zenia knew a woman called Lindy Trevett. Don't tell me. That's somebody else you've never heard of. Never mind. Eric Shernholm, whom I've mentioned before, was staying with Abigail at the Royal Lancaster hotel. Okay? Then a few days back she goes to see Lindy Trevett and then she vanishes. Next thing is Abigail turns up in Harding wheeling the old bloke around. And the only thing I can tell you about him is that when he's not doodling through the streets of Harding, he lives in Tottenham with Lindy Trevett.'

Lanche actually laughed. 'What an utterly ridiculous story.'

I wish he hadn't said that, because I'd just played it back to myself and it *was* total gibberish.

Leonora was enjoying herself too. 'Oh, I can't wait to read it in the paper: "Mysterious Chinese woman flees London to push a mysterious old chap in a wheelchair." What a marvellous scoop.'

Nobody in newspapers calls an exclusive a scoop, unless they're taking the mick. So that rankled even more. I fetched out the Bensons again and let the Lanches enjoy their brief moment. Time up. I said, 'Let's forget I ever mentioned Abigail. We're still left with a terrific story, "MP and wife jailed for effing up murder probe." '

Lanche went back into hibernation. Leonora hooded her eyes at me. Somewhere behind them she was figuring the odds, and they weren't all that wonderful. But she was still refusing to call it quits.

She said, 'Mister Chard, you are in possession of a few fragments of what you might term a terrific story. I quite understand that were you to publish these fragments, you would make life rather difficult for us.'

I said, 'Who knows? You might even get to like Holloway.'

She pretended I hadn't spoken, 'But I, or rather, *we*, are prepared to give you the complete story on certain conditions. The first is—'

I stopped her there. 'If anybody makes conditions around here, it's me. And if you don't like them, tough. I just go ahead and run what I've got. Then I tip off the Old Bill.'

She said, 'The first condition, in fact the sole condition, is that you give us five days. A week at the very most. Then, I promise, we will provide you with all you wish to know, and you will have an infinitely better story.'

I had to hand it to Leonora. Here she was with her back hard against the wall and she was still talking terms.

I said, 'No. That way I'd also be guilty of obstructing the police.'

She wasn't giving up. 'But Mister Chard, how would the police know?'

Lanche woke up. 'We wouldn't tell them.'

I skirted round the offer, and I was sorely tempted. Tell any God-fearing hack that you'll give him a humdinger of a story on the strict proviso that he first sells his granny, and old granny will be down the car boot sale in two shakes. But that's only if the hack *trusts* the would-be storyteller. And so far the Lanches had lied their heads off to me.

I said, 'So what is this great story?'

Leonora sliced out a smile. 'Let's freshen the drinks first.'

Oh, all right. While she was away her husband suddenly started talking. 'We are absolutely sincere. I appreciate it seems odd that we have not told the police that we knew Zenia, but there were very good, very *honourable* reasons why we refrained. If you give us the time we ask, I will answer every question.'

I said, 'Tell me about Tom Davies.'

He looked surprised, or maybe just vague. 'Tom? Tom is what you might call a militant Tory. I really have nothing to do with him.'

I said, 'Then why does he hate your guts?'

'Does he? I really couldn't say.'

Yes, he damn well could. I said, 'Have a guess anyway.'

But Leonora steamed to the rescue with our drinks. She was back on the fifty-fifty mix. She was also back in the happy hostess routine of the day before. She said, 'Howard, tell me if you agree, but this is what I suggest: we invite Mister Chard and his er, colleague for drinks tomorrow evening. Perhaps we will be more at liberty to talk openly then.'

Howard agreed. I didn't. I said, 'I've got a mean-tempered boss waiting for my copy. When I phone her this afternoon to say I've nothing to write about, she'll roast me alive.'

Leonora didn't ruffle. 'I'm quite sure that someone as shrewd as you could fob her off with a good excuse.'

That was easy for her to say. She'd never met Crazy Horse. I said, 'Just how big is this story?'

Huge. Absolutely out of this world. At least that's the way Leonora tweaked it. Her partner didn't contribute anything.

I drank deeply of my gin. Hell. I felt like I'd just been dealt a poker hand in the Last Chance saloon and my two face up cards were a jack and a queen. Leonora was showing a pair of jacks. For all I knew I was sitting on a run, even a flush. The smart money was on her hand. I could fold now and take what winnings I already had, or I could hold out for the flush. I am a vain and foolish man. I took the bet. But I hedged it just a little.

I said, 'This is as far as I'll go: you've got three days maximum. After that I run what I've got.'

The Lanches chewed on that while I amused myself with the gin. Finally Leonora said, 'If that's the best you can do, I suppose one must accept. I think we understand your position, that is, with regard to your superiors . . . we can only pray that we are able to meet your deadline.'

And I could only pray I was betting on the right hand.

Leonora said, 'My suggestion that you come round for drinks tomorrow still stands.'

I suppose that was meant as a goodwill token. I needed a little more. I said, 'In the meantime, Frankie is going to take some shots of you together.'

She agreed without a murmur. She even agreed to go off and change into something more photogenic. And after that she and Lanche posed sunnily in their back garden while Frankie squeezed off snaps by the hundred.

That was when I should have known I'd lost it. I'd find out soon enough.

Chapter Eighteen

I'd deliberately left my mobile at the hotel so I didn't get any stupid calls in the middle of the Lanche summit. When we got back, there were messages for me everywhere. All from Miranda Briel. Odd. News execs never work on Saturdays. They just lounge around sharpening their claws for the week ahead. Why was she still on the case? And what did I have to tell her? Nothing. Absolutely nothing. I didn't even have a game plan on how to break it to her. I'd just have to play it on the hoof. I put a call through to the main office number. Some dipstick on the switchboard, unaware of Miranda's sudden elevation to sort-of Exec. Ed. promptly banged me through to Features. My mate Oscar picked up the call. He'd been hauled in on his day off to rewrite some gunge for Monday's spread. He moaned a while about that and then he said, 'Howdy, paleface. Crazy Horse is on the warpath again, and she's after your scalp.'

'Thank you for that, Oscar. You've cheered me up no end. Now, can you transfer me . . . no, wait a moment. Remember when you were doing a profile of that MP, oh, what's his name, Howard Lanche?'

He remembered.

I said, 'Did you ever meet a woman called Abigail?'

He wanted to know why.

I said, 'I'll tell you next week.'

He thought for a moment. Then he said, 'Alibi cooked up in Georgia for the maid.'

Dear God, he must be back on the razzle.

I said carefully, 'Would you mind repeating that, only in English.'

He repeated it. He went further. He explained it. I'll try and keep this short. Oscar is a fiend at crosswords, the cryptic variety. Give him ten minutes of a morning, and there's the *Telegraph* puzzle done, across, down and sideways. Another ten minutes, and there goes the *Times*. But the pleasures of filling in empty squares have begun to lose their sparkle for Oscar. So recently he's taken to making up his own crosswords which can be solved only by someone with a brain as warped as his.

He said, 'You mentioned Abigail: all I did was turn her name into a clue.'

I still wasn't following this. 'I don't get it.'

Patient sigh from him. 'Think it out: "Alibi cooked up".' 'That's a way of saying you mix up the letters of alibi. " . . . in Georgia . . ." That means you put Georgia in. Well, you use the Americans' abbreviation for Georgia, which is . . .?'

'GA,' I said smartly.

'Very good, Max. So now you have an anagram of Abigail. Get it?'

Sort of. I said, 'You've given me a headache. All I want to know is—'

'The answer is no. Never heard of her.'

'Thank you. Now stick me on to Crazy Horse.'

Miranda Briel snatched at the phone. There

followed the usual tirade of abuse and cheap cracks. I let her rattle on until she was feeling better.

I said, 'Howard Lanche knows who I am and what I am doing. And don't ask me how.'

'How?'

I said, 'Doesn't matter. Yesterday his wife let it slip. So this morning I saw them both and asked them all about Zenia Evans.'

Crazy Horse began jumping over desks, 'You did *WHAT*?'

'They both deny knowing her. But—'

'—You bloody *moron*. What was your brief?'

I said, 'I was sent out to get a story. That's what I'm—'

Crazy Horse already knew all the answers. 'You were told that on *no* account were you to let Lanche know we were on to him. How the hell am I to explain this to the Editor?'

With tremendous glee, I imagine.

I said, 'Miranda, they know exactly who I am. There's no point in me pretending to be somebody else.'

'I just don't believe you, Chard. You're supposed to be a professional journalist, yet you cock up a major exclusive. I can't tell you how angry the Editor'll be, but I *can* tell you one thing: you'll be very, *very* lucky if you still have a job tomorrow. Get back here this very minute.'

I lit a Bensons. 'No.'

I had to say it twice more before it got through.

She screeched, 'Are you defying me?'

'You could put it that way. You're not my boss. The Editor is. Or my News Editor, or Tony Belker, or anyone on News Desk. If they tell me to pull out, I pull out. I'm in my hotel room right now and I'll stick by this phone until I hear from someone in a position of authority.'

And I slapped the phone down.

Frankie, who all the while had been lying with his boots poking off the end of my bed, sat himself up and eyed me sorrowfully. 'It was nice knowing you, Max.'

I ignored him. I pulled out the mobile and dialled Belker's home number. Please, *please* let him be in.

This was my lucky day. He answered after only about seventeen rings. He sounded tetchy, snarly, brutish. I could have hugged him.

I went straight into it, telling it more or less as it happened, except every now and then I introduced an evil chunk about Crazy Horse trying to sabotage *his* story. I also took an off-the-wall gamble and told him about the Lanches' promise of a deal.

I wrapped it all up and waited. I waited a bit longer. Then Belker said, 'What is your gut feeling on this one?'

Butterflies, mostly. I said, 'Whatever they are holding back has something to do with Zenia's death.'

'That's not an answer. Did they kill her?'

I said, 'Leonora might have. But not him. He was in London.'

Belker picked at that for a while. 'Max, what I need to establish is that we have a story. If not, I don't intend to stick my neck out for you.'

The fool doesn't even have a neck to stick out. I said, 'They have three days to deliver. If they welsh on the deal, we still have a copper-bottomed exclusive on them keeping information from the Old Bill. What I'm saying is we have insurance. But . . .'

He picked up on it. 'But?'

'If Crazy Horse pulls the plug today, then I won't find out what the Lanches are really up to. Somebody else gets the story.'

I could hear Belker sucking on his teeth. So far all he had done was ask me questions. I knew exactly what was giving him pause: if he managed to win me breathing space, I just might deliver a scorcher. And he would earn all the brownie points, for that's the way it goes in newspapers. He would be reinstated as the Editor's Chief Imbecile, and Miranda would be cast onto the shores of oblivion, otherwise known as Features.

But if I failed to come up with the goods, Belker would be down the greasy pole faster than a speeding fireman smeared with butter.

He said, 'If I were to phone the Editor at home and make a special case for you, I would need your assurance that you will not foul up.'

No problem. I said, 'Have I ever?'

'What about that time in Naples?'

Every time I think that's all forgotten, somebody just has to go and dredge it up again.

I said, 'You have my promise.'

He still wasn't convinced. But by and by, with sweet words and buckets of oil, I won the bugger over to see it my way. This is less than true. Belker didn't care a toss about either me or the story. All that mattered to him was kicking Crazy Horse out of his office. I was but a pawn in the game, to coin a phrase.

I clicked off and grinned at my monkey. 'Come on, Frankie, it's time we had a drink.'

We breezed down the stairs. I paused only to tell the receptionist to page me in the Saverley Suite should anyone call, and then we assumed the thirsty man's position, propped against the bar, waving a crisp tenner. Well, I was doing the last bit. The round-the-world backpacker was playing mummy and she flashed Frankie a big one. I was going for broke today so I let him have a large malt. A bubbling Gordons for me. I suppose I should have been feeling twitchy, but I remember this bloke once telling me never to worry about anything which was beyond my control. Sound advice, that. He never worried about the truck which smacked into him on the M62, thereby ending all his worries for ever. If there was a truck heading my way, well what could I do? So I just savoured the moment. Or more likely the gin.

Anyway Frankie was doing all the worrying for both of us. He said, 'You don't really believe she's going to snitch on her husband?'

'Leonora? He didn't kill Zenia. He was in London.'

'Jeez, Max, you really ask for it. What makes you think he was in London?'

He was spoiling my drink. I said, 'The night Zenia cleared off, I phoned him. And Lanche answered. Okay?'

Frankie went, 'Har!' I ignored him. He's just another speeding truck you have no control over.

He made that 'Har!' noise again.

'Frankie, if you don't belt up, you can buy your own drink.'

To my eternal astonishment, he sacrificed the prospect of free liquor. 'Never hear of a phone relay?'

Sure. Everybody knows about them. If you're not at your usual phone, the relay is the gizmo which patches you on to some other one . . .

Oh rats. I pulled up the memory of my call that night to Lanche's Dolphin Square flat. The first thing I had heard was a mechanical woman saying. 'The person you are calling knows you're waiting. Please hold.'

And I, the pinheaded cretin that I am, had simply assumed he was in his flat and on the phone to somebody else. But what if it was a relay job? What if Howard Lanche was back down in Harding and my call was redirected?

Frankie said, 'Bet you never thought of that.'

I looked at him with a new-found hatred. 'Go away.'

But he just hung there over the bar drinking the whisky I'd bought him and doing his wolfman smile. 'And how do you know where he was when Zenia was murdered? Just because you *thought* he was in London when she disappeared, you're assuming he was in the clear the night she was killed.'

Assuming? That's an awfully big word for a monkey. Somebody must have been teaching him new tricks.

I said, 'I have made one very stupid assumption. I have assumed that the photographs you took today are in focus, and, when printed in our great newspaper, will be vaguely identifiable as those of Howard and Leonora Lanche. But I suppose that is too much to assume.'

I know, I know. I should have said presume.

Frankie growled into the empty glass. But life's too short for fighting. So I bought him another biffo Scotch and told the barmaid to have a shot too. She gave me a muscular smile. I'm guessing she did. That was just another of my assumptions, for my eye was on the far horizon. All I could see was a whole fleet of uncontrollable trucks heading my way.

The first one came thundering down out of nowhere, from the very quarter I would least expect it. From Rosie's place, down in Battersea, to be exact. That was around five o'clock. Before then all was sunshine and light. Nothing from Miranda, but Belker had phoned me thrice. First to tell me he'd won me another three days in the hellhole. The others were comfort blanket calls where I guaranteed him the world and ten per cent of all else. After he tailed off I was left with nothing to do. Except to rake through the ashes of my own ineptitude. Yep, Frankie was right: Lanche could have slung Zenia sea-wards. Lawdy Lawd. I'd been outsmarted by a monkey. Not many people can say that.

I left Frankie fermenting in the bar and faded back to my room. I'd gone right off drink. What I needed was someone to share my gloom and despond; to tell me I was nowhere near as dumb as I feared. Therefore I pulled the bedside phone towards me and rang Rosie.

'Can you call me back?' said she. There was a radio or TV racketing away in the background. 'I'm doing a hundred and one things at the minute.'

'Make it a hundred and two.'

She said, 'I'm listening.'

Now wasn't that something? I didn't exactly reach for the Kleenex, but my soul blew its nose loudly and shuffled its feet. I said, 'I've landed myself right in it.'

A lesser woman might have said, 'Again?' Not Rosie. She went straight to the heart of things. 'Whatever it is, it's not your fault, Max. Don't let it get you down, darlin'.'

Rosie had stacks more calamine lotion on offer, and I happily wallowed in it, washing away all woes and cares. I listened to her smoky voice and felt my fretted nerves cease jangling. Do you know, that woman could make a bundle as a psychoanalyst.

So there I was, mellowing out when Rosie said, 'Did you hear that?'

'What?'

'The news on the radio.'

I couldn't have cared less.

She said, 'That MP you're chasing; isn't he called Lanche?'

I sat up. I couldn't have cared more. I couldn't have been any jumpier either. I asked warily, 'What about him?'

'Nothing much. He's just resigned.'

Ohhhh *bugger*!

Even as the words zapped across my brain, my mobile began chirping and the bleep bleeped.

I said, 'Rosie, I've got to go. The office is screaming for me.'

Her parting words were, 'Don't worry; it may never happen.'

Too late. It had already happened. I looked at the bleep first, mainly because I wanted to hold off talking to anybody for as long as I could. The message was from Belker. I didn't know you were allowed to use words like that on a pager.

Next the mobile. Crazy Horse. Who else? It was hard to tell whether she was incoherent with rage or joy. Probably both. After a while I began to make out whole sentences. 'Your head is on a plate, Chard. Not only have you disobeyed me *and* the Editor: you've also missed the story. I *begged* the Editor to give you one last chance today, and look what you've done with it. He's tearing his hair out.'

A neat trick, considering the state of his bonce. She stormed onwards and upwards, throwing in my teeth various past outrages which I don't want to talk about. But she did toss in one good line, ' . . . and when it comes to fiddling expenses, you're another Yehudi Menuhin.'

Then a break for breath. I could just picture her pointy boobs bopping about all over the place. This was the moment when I was supposed to prostrate myself before her and plead for my miserable life. Or that's what she thought. I said, 'I'm not taking the rap for this.'

Snort. 'Oh, so you're not to blame, is that it? Well who is then?'

Personally I blame El Nino. But I just said, 'Lanche lied to us. That's the—'

'—He lied to *you*. And you believed him.'

I said, 'Miranda, aren't you missing the point here? Tomorrow all the Sundays will carry a story saying Lanche has quit to spend more time with his family, or because he has an ingrowing toenail or something. But we have a better yarn.'

For once she was listening.

I said, 'We will have an exclusive detailing precisely why he chucked it in – because he *and* his wife deliberately screwed up a murder investigation.'

Oooh. She hadn't thought of that. I moved briskly on, 'Now, if you get off the phone I can write the story. Okay?'

Nearly. She just had to get in a few sharp ones about it being a rubbishy story anyway and she'd probably have to get someone with brains to rewrite it. But at least she cleared off.

I lit a Bensons. Now for Belker. I was expecting a similar burst of sound and fury from him. But no. If anything, he came across as a deeply hurt human beanbag. 'You gave me your word, Max. I went out on a limb for you and I'm left with egg all over my face.'

He's good at mixing his metaphors. I acted all open and honest so he wouldn't notice the lies. 'Tony, you are the most respected news executive on the paper. You run the whole news operation. If Crazy Horse weren't squatting in your office, this mess would never have happened.'

He couldn't help himself. He believed it.

I said, 'I still have to run with my instincts, and I still believe there's a stonking great story in here. That's why I want to stay in Harding. But if you tell me to leave, I'll be out of here in five minutes.'

Since his boardroom balls-up, Belker was in no position to tell any hack what to do, but the illusion of power appealed. He cradled it in his foul bosom for all of five seconds before he reluctantly cast it aside.

'No can do,' he said. 'The Editor has already let it be known that he thinks I made a bad judgement call. You'd better leave.'

Down the days Belker has bawled many cruel words at me. But those last three, spoken in nothing harsher than a grumble, were the cruellest of all. He was telling me to kiss my story goodbye. No. He was telling me to kill my own blue-eyed baby. I just couldn't do it. There had to be some way out, some deal I could make.

He said, 'Did you hear me?'

Hush. I'm thinking.

'Max?'

I said, 'What can I do to make you change your mind?' My God, it sounded like a love song.

'Nothing. This isn't just me. The Editor wants you back. This is a no-option situation. Disregard his instructions, and you'll be sacked.'

Got it!

I said, 'Just say, Tony, I send you my signed resignation, to take effect if I fail to produce the story.'

'Urkk?' That's the sound he makes when he gawps. He must have hungered for such an offer so many, many times. At night, as he heaved and sweated in his stinking pit, how often had he dreamed of me offering to quit? And how often had he screamed out, 'Yes! Yes! Yes!' until his missus bashed him with the alarm clock?

And now the very moment had arrived, and all he could say was 'Urkk?'

I repeated the terms.

Finally he gave voice. 'Do you really mean this?'

'One thousand per cent. I have a story to write, but as soon as that's through, I'll e-mail you at home with the exact wording. Then I'll type it out properly, sign it and post it to you tonight. It will be on your desk first thing Monday.'

Belker was as silent as a stuffed dugong. I expect he was marvelling at my raw courage.

He said, 'That is the stupidest idea you have ever conceived . . . but . . .'

'But?'

' . . . and I can't say whether the Editor will deem it valid, or even if he would agree to let you stay on the story. You'll have to put a clause in there, to the effect that it is *not* written under duress, and it might even be wise to have it witnessed. I must warn you now, I have no intention of doing anything until I have the e-mail.'

'You'll have it. Give me an hour.'

I put down the phone so softly it made only the faintest of clunks. I pursed my lips and pumped out a long stream of air. What on earth had I let myself in for? I must be absolutely barking. I mean, there are only nine other people doing the crime slot in national dailies so there's not much in the way of job offers. I mentally reviewed the other nine. Nope, none of them looked the type to get in the path of a runaway truck. So I just had to bring home the Lanche story. Otherwise . . . I didn't feel like thinking about an otherwise. Instead, I dragged out the laptop and started hitting the keys.

Somewhere in the middle of my labours Frankie showed up. 'Hey, have I got some news for you,' he yammered happily.

I gave him a tenner and told him to go play with the bottles. He didn't take offence. And so I picked away at the story. You already know it so I'm not going

to give you a rerun. I shuttled it off down the modem
and I turned to my formal letter of resignation. There
were only three paragraphs, but I swear it took me
twice as long to hammer them out as the twenty pars
I'd dished up on Lanche & wife. I e-mailed it through
to Belker and copied every word down in my notebook
so I could type it later. I folded my notebook with a
deep and doomy sigh.

Just when I was about to charge downstairs and
flood myself with drink, Miranda Briel came on. 'You
told me this woman was murdered.'

'No,' I lied. 'I said police were treating it as a suspicious death.'

'That's the same thing. I want a correction.'

Like I said, Miranda knows nothing about the
secret art of hackery. I talked her through it. 'Suicide
is a suspicious death, so is manslaughter. Murder is
just another one. My police contact down here is still
wavering.'

She said, 'Why haven't you inserted a quote from
him?'

'Maybe you haven't got as far as the line which
goes, "A police source last night said." '

'Oh. That's him?'

'That's him.'

There were a couple of other things she wanted to
bitch about but I shut her down, saying I was off
to meet my secret contact. She still couldn't leave it
alone. 'Just remember; I don't want to see your usual
outrageous expenses. You keep them to the bare
minimum, or I'll chop them in half.'

Expenses? As if that was all I had to worry about.

I broke free from her clutches and got out of the

room, which by now was a bit too smoky for comfort. I heroically ignored the bar and cajoled the receptionist into letting me have a go on her word processor. Out came the notebook. I fed all the words onto the screen. They stared back at me. I read my resignation through again. It went like this:

'You are a drink-raddled loony with the brains of an amoeba. Do you realize what you have done, you dolt? You've stuck a loaded gun in the hand of Belker, Crazy Horse and that toad who calls himself an editor, and you've begged them: "Shoot me. Please." '

Actually it didn't read at all like that. It just seemed that way. I pushed a button and ran off three copies of my death warrant. Done. *Now* for that drink.

Frankie wasn't missing me. He was half over the bar, dribbling all down the barmaid's frontage. By the shape of him, there wasn't much left of my tenner. I pulled them apart and slapped in an SOS for a monster gin *and* a pint of lager. I was feeling reckless so I told Frankie and the barmaiden to enjoy themselves too. Alcoholically speaking, that is. I led him off to the window seat and hauled out my suicide note. 'Sign that, Frankie. Right there by the X.'

'Wot's this?'

I told him. There's a certain species of monkeys you get in any reasonable zoo. They're small and sort of greenish-grey. That's not the interesting point. What is, is that if you bare your teeth at them, their monkey mouths plop open and their eyes go big and round. Well, I can tell you now, my monkey is directly related to them. The main difference is he talks.

'You're nuts. This is just what Belker has always wanted.'

I know, I know, I *know*.

'Just sign it, Frankie. And print your name underneath.'

In straggly joined-up writing he signed Frank G. Frost.

'What's the G for?'

He wasn't telling. He said, 'Want to hear what I've got?'

'Later. Lanche has gone and quit as an MP.'

Frankie called Lanche by all the names I'd already thought of in the past couple of hours. When he was done, he said, 'Lucky I wired off the pix, then.'

'What?'

He enlightened me. 'Remember you dumped me in the bar this afternoon? Well I'd no money so instead I went back to my room and sent the smudges back to the office. Hey! Think about it; I'm the only photographer to get the last pix of Lanche before he resigned.'

I smiled for him. But what I was really thinking was I had never been such a half-witted amateur as I'd been today. Rule Number Seven in Chard's book, is always, *always* protect your photographer, for you are smarter than him. That meant when I heard of Lanche's stunt, I should have warned Frankie right away to wire his pix. I hadn't, but he had. Doesn't your heart warm to him?

I said: 'You got room for another large one?'

'Oh, all right. Then I'll tell you what I found out. It'll blow your mind.'

Way too late. I'd already blown all the fuses in there and Brain was sitting shivering in the dark. Anyway, before Frankie could begin to rattle off his tidings, my mobile cut in. Belker. 'I have your e-mail and I am about to call the Editor. I feel it only fair to caution you now, it might be well be redundant in light of the latest developments.'

What light? What developments? I just said, 'Uh-huh?'

Belker said, 'You mean you haven't heard? Christ, Chard, you've really taken your eye off the ball on this story. Teamwork is the name of the game, but you're not even in the same ballpark.'

I still had no idea what this was all about. 'What developments, Tony?'

He said, 'If you had taken the time to ring the district man, Hughie Gall, he'd have told you. Thank God at least he's on the ball, or we would have been the laughing stock of Fleet Street.'

'What developments, Tony?'

By way of answer he snorted derision. But he got there eventually, 'You had an exclusive on how the Lanches kept evidence from the police. Right?'

I stayed quiet.

He said, 'Well you might like to know your story has been spiked.'

'Why?'

'Because this afternoon Howard Lanche and his wife told the police they knew Zenia Evans.'

The hellhounds. The *evil*, two-faced, backstabbing, double-crossing, Zenia-killing, slimeballs. I said, 'They've gone to the Old Bill only because they knew I had the story.'

Belker accused, 'Yeh, and by telling them, you gave them the chance to be proactive. They got their pre-emptive strike in first.'

That often happens with pre-emptive strikes. I said, 'We can still run an exclusive, saying we forced them into it.'

'No. The lawyers wouldn't let it through. Lanche has issued a statement, explaining the delay in coming forward. So you can discount any exclusive there. Now, I want to read your e-mail to the Editor. But I wouldn't hold my breath. Even you must realize you've bungled this one.'

He went off without wishing me luck. I rang our Saturday News Desk and talked Louise into pulling up Lanche's statement. A good brief must have written it for him. It covered all the bases. The first bit said he was 'reluctantly' leaving politics to concentrate on 'outside interests'.

Like pushing people off cliffs.

He went on to ramble about what a wonderful human being the PM was, and how much he had enjoyed serving in his government.

So much so that he'd felt the need to jump ship.

He wished unconfined joy to his successor, and the Party, and the PM and anyone else he could think of, blah, blah, blah. And then he got down to what all this tosh was really about.

In a separate issue, which I must stress is in no manner related to my decision to resign, I have today been informed that unbeknownst to us, a young woman, who performed occasional duties for my wife and also for myself, was recently the victim of a tragic accident.

The woman has a common surname and I was unaware at first that the victim was in fact our acquaintance. Although we knew her only slightly, the news of her death was a shock to us. My wife and I have passed

on to the police what little information we have. We ex-
press our sincere condolences to her family on their
bereavement.

Neat, huh? I particularly liked the way Lanche
made it sound as though Leonora knew Zenia better
than he did. And how about knowing her 'only
slightly'? He even left out Zenia's name. I was griev-
ously tempted to ring Belker and talk him into running
a story exposing all the half truths and downright eva-
sions in Lanche's yarn. But I knew I'd only cop another
earful of grief. So I just grizzled into my drink.

Frankie said, 'You ready to listen to me yet?'

This was hardly the time to hear the chitterings of
a deranged monkey, but I'd nothing better to do. 'Fire
away.'

He began way back in the afternoon. 'I thought I'd
have a shufti around town to see if I could get a snap
of that Abigail bird, right? I looked all over, but not a
sign of her. I was about to give it up as a lost cause
when I saw that old bloke in the wheelchair. You know
who I mean?'

I knew. But I was past caring.

Frankie said, 'Just guess where I spotted him.'

'Climbing up the church spire.'

'Max, do you want to hear this or not? It might just
save your bacon.'

'Oh, all right.'

Frankie said, 'He was just down the road, going for
a stroll.'

'He was *walking*?'

'Don't be a plonker. He was in his wheelchair,
wasn't he. But it wasn't the Chinese girl pushing him,
it was another babe. Another right little rascal.'

So the old bod had a harem of stunners. Zowie.

Frankie said, 'I got out of the car and followed them to this big house. And you'll never believe what he said when they got to the gate.'

I wasn't even going to try.

Frankie squinted up his eyes at me so he looked like a Picasso portrait. He said, 'Check this out: the old codger said, "We're just in time for tea." And he said it with an American accent.'

I goggled. 'That's it? That's going to save my bacon?'

He had on his big loopy smile now. 'You haven't heard it all.'

There was an empty tonic bottle on the table in front of me. I suddenly felt an overwhelming urge to grab it by the neck and blatter him to death with it.

Frankie said, 'What he said *exactly* was, "We're just in time for tea, *Abigail*." '

Chapter Nineteen

My fingers froze on the tonic bottle. I slowly repeated, 'Time for tea, *Abigail*. Are you sure that's what he called her?'

'No mistake. I was walking right behind them. She said something back to him but I couldn't catch it. But one thing I can tell you is she was talking with a jock accent.'

Two Abigails in one little town. Two Abigails, one Scottish, the other Chinese, but both linked with the wheelchair man. What did it all mean? I couldn't take it in so I went and rustled up another round of drinks while I pulled it this way and that.

I handed Frankie his whisky and said, 'The bloke in the wheelchair looks pretty doddery to me. Maybe he just got her name wrong.'

'Maybe that's what she's called.'

Unlikely, but not out of this world. I said, 'And this house she went into, where is it?'

'I told you – the road out front. It's the big, flashy place.'

I said, 'Ah, Jordan House.'

'How did you know its name?'

Because I can read, Frankie. I said, 'Did you grab a snap of her?'

'What do you take me for? I used the telephoto and got her as she was going in the door. The pix are a bit grainy, but they're okay. Want to see them?'

Too right. They were contact prints, just four of them, and two were miles off focus. The other couple were bang on, not that I could make out much, for the Saverley Suite is one of those places that goes in for low lights and high prices. Fortunately Frankie had come tooled up with his pocket magnifier.

Definitely the same wheelchair passenger, definitely a different girl. This one was blonde-ish. Like Frankie had said, she was an all right piece of crumpet, even though she was rather dressed down in a long, dark, wide-collared coat. But give her a glam makeover and she'd be quite something.

I said, 'Care to explain just how Abigail Mark Two is going to save my bacon?'

He had it all laid out. 'Don't you see – this means we've found his *real* girlfriend. Why don't we go and show him what we've got? I'll lay you evens he'll own up.'

Frankie has a touching faith in picture power. 'The camera never lies,' he tells anyone daft enough to listen. Don't you believe it. Still, I would have liked to see Lanche's face – and Leonora's – if we showed up on their doorstep and waved the snaps at them. I summoned up a minicab, for I was strangely averse to Frankie driving me with all that whisky sloshing around inside him. While we waited, I stuck my resignation offer in an envelope and gave it to the receptionist. I marked it First Class.

We went ready for battle. Camera, flash units, tape recorder, the works. And all for nothing. As we crested the down on which The Maltings parked itself, the house was in utter darkness. Just out of habit we banged the door and had a good snoop out the back. Still nothing. I don't know why, but I got the feeling it might be deserted for some days.

Frankie said, 'Where now?'

To Alex Hartiwell's place. It was empty too. I used the mobile and gave Lanche's London number a shot. All I got was an ansaphone. I didn't leave a message.

Frankie prompted, 'Let's try that Jordan House place.'

No. Not yet. I needed to know what to ask before I went calling there. I said, 'I want a look inside Red Gables.'

'We've already done there.'

I wasn't in a mood to argue. I just told the cabbie to hang about and off I went into the darkness. Frankie let me get twenty yards before he joined in. The back door which I'd left open was locked. But I was all out of scruples. I elbowed in a side pane and sprung the latch. Frankie said, 'This could be trouble, Max. Serious trouble.'

Trouble? Tell me about it. My job, my entire career was on the line. If I had to bust every window to come through this, I'd do it singing. Frankie couldn't help himself. He shambled in to the kitchen after me. Without torches we made slow going of it, but we got there in the end. There weren't any police notices on the tower room door. That meant they were plain sloppy, or that Lanche had not told them about Zenia's last resting place. It was unlocked. I used my bootleg Dunhills lighter to guide me through the junk.

And so to the bed. No rucksack. So Lanche or the

Old Bill had it. I cast around looking for tracks of flat feet in the dust, but by now my lighter was close to meltdown. Also my fingers were beginning to yowl. I gave up and got out. Back down through the rackety house. I closed the kitchen door behind us, hooked up the latch and dusted everything with a nice clean hankie.

The minicab was ticking away out front. It offered express transport back to the hotel bar and all its comforts. But I hesitated. There was still work to do. I said, 'Let's have a go at Tom Davies.'

'The big nasty guy?' Frankie was less keen. But then his resignation letter wasn't in the post. He dragged his heels.

Davies opened the door. You could tell he'd recognized us by the way he stopped smiling.

'Huh,' he said.

I didn't have time for small talk. 'Mister Davies, my name is Max Chard. I'm a reporter and I'm trying to find out what connection there is between Howard Lanche and the woman who died out the back of your house.'

He was not the trusting type. 'Yeh?'

I said, 'He admits he knew her. He admits he let her stay in Red Gables. But he did not tell the police until today. And I think there's still a lot he hasn't admitted.'

Davies was getting interested. 'Oh yeh?'

I said, 'He may not have told them of how he used to spend nights with her in a mews house in Bayswater.'

Davies said, 'Come in.'

His was a neat house, but not a loved house. In

the hall there was a clear plastic runner over a buff-toned carpet. Lighter walls. Two little framed multi-colour things that looked like they'd been knitted. The living room was equally daring. Mrs Davies was at home, a teak-effect fireplace to her left, a matching TV dead ahead. Davies made the introductions, 'Barbara, this is . . . what did you say your name was again? . . . Oh, yes, Mister Chard . . . he's a reporter and he's doing an exposé on Howard Lanche.'

Yes, well. I flashed her a pearly one. 'And this is my photographer, Frankie. Frankie, give me the contact prints. And the magnifier.'

I offered them first to Mrs D. I said, 'I *know* that Lanche is also involved with a woman called Abigail and that's what the woman in these pictures is called. Frankie took them today. Have you seen her before?'

Naturally she just had to look at them upside down. She got them the right way up and squinted at the magnifier. 'Oooh, that's Jordan House.'

Forget the house. Look at the girl.

She said, 'And that's the man who owns it. But I don't know his name.'

Somehow I kept my smile in place. I prodded, 'The woman?'

Time took itself off on holiday while she frowned again at the print. I think she liked it better upside down. At last she said, 'I can't be sure. I'm sorry. You see, there are so many young people coming and going at the Jordan House. She might be the old man's nurse, but, you know, they're not like neighbours. They're more like the guests at the Reen Court. One day you see them, the next they're gone.'

And a fat lot of help that was. I turned the prints

over to her husband. He said, 'He must be seventy if he's a day, but he always has these dishy young nurses. I reckon he's got stacks of money so he can hire who he likes.'

I said, 'I thought Jordan House was some sort of religious charity for drug addicts.'

'Aye. Rich ones. They've all got a plum in their mouths and they turn their noses up at the rest of us.'

This man and Belker should get together to mix metaphors. I said, 'You ever see her before?'

'Like Barbara says, we can't be sure. But she looks familiar.'

So much for Frankie's bacon-saving smudges. I said, 'Have you ever seen Lanche with *any* young woman?'

Not that he could think of. Well, not anyone called Abigail. Or Zenia.

I said, 'Lanche hid Zenia in the tower room of Red Gables. Did you see him – or his wife, or even their car around here recently?'

Barbara Davies slapped her cheeks with her hands. 'No! You mean that poor girl was only living next door?'

No. She was living *only* next door.

If anything, Davies was enjoying the yarn. 'So this is a sex scandal, is it? I'm surprised. Lanche is always up to some dirty business, but I never expected that.'

I said, 'What dirty business?'

He flapped a hand. It could have meant anything.

I said, 'You may not have heard, but Lanche quit today.'

I was expecting them to holler Hallelujah and hop around. But Davies just muttered, 'Good riddance.'

I said, 'So now he's gone, you might want to tell me what you had against him.'

Barbara took up that one. 'It's a long story, Mister Chard, and it won't do any good to go dragging it up again.'

Try me. I turned to Davies, 'I thought you'd be delighted by the news.'

'I'm not. For I'll tell you now, and you can bank on it, that slippery pal of his will take over.'

I took a stab at precisely which slippery pal he had in mind. 'Alex Hartiwell?'

Got it in one. Was there anybody on this earth Davies liked?

I asked, 'What's wrong with him?'

That had them both laughing. He sobered up first. 'You're a stranger and I expect you come from London, so you wouldn't understand small town politics. But I'll tell you this, between them, Lanche and Hartiwell have Harding sewn up tighter than a duck's arse.'

'Tommy,' Barbara Davies reproved.

'Sorry, love, but it has to be said. Hartiwell sells his uncle's house to the charity people, even though everybody along the road wanted it to stay a private house. But we didn't say anything, and of course the council rubber-stamps it. Now Lanche is selling next door, and if we're not careful, that'll be bought by a developer and we'll have building work going on night and day. He puts on a big show, but . . .'

'But?'

But nothing. Davies wasn't telling. I waited in case he changed his mind.

His wife said, 'I'm sorry, I haven't offered you both a cup of tea. Can I get you something?'

'They might like a glass of beer instead, love. I know I'm having one.'

No. We'd pass on that one. But thanks for the offer. And good night.

And home to base. No messages, apart from Rosie's ten-thirty cheer up call. Some other bloke and his beloved were in our special seats, so we just had to lounge against the bar.

Frankie asked, 'Why didn't we turn over Jordan House?'

'Because it is dark. You'd have to use flash and you couldn't snatch any good pix.'

This was a whopping great lie. The real reason was I still had no idea what was going on. But Frankie fell for it anyway.

'That's why I like working with you, Max; you always think of your picture man.'

'Oh, all right. Another large one?'

Seven nights a week I hurl myself into bed and let the world go hang for six solid hours. Maybe more, if I've been enjoying myself beforehand. I sleep sound as a baby hedgehog in the cradle of snowy winter, and if perchance I dream, my dreams are unclouded.

But not that night. I flumped around amid the pillows, kicked off the duvet, dragged it back on board again, and I listened to every click of the clock. That was the worst part. By far.

Each time the grim green numbers flicked over another minute, they were pushing me closer and closer to the speeding juggernaut. What had I done? Oh, why, *why* had I done it? If I'd just shut up and let

Crazy Horse/Belker/the Editor beat me to a pulp, the chances were that would have satisfied them. All right, they might have shredded my expenses too. But at least I'd still have a job. Now here I was in the back end of nowhere without a future. And most of all, without a story. I could see the truck's blazing head-lights. I could even make out the teddy bear tied to the throbbing chrome grille. Worse, oh, far worse, I could see the driver.

And it was *me*.

I sat up fairly swiftish. This was light on the road to Damascus stuff. But what did it mean? I flipped on the lamp to give it serious thought. The clock ticked off another four minutes to doomsday and I hadn't got anywhere. So I hopped out of bed, unchained a mini Gordons from the minibar, lit up a Bensons and tried again.

I started from the point where only this morning I'd told the murderous Lanches about Abigail. I'd said, 'She drives a big white minibus.'

And he, amazed, or something like that, had said, 'She drives a minibus?'

And that was the moment the Lanches thought they were safe. No. They *knew* I couldn't touch them. I remember that bit so sharply. Also I remembered thinking, 'Why has he left out the colour of the minibus?'

Because it wasn't important, that's why. The minibus might have been striped like a tiger but it still wouldn't have meant a thing. It was the *driving* that threw him. For *his* Abigail couldn't drive. His was Abigail the Second. Oh boy. Terrific theory but nowhere near enough. I needed back-up. I ran it through again, only this time I heard Leonora's voice laced with sarcasm. 'A mysterious *Chinese* girl.'

A different Abigail. It all hung together. But where did it get me? It got me back to the minibar for the last Gordons, that's where.

Meanwhile, my brain, which isn't into pro drinking, was pulling away at something else. The voiceprint.

You may not have heard of it, largely because I've just invented it, but here's the score. Everybody has his/her own way of chopping up the English language when they talk. It's as personal as your fingerprint. A good hack listens carefully to what people say. He gets to know their speech patterns. That way he can invent a quote which reads as if it belongs. Sometimes even the bloke you've been turning over thinks he might have said it.

But if you don't take the time to know your target, you can bloop out big time. Here's a quick f'rinstance, sadly allegedly true. A girl has a wonder operation which saves her life. A hack, following up the story, and unable to con her way into the intensive care unit, makes up a quote for her: 'Thank God for the miracles of modern science.' An all right quote, in its place, but not when you stick it in the mouth of the miracle girl. For she was only two years old.

Where was I? Back to the voiceprint on the Lanche story. This morning I'd listened to both of them. Leonora particularly. She talked as if she was lecturing the girls at Founder's Day and she used the word 'quite' at every chance she got, so, when I made up a couple of quotes from her, 'quite' figured quite strongly.

I was getting somewhere. Other fragments came drifting back. I remembered one tiny background detail that didn't belong and one thing which did belong but wasn't there. And then the name of a place. Pure coincidence? Hardly. What else was there? An apparently innocent connection between two people. So now I had something. I knew that someone had done something totally out of order, I could even guess why. And that gave me the who. But ... I smacked my head into a full stop.

Back to the minibar. Some loon had piled it with Bacardi Breezers, orange juice, even a couple of cans of tomato juice. There remained the Scotch and the vodka miniatures. Maybe later, if things got desperate. All I wanted now was a decent gin. I stuck on shirt and trousers and padded along to Frankie's kennel. Blat, blat.

He yelled, 'Who's there?'

'Knock, knock.'

He opened. He had the TV flickering away and his tongue was down on his lap. 'Hey, are you watching this too? See the bristols on the blonde babe?'

The room smelt of dead socks and Frankie. I said, 'Give me your minibar key.'

'What for?'

'I'm all out of tomato juice.'

Whereupon Frankie forgot his pleasuredome movie. 'Clear off. You want my gin.'

He doesn't even drink the stuff. I said, 'You have a choice: either you hand over the gins, both of them, or I will never buy you another drink. Ever.'

That was a toughie, for all cameramen are into short-term investments. I said, 'It's two in the morning now. In nine hours it will be eleven. Who's going to buy you drink then? It certainly won't be me. The key.'

Long tussle as poor monkey tried to sort following into correct order: money, bare-breasted rascals, future prospect of unlimited drink. He chose wisely, chucking the key on the floor. 'Just this once. But you owe me.'

There were *four* happy little bottles of Beefeaters in there. The maid had left me only two. I trousered them all. He had his boogly eyes on the TV. 'What did you take?'

'Two gins, and all your ice,' I said.

'What about the tonics?'

Thank you Frankie, I'd forgotten them.

I was closing the door on him when he said, 'This has been a bad job for drinks.'

Eh?

He was still glued to the box. 'I mean, a lot of jobs people say, "Like a drink?" and, you know . . .'

A woman with boobs as big as Belker's burst onto the screen. I'd lost him. But on the way back to my own room I thought about it. Frankie was right. I'd done a string of cosy interviews, from Eric Shernholm to Howard Lanche, and sundry others besides. Only Lanche and Tom Davies had offered up drink. But all those other people . . . something strange there . . .

I pushed that aside and returned to the main feature. Okay, I'd nailed down one corner of the story. The rest of it was flapping around in the mists. And its name was Abigail. I still couldn't make her fit into the picture. Well, let's see how she pairs with any of the other riff-raff.

Eric Shernholm knows her. He was the one who coughed up to her very existence. He was the one who told me he'd lost her. No. Stop. His actual words were, 'I'm missing an Abigail.' And I hadn't picked up on it. *An* Abigail. Which particular Abigail was he prattling on about?

So who else knew this Abigail? Zenia must have been in on the secret. What about the Man in Black? Yep, him too. Then Lindy Trevett. And old Mister Moses who gets wheeled around town by Abigails. The Lanches had jumped when I threw out the name. Except I'd got the wrong Abigail. So, apart from me, who didn't know her? Alex Hartiwell and Tom Davies plus wife.

Frankie must have watered down those gins because I was still thinking backwards. The only thing you can do when this happens is to drop the whole damn thing and think about something else. I thought about the office. I pushed the nightmare vision of Crazy Horse out of the way and tuned in to that long, long ago Sunday briefing. The day the Editor and Belker had dumped this on me. Even then I knew it was iffy. And there was that bit afterwards when I read up our files on Lanche. I'd skimmed through it at the time. Now I knew it meant something. But I was still only guessing just what.

I poured out the second of Frankie's gins. I put the two unopened bottles back in my minibar. There was a small satisfaction in knowing that when we came to pay our bills, Frankie would cop it for four gins, and I was down just a couple of tonics.

I swung the chair window-wards, flushed wide the curtains and sat in the little tubby armchair, looking out onto a star-flecked sky. I sat there, smoking and taking the occasional sip until it was time to ease my bones. And sleep came easy. I dreamed too. Mostly of the office. Little things floated in and out of my mind as the clock counted off its green minutes.

And somewhere in the soft limbo hours my soul whispered, 'Thank you, Oscar.'

Chapter Twenty

Sunday dawned a shade early, but I embraced it anyway. Even before I showered I went and kicked Frankie awake. He scratched his various cubby holes and whinged, 'What's the rush?'

I said, 'I have been thinking.'

'Oh yeh?' He's interested in unusual hobbies.

I said, 'They've got the jump on us. But if you pull your finger out, we might just get ahead of them.'

'Then we'll have the jump on them.'

And people say monkeys can't think for themselves. My duty done, I cleared off because I didn't want to be around when Frankie hauled himself out of bed. The day ahead was not one of your usual jobs. Today was the day I had to grab up all the main characters and stickyback them into the frame.

But first a burst of shower power. The morning shower is an ace invention. Not only does it blast away all the aged skin cells which died in their sleep: it also helps you strip down whatever crazed ideas you came up with in the night. I exposed my several notions to the pulsing jetstream. All right, it stripped off some of the more fanciful theories, but it left the main body intact.

As soon as I was dried and dressed I got busy on

the phone. The local police first. I introduced myself as Jim Mumflepumfle of Radio Nifferdiff. A complete waste of mumbles there, for Harding nick simply fobbed me off on county HQ. I was put through to the press office and I tried out my pantomime again.

A woman said, 'That's a bad cold you have there, Jim.'

God bless you, ma'am. I gave my nose a honk and got on with the questions. Yes, they were treating Zenia's plunge as a suspicious death. No, the Old Bill could not disclose whether Howard Lanche had given them a statement.

I said, 'There's a rumour going round that you've found the woman's rucksack.'

'Wait a mo.'

I lit my first of the day and prepared myself for a long wait, because that's what you have to do when you ring *any* police press liaison bureau. She came back on stream. 'I have the latest update here . . . what was your question again?'

I reminded her.

She said, 'Umm . . . certain items of personal property which we believe may have belonged to the victim were recovered from premises in Harding during the course of yesterday evening.'

'Does that mean you've got the rucksack?'

Well she didn't know, did she? All she had to go on was this two-line update from the main woodentop in the investigation.

I said, 'Is there a press briefing today?'

'Don't think so. If there is, they haven't told us.'

And that was all the Law had to say for itself. Yet people, Rosie especially, think my job is a doddle. I tried the Lanches, placing a one hundred to one bet that they wouldn't answer. I won, but I still felt like I'd lost. Hartiwell next. He was actually there, live on line.

'Alex, this is Ed Stonelight.' I threw in the fake name hoping for a reaction.

'Ed! How are you today? Still house-hunting?'

No chill edges in there. Maybe they hadn't told him. I said, 'We're both in the pink. Didn't think I'd catch you in. Thought you'd be out fishing.'

'Wish I were, wish I were. But, you know how it is, work builds up and you have to put your head down and get on with it.'

So far all was briskish and bright. Let's see how long he could keep it up. I said, 'We were hoping to stop by later, but if you're too tied up . . .'

Only slight hesitation. 'Well, if you could leave it until this afternoon, say four o'clock. How does that sound to you?'

It sounds like four o'clock.

I said, 'Great. Four it is.'

So much for Hartiwell. It was still only a smidgeon past eight. I called Belker at home. His old woman answered in tones you could use to grind rocks. Mind you, if I was married to the Blob I wouldn't sound too chipper either.

He opened on an encouraging note, 'I have nothing to say to you. Talk to the Editor, or Miranda.'

Not so fast, my elephantine friend. I said, 'Two things are true: I'm headed straight down the pan, and so are you.'

'Your balls-up has nothing to do with me. The Editor knows that. He knows my role in this has purely been one of a facilitator. So don't try tarring me with the same brush.'

I said, 'I wasn't talking about the story; I was talking about your sell-out comedy act in the board-room. Particularly that crack about the chairman's ugly daughter.'

He went unusually quiet. In the background you could hear the squeals of something horrible. I tell you, it fair churns your stomach, knowing there are baby Belkers out there.

He tried to bluff it. 'You have the wrong end of the stick, Chard. The chairman *personally* appointed me to head up his special project.'

I said, 'You've got Crazy Horse in your seat. You're stuck out in airy-fairy land. Can't you see, they're trying to tell you something, Tony.'

Silence. Apart from that thing in the background carrying on like nobody's business.

Belker said, 'I've done all I could for you, but you're in a zero gain scenario.'

Do they find these words lying about in the street? I said patiently, 'Fine. I'm for the skids. But what about you? This story could get you back in your chair. Think of yourself.'

Considering he's spent his entire life doing pre-cisely that, it wasn't hard.

He warned, 'I'm not taking any flak for this. You call me when you have the story written, confirmed, and ready to go. Until then—'

'Until then I need somebody to keep me posted of what's happening politically. I mean our Parly boys might get to hear whispers about the real reason why Lanche chucked it in. I'm like a leper down here.'

Belker said, 'Your crony, Dinesh, I'll keep him abreast. But don't even try to talk to me.'

I said, 'You'll only get one call. That's to tell you I've cracked it. That's when you drop it on the Editor.'

He tried for a laugh but couldn't quite make it. 'We'll see.'

And there we left it. I'd been sparky and stone sure of myself throughout. But now a double measure of doubt surfaced. Also, I was wondering why on earth I was rescuing his fat hide from a well-earned fate.

My phone rang, answering the question for me. Miranda Briel. It's hard to credit, but she was acting editor for the day. She shrilled out the usual terms of endearment while I thought of other things. I suppose breakfast was uppermost in my mind. Then she was gone and I went and scooped up Frankie and we hoofed off to gorge. Over dry scrambled eggs and wet mushrooms I plundered all the Sunday papers. Nobody had made a big deal out of Lanche's resignation and his 'slight' knowledge of a dead woman.

Frankie reloaded his plate from the brekkie buffet. Do you know, he packs away more carbohydrates at a single sitting than a whole herd of hungry Herefords scoff in a season. But he's skinny as a hosepipe. Rosie says it's all down to a fast metabolism. Therefore, after he'd finished off his third helpings I was reasonably sure he'd burned up all the liquor from the night before. That's why I let him drive. But not too far. We eased out on to Maidmont Road, turned hard right, and stopped with two wheels up on the kerb. Ahead of us the road tilted left in a long slow sweep, curling away inland. You could see the big clump of evergreens bracketing Hartiwell's house. Between here and there you had all the rest of it – Red Gables, Chez Davies, the Capthorne spread, and the Jordan House.

The Jordan House.

Somewhere behind its silent walls was a woman called Abigail. And only she could tell me the full bit. The big question now was *would* she?

Frankie said, 'What're we waiting for?'

'For Abigail.'

'Which one?'

Good question, Frankie. I said, 'Not the one you snapped yesterday.'

'Oh the other one.'

I turned away and stared out the window. Nothing to see there. But at least it meant I didn't have to look at Frankie. All snappers get fidgety when they're not pushing buttons and scrambling up and down their little ladders. Frankie gets more fidgety than most. I couldn't see him now, but I could hear him all right. He was tip-tap-tapping 'Take Five' in three-four time on the steering wheel, stomping his right hoof to 'Satisfaction', and making weird noises thus: 'Dukka-dukka-*dukka*-Donnnnggg!' I'm guessing that was his vocal intro to 'Layla'. He's a regular one-man band, is Frankie.

He vandalized half the great songs of the millennium before the racket suddenly halted. 'Here they come. No. It's not her.'

I said, 'Don't even look their way.'

'Wot?'

I unfurled a map and spread it all over the dashboard. 'Pretend you're reading it, Frankie.'

'It's upside down.'

'Just bloody pretend.'

I risked a glimpse over the edge. About eighty yards away was the Moses character, rolling slowly towards us. Behind him walked a heavily-wrapped up young woman. Frankie whined, 'It's not the Chinese babe. And it's not the jock one either.'

'Keep your stupid head down.'

The wheelchair pusher was older, taller and not in the same league as the others. She still wasn't bad. The pair wheeled past and off down the road towards Harding. They took no notice of us. I watched them in the rear-view mirror until they went over a dip and vanished.

'Okay, Frankie. It's time we got ourselves acquainted with Jordan House. So we're on best behaviour.'

He actually drove up the driveway like a normal person. Even so, I could tell by his silence he was missing the squeal of brakes and the stench of burnt rubber. The house looked at us stony-faced, but a snoopy little spy cam hanging off the porch watched our arrival with interest. I pressed the bell and way off in the distance I heard a chime. The trouble was nobody else seemed to hear it and I had to lean on it again.

The big cream door was opened at last by a small dark woman. She could have been a kid sister to Zenia Evans. She was wearing those big 1930s librarian specs. One eyebrow was hitched up. 'Yes?'

I smiled upon her fondly, 'Good morning. Just thought we'd stop by to introduce ourselves to our new neighbours. I'm Ed, this is Frankie, and we're buying Red Gables, you know, the house further along the road.'

No response. So I breezed onwards, 'Yes. We're hoping to set up a residential arts college, and we wanted to make sure that you, and of course the other neighbours, have no objections.'

Long pause from her. 'Perhaps you should speak to Dr Regis.' She stopped herself there and looked at me thoughtfully. Nope. I didn't look like trouble.

She said, 'Come in. Wait in the hall and I'll find him for you.'

But before she went in search of the doc, she closed the door and bolted it behind us. We were left standing in a wide open square hall with too much ancient wood on view. We watched her trip neatly up the stairs.

'Great legs,' Frankie said in a whisper you could hear a mile off. God knows how he knew what her legs were like. All you could see of them under a long grey skirt was a matching pair of ankles. Anyway, I was more concerned with the surroundings. Every door leading off the hall was closed. Outside one of them was a metal ramp, indicating that this was where the wheelchair bloke rested between his rolling romps around Harding. The walls were empty of pictures. But over an archway leading towards the back of the house was a small silver cross, edged in purple. The crossbar was slanted so it pointed up to the right. Underneath it were three silver letters U. L. T. Whatever they might mean. I listened for stray sounds. Nothing. Now we were inside, I was beginning to have serious qualms. What if I'd jumped to the wrong conclusions? Like my own.

But I switched on the smile again as a bloke in a dark suit, buttoned-up white shirt, no tie came down the stairs towards us with the woman tagging along behind. I'd say he was forty, and a bit more besides. The hall was too dark to make out his face. He came down to our level and stuck out a hand. Now that was interesting. Not the fact that he did it, but the way he did it. You watch. When an Englishman shakes hands, he produces his mitt as if he's been hiding it in his trouser pocket for the last three years. But an American pokes it out straight at you. And that's the way he did it.

He had a smile that didn't stretch very far. 'Good morning. What can I do for you?' His delivery was stilted.

I said, 'I was explaining to your . . .' A nod here at the blabbermouth door-opener . . . 'about our plans to turn Red Gables into a residential arts centre.'

'Yes?'

Dr Regis had grizzly grey sideburns with like-minded hair up top. His face had nothing written on it, least of all curiosity.

I said, 'Naturally we want to be on good terms with all our neighbours. So if you have any objections . . .'

If he had, he didn't feel like sharing them. My story was too flat. It needed a bit of spin. I said, 'The estate agent told us that Jordan House is a charitable institution: this morning my colleague, Frankie, who is our head of photographic studies, came up with an idea which I thought might appeal to you.'

Regis showed not the slightest interest. He hadn't even asked our names.

I said, 'Frankie suggested that in the spirit of charity we might offer arts courses to any of your residents who might benefit from them. Free, of course.'

Regis opened up with a full sentence, 'Generous of you, but that would not be suitable.'

I blinked innocent eyes.

Regis said, 'The programme we follow at Jordan House involves intensive one-to-one therapy. But I wish you every success with your project.'

Definitely an American accent hidden in there among the wooden English words. Yet what did that give me? Any minute now we were going to get bummed out. I could sense him already switching off. I said, 'Such a shame about Zenia.'

'Zenia?' Just a touch too casual. He'd lost his smile too.

I said, 'The one that thought she'd got away.'

He was stiff as a tree and he spoke like one. 'I . . . have . . . cases to . . . attend to . . . Good day . . .'

He looked over his shoulder at the waiting woman. 'Show these people out.'

But I lingered, watching him climb up the stairs. He didn't look back. The woman with the round specs had the door open and Frankie rambled through. I stayed put. I still had my eyes on Regis. He was just a step short of the landing when an upstairs door flipped open and three people appeared. Two were blokes. Between them was a young light-haired woman. I wouldn't bet on this, but they seemed to be holding her at the elbows. The trio were walking directly across the landing to a door opposite. They got halfway there when the girl suddenly stopped and pivoted so that she was facing Regis.

She opened her mouth to say something and then

she looked past him straight at me. I was standing in the sunlight of the open door, and Frankie had come back to see what was holding me. The two men closed in on the woman and hurried her across the landing. But not fast enough. Just before they got her away, she shouted. No, it was more of a wail than a shout. There were only two words. She said them twice, and I heard them distinctly: 'Help me. *Help* me!'

Regis watched her go before he turned to me. He wasn't giving anything away.

I said, 'Want to tell me what's going on?'

He leaned both hands on the bannister rail. 'Jordan House is a rehabilitation unit. Naturally some of our residents are troubled.'

That's all he had to offer. I said, 'They might be. I'm not. She called out for help. Why?'

Regis ignored me. He turned to the librarian type. 'The door.'

He cleared off. The woman said, 'I think you should go.'

I got one foot past her and I stopped as if I'd remembered something.

I said, 'Oh, Abigail?'

'Yes.'

'Never mind.'

We were back in the car. I was expecting at least a spark of excitement from Frankie but I was in for a disappointment. He just sat there looking through the windscreen with furrows chasing each other across his forehead.

I said, 'Didn't you hear that? She answered to

Abigail. And the one upstairs is another Abigail. I'd bet the farm on it.'

He was still locked up in his own strange musings.

I shook him by the shoulder, 'Don't you get it? They're *all* called Abigail.'

'Yeh.'

Well, if Frankie wasn't going to pat me on the back, I'd have to do it myself. I said, 'But I knew that before we even knocked on the door.'

'Balls.'

'I'm serious. "Alibi cooked up in Georgia for the maid." '

This time he turned to look at me. He said, 'What are you on about?'

There followed a brief explanation of Oscar's cryptic clue. When I'd finished he was none the wiser. 'So?'

I said, 'Think it through. Alibi in Georgia for the maid. I thought it was only a stupid anagram of Abigail.'

He was getting a headache. 'But you just said that's what it was. I mean, you're not making any sense. One minute you say it means Abigail, the next you say it's something different.'

I took a deep breath. 'The *real* clue is "the maid". The *maid*. I'll lay you ten to one that Abigail is another word for a maid.'

'So what?'

This was turning out even harder than I thought. I said, 'That means all of the young rascals in Jordan House are maids. The Chinese bird, the Scottish blonde, the one who opened the door, even the one who called out for help.'

Frankie said, 'Yeh. She's the one I'm thinking about.'

That stopped me. I looked at him hard. 'Well, don't keep it to yourself; let me in on the big secret.'

He said, 'I can't be sure. We've got to go back to the hotel to make certain.'

And that was all he would say. Even when we were back amid the pong and clutter of his room he still wasn't talking. He was down on his knees rooting around among his piles of aluminium camera boxes. I kicked a pair of boxer shorts off a chair, flipped over the cushion and sat down to watch.

Frankie was in no hurry. I smoked my way through two Bensons before he cantilevered himself upright, holding several strips of negatives. He took them to the window and began peering at them with a rare thoroughness. This was all very entertaining, but didn't mean anything to me.

And then he said, 'Got it.'

'What you got?'

Frankie was smiling in a gloating sort of way. 'Have a butcher's at this.'

He stabbed his bony forefinger at one of the negatives. I looked. All I could make out was a woman's face in black and grey and white.

I said, 'Who is it?'

'It's the bird at the top of the stairs.'

I looked again. 'You're guessing.'

'Naw. What about the cheekbones. And the hair. It's the same one. Here, have a go with the lens.'

I tried again with the magnifier. It was still just a patchwork of shadows. I shook my head.

273

He said, 'You wait till I run off a print. Then you'll see. But I'm betting you anything you like it's her.'

I suppose I was still a non-believer. He pulled out a twenty quid note and slapped it in my hand. 'A score to a pint it's the same one.'

Frankie *never* bets cold cash, and definitely not at those odds, unless he knows he's already won. Suddenly I believed.

I said, 'Where did you snap her?'

And he told me.

I got offside after that because Frankie's room is ripe enough without adding his various picture chemicals to the mix. I went down to the bar and lined us up a pint apiece, for I always pay my bets promptly. I was sitting there trying to work out where this new stuff got us when Dinesh rang me. 'Belker's just come over and he's told me you might like to know that the man you're writing about is supposed to be still down there.'

'Okay. Anything else?'

'Yeh. His likely successor is his agent. What's all this about, Max?'

'It's a special.'

'Oh.' Dinesh is too well brought up to pry. He switched track and rattled off the latest office tittle-tattle. I cut him short. 'Do me a favour. Get out your dictionary and look up the word Abigail for me.'

I could hear him thumbing through the pages and talking away to himself, 'Abbess . . . abbey . . . abbot—'

'Try it with one B.'

Off he went again. 'Abide . . . abiding . . . abiet . . . here it is: "Abigail, a maid, usually lady's maid. Biblical." Is that what you want?'

'That's exactly what I want. I'll tell you the whole thing later.'

As I tucked the phone away Frankie appeared, wearing a wall-to-wall smirk. 'Right, mate. That's twenty quid you owe me.'

'The bet was a pint. Now let's see this snap.'

He chucked the print down in front of me and reached for the glass. I concentrated hard on the little oblong. It was in black and white, and that didn't help matters. Frankie slid me the magnifier and I screwed up an eye. The picture showed a girl in her early twenties with long blonde hair and wide awake eyes. She was grinning straight into camera.

Frankie said, 'See?'

Not quite. The woman I spotted in Jordan House looked thinner, older. And certainly a damn sight less pleased with herself.

I said, 'You're certain?'

'I'll bet you an even hundred.'

No. Just this once I'd take his word on it, for snappers are red-hot at remembering faces. I said, 'How come you were able to pick her out?'

'Cheekbones. When we saw her today she didn't look anything special to you. But just by looking at a bird, a photographer can tell if she's photogenic or not. This one has the cheekbones. She takes a good snap.'

I said, 'So now we know who she is and where she is. All we have to do is get to her. And somehow I don't see Regis and his boys fixing us up with a date.'

Frankie bobbed away at his drink. He came up for air. 'What I need is a good clear pic of her. Then we can confront Lanche. Just say we broke into the house.'

'Yeh. And just say we ended up in jail.'

Frankie shut up. I ran through the options. I supposed I could always call the police. But then how would I pitch it? They'd want to ask me all sorts of questions which I didn't feel like answering. Besides, they might be inclined to go leak *my* story to every hack in the neighbourhood. So the Old Bill were not on. What did that leave me? I could try threats. Another no-no. Regis & Co. would simply stonewall me and in the meantime they'd whisk her off somewhere else. Oops. That one should have occurred to me sooner.

I said, 'They'll get her out of the way. They'll move her tonight when no one's around. Then we're left with nothing.'

'We could doorstep them and follow her.'

I shook my head. 'They'll be watching. We'll wind up chasing a decoy while they sneak her off after we've taken the bait.'

Frankie emptied his glass noisily. 'If only there was some way we could smoke her out.'

'Yeh.' I lit a cigarette and watched the smoke drift upwards.

Smoke!

I grabbed him by the arm. 'You've hit on it. Frankie G. Frost: you, my son, are a true genius.'

He looked more puzzled than you might expect of a genius. But he grinned anyway. 'Oh yeh?'

And so I explained. His mouth gawped wider and wider as I ran through the masterplan, and by the time I hit the end he was full of nitpickety objections, such as how many years in jail we'd cop.

I said, 'You leave the criminal bit to me. All I want you to do is hang around with your camera. And, well, just follow my lead. Now, first I need a whole stack of papers.'

I scooped up a couple of books of matches and went out to reception to collar every single newspaper on show, including the entire pile of unsold *Guardians*. The receptionist blinked in bafflement, and who could blame her. Frankie was standing way off by the door, pretending he didn't know me. I'm not sure what bothered him more: being seen in the company of a criminal, or being seen in the company of a *Guardian* reader.

Chapter Twenty-One

We hopped in his motor and headed for the nearest petrol station, a Texaco place on the road into Harding. Frankie slewed off the road a clear quarter of a mile short of it.

'I'm not buying the petrol,' he said.

This was no time for wishy-washyness. I said, 'Just drive us up to the pumps and I'll pay.'

'You take the petrol can. It's your idea.'

I said, 'No, it's not. You came up with it.'

Bicker, bicker, snarl and bicker. All the while there was a sergeant-major voice in my head, shouting above the row. Leaving out the more colourful words, it was saying, 'Just get on with it before they sneak her out.'

I gave in. Frankie tossed me the keys to open the boot. Just as he'd promised, there was a red plastic petrol can in the back. I trudged down the hill towards the service station. I glanced back. Frankie had his sun visor clamped down to hide his eyes, but his bumpety nose was in plain sight.

There were about eight different pumps. I went straight for the four-star, a frisky little vintage. I know this because it squirted all over my shoes and trousers before I managed to get the nozzle in Frankie's can. It was in there only seconds before the petrol gushed over the top and gave me another drenching. I clunked the nozzle back in its slot and made a mental note to refrain from smoking for a day or two.

The geezer behind the till let me know he was richly amused by it all. You could see a bubble floating out the top of his head with the words 'What a pillock.' And this from a man kitted up in a red boiler suit.

I trudged back up the hill with the petrol can banging against my leg. Frankie had swung the car around for a fast getaway. He pushed open the door, 'Get in quick, before anybody sees us.'

Just out of badness, I dawdled. Whereupon he thumped the car into gear and began to pull away so that I had to jump in or get left behind. I gave him a scorching and he came right back with more of the same. Honestly, I don't know why I hang around with the idiot. Must be my soft heart.

We rolled up at the hotel car park again with Frankie still mouthing away. I said, 'Shut up and listen. Here's the plan—'

'Here's *your* plan, you mean.'

I ignored that. 'I'm going to sneak through the hotel gardens and find a way round the back of Jordan House.'

'I'm not.'

There are times when I could really use ten yards of surgical tape to gag the man. I said, 'You, meanwhile, will be close by, so that when people come running out of the house, you can snap them all.'

He had a more chicken-hearted idea. 'I'll doorstep the front and shoot them with the long lens.'

'Just remember, if you miss her, bang goes my job.'

He generously offered, 'I'll come and see you in jail.'

Growl. I didn't want to think about that. I got out of the car and straightened my tie. To all the world I was merely a well-dressed man without a care in the world. Minor correction. A well-dressed man whose trousers stank of four-star. I swathed the petrol can in reams and reams of newspapers. Now I didn't look quite so casual. Let's just hope the Reen Court people had better things to do with their life than snoop on innocent arsonists. I walked without hurrying round the back of the building. No one in sight. The gardens stretched off to my left, stopping dead at a line of wind-whipped trees. They were firs or something of that ilk so I couldn't see if there was an electrified fence behind them. There was only one way to find out. I breezed straight up to the foilage and vanished from sight. I stopped and took one quick look back. Sunlight sparked off the windows of the hotel. The entire staff might have been lined up behind them watching me for all I knew. Still, it was too late to stop now.

I turned about and parted the branches. Ahead lay a cordon of chest-high prickly bushes and twenty yards beyond was the side wall of Jordan House. Only four windows, and two of them had bobbly bathroom glass. From this range the other two were happily lacking in spectators. Okay. So what about closed circuit cameras? I went over the side wall from tiles to drains. Nothing. Maybe the cameras just covered the doors.

Holding the petrol can out in front of me I shouldered through the bushes and straight up to the wall. I ran another check for cameras. Still nothing.

Now that I'd got to the target I was somewhat at a loss. The main idea was to start a fire big enough to scare Regis and all the Abigails into flight. I could manage that all right. But just say the fire got ideas above its station and roasted everybody alive? Ur. The alternative was to start the blaze here against the side wall. But then they'd probably not even notice it.

I edged towards the back of the house and stuck one eye round the corner. Damn. There was a door with a camera on top. I pulled my head back in sharpish and thought about this. The only bright spot was the camera had its eye facing off towards the cliff, so it probably hadn't seen me. But if I tried to get anywhere near the door, it would catch me. No question.

I kicked a brick in frustration. A brick. Now that just might come in handy. I squinted round the corner again. The camera was mounted on an angled bracket so that you could adjust it to point any old way you wanted. I beamed fondly on the brick. It was just lying there begging you to chuck it at something. I put the petrol can down and weighed my friendly brick. A heap of its mates were loitering nearby shouting, 'Me too! Me too!'

Oh all right then. I chanced another look at the camera and worked out how much of myself I could show round the corner before it copped me. I reckoned one eye, one arm and one leg was just about the maximum. I took a deep breath and hefted the brick as hard as I could. When last seen it was heading towards France. Bugger.

But its mates had caught the general idea. The first one thumped against the wall a bare inch north of the camera bracket. Number two hit the side but only made it wobble. Somewhere around brick six I got my eye in. There was a Glonk! and the camera suddenly changed its mind and started ogling the seagulls. Ha!

I hung around waiting for five long minutes until I was sure that no one inside Jordan House had twigged. All was tranquil.

I eased round the corner and had a full look at the layout. The white minibus was parked on a gravel stand. Behind it there was a ramshackley wooden shed that looked like it wasn't long for this world. Both minibus and shed presented themselves as burnt offerings. All very tempting, but they wouldn't force the Jordan House mob to flee for their lives.

Which brought me to the back door. It was plain and wooden without a pane of glass or even a keyhole to snoop through. To its right there was a window, but it was set too high in the wall and I didn't feel like pogo-ing up and down to get a dekko. It had twin fanlights and they were both wide open to the ozone. I looked the door over again. Under it there was a narrow gap. I knelt down and had a peek. It was a kitchen, I guessed. Red-brown tiles, bottoms of cupboards. No feet. That didn't make me any happier. There was enough old wood in there to trigger a replay of the Great Fire of London.

I cast about for other things to set ablaze. Further along the house was a built-on conservatory affair, as far as I could see unoccupied. But it posed the same risk of barbecuing the entire guest list. The only other things on view were a marble-topped garden table and a tin dustbin. And there wasn't much I could do with them.

I pulled back round the side of the house and

got out a Bensons to help me think better. I had a matchbook in my hand, a red-headed match on the sandpaper all set to strike when my senses kicked in. My sense of smell, to be exact. And only just a split second off self-combustion I remembered my petrol-drenched condition.

Wow! This arson lark isn't all it's cracked up to be. I put away the matches with trembling fingers. I'd gone right off the idea of blazing fires. I stood there breathing deeply, but not too deeply, on account of the fumes, and started reviewing my wizard wheeze again. Frankie's words came tumbling into my head: 'If only there was some way we could smoke them out.'

That's it. That's where I was going wrong. I didn't need fire. I needed smoke. Lots of it. And once I'd got that sorted in my head, the rest was simple. I nipped round the back and pinched the dustbin which seemed to have cornered the market in potato peelings. I sploshed some petrol onto them and then started ripping up papers. I stopped for a moment to read the splash in the day's edition of the *Sunday Mercury*. The intro was the only bit of note.

Police are treating as suspected murder the mystery death of a young Canadian tourist whose body was found last week at Raglan Cove, Harding.

Following a second examination of the victim by a Home Office pathologist, a police spokesman confirmed this. 'There is evidence to show that this woman's death may not have been accidental, as first appeared.'

Can't say I was surprised. I got on with my labours. The bin was now half-full and looking good, but I needed that extra something. The fir trees supplied it.

Nice green branches that would give off more smoke than the *Flying Scotsman*. The only snag was they were singularly reluctant to part company with the tree. In the end I virtually had to gnaw the things off.

And all the while someone was watching me. God only knows what the watcher thought I was up to.

I filled the bin to the brim and added a few more branches for luck. Glug-glug-glug. There went more petrol gravy. Now for the masterstroke. I sneaked another look round at the conservatory. Still empty. I grabbed hold of the table and lugged it towards the kitchen window. The thing weighed about as much as a fully-loaded jumbo jet. But desperation gave me the strength of ten lunatics. Another brief pause to see whether anyone had sussed me. All clear. I hoisted up the bin and parked it on the table. The top branches were just off the open fanlights. Maybe a little too close. I hauled the bin back six inches. Yep. That should wipe a good two years off my sentence.

Now to light the thing. I rolled up a *Guardian*, dipped it in the petrol can, and reached for the matches. This was the hairiest moment of all. I was half inclined to whip off my trousers, but I suddenly had this vision of me scurrying around in my boxers, setting fire to dustbins. No. That did not meet the Chard standards of dignity. Instead, I was just very, *very* careful. I placed the *Guardian* on the ground about a yard away and tossed a lit match at it. It flickered and died. This wasn't going to work. I tried again, only this time holding the paper way up like the Statue of Liberty. It took. But only just. I waved it about in the breeze until there was a lick of flame eating away. I held it up against the bin. Do you know, I reckon that pump attendant must have watered down his petrol it took so long to get going. A billow of dirty grey smoke seeped out of the bin and jumped on top of me. After I was done coughing and wiping my eyes, I had a look to see how the bin was behaving and I must say I felt a stab of pride. It was chuffing out smoke by the gallon and a fair whack of it was climbing through the windows. I would have liked to have stood there admiring it, but phase two of the plan meant I had to scoot round the front and count the survivors. Before I left I went and let down all four tyres on the minibus. Let's see them try to get Abigail out in that.

And so to the front. Frankie, as promised, was miles from the scene of the crime. He was standing in Maidmont Road with his mug peering through the bushes. I walked up to join him. He said, 'Where's my petrol can?'

Ooops. I legged it back round the side, grabbed the damn thing and pitched it deep into the firs.

Back at the front you could see occasional puffs of smoke. But nowhere near enough. Anxiety began to tug at my nerve ends. And then from somewhere in the well of the house came that most welcome of sounds: the beep-beep-beeeeeping of a smoke alarm. I was hoping for the door to fling open and all the assorted inmates to come charging out. They had other ideas. A tall bloke emerged, looked up at the front of the house, scratched his head, prowled away and looked down the left side, came squelching all the way across the gravel and checked out the side where I'd been. That's when he saw the smoke. He returned to the front door a few mph faster. All the time Frankie was taking shots of him. The bloke stood in the hallway talking to someone out of sight. And then they came. Men first. Four of them. No sign of Regis yet. Gap in proceedings here. Next on stage was the wheel-chair man, closely pursued by Lindy Trevett. Aha! And finally came five women, all called Abigail, with Doc Regis chivvying them along.

The one we wanted was at the tail of the queue, another girl holding her hand. Frankie's camera was already on her. The whole congregation were in a straggly semi-circle, their backs to us. I said, 'Okay, Frankie. This is it. Keep snapping her. If anybody stops me, you know what to do.'

I marched up the drive and nobody even spotted me until I was right up to her. I said her name and she turned round so fast her hair swirled back behind her ears. She said, 'Who—?'

The woman with her was the taller, older one we'd seen that morning. I saw her mouth tighten as she reached for Abigail's arm. But I just grabbed the blonde girl and yelled, 'Run!'

Too late. A couple of the blokes were trotting our way and blocking off the drive. I faced about and pointed down the side. 'Run!' I yelled again, only a bit louder this time.

The blonde still wasn't moving and now the pack was closing in. They were between me and Frankie and he was just twiddling with his cameras. I shouted out, 'Frankie, *shoot* them.'

I think they must have taken 'shoot' literally because they all stopped and looked behind them. That gave me all I needed. I hustled the blonde down the side to the spot where I'd sneaked in from the Reen Court garden. We might have made it and all, but for this geezer who stepped out of the smoke and thumped me in the chest.

'Butt out,' said the Man in Black.

I had the choice: I could hand her over or I could batter him witless. I got the impression he might be the better batterer around here. But did he know that?

I said, 'You touch her and I kick you clear off the cliff.'

He said, 'I told you to butt out. Next time I make you.'

He stared straight at the blonde, 'Come on, we're out of here.'

And without another look in my direction he took her away from me. The fool. The moronic, muscle-bound, iron-pumping macho man. My entire future depended on me winning this battle. What did he have to lose?

He had his back to me. A last lonely brick lay down by my right shoe. So I picked it up and brained him good and proper. He went down faster than a pint on a summer's day.

'Ooh,' said the blonde, 'you shouldn't have done that.'

And then she proceeded to tell me why, which was a bit embarrassing. In the meantime I'd got clear through to the Reen Court and the only sounds of pursuit came from Frankie as he fought his way through the firs.

'Max!' he shouted, 'Max! There's a dead guy here.'

With deepest foreboding I waded back in among the pines. The happy news was the Man in Black was less dead than originally rumoured. You might have thought that would have made his day too. Not quite.

He was all set for tearing me to shreds. But there was blood dripping off his left ear and he was a touch shaky. Also, he was half expecting me to bat him with another brick. I played peacemaker instead.

I said, 'She's just told me who you are. If you'd had the brains to tell me you wouldn't have a headache now.'

He growled way down in his throat and rubbed his aching bonce. In a quiet way I was enjoying myself. I said, 'You ever try any tricks like that on me again, and I *will* kick your backside off the cliff. Now, do you want to talk, or do I have to bang some sense into you?'

A dead easy question, you might think, but he was still looking murderous. I said, 'My name is Max Chard and I'm a reporter. I'll make you an offer: you tell me the story and I give you Abigail.'

The Man in Black – though now I come to think of it, he was wearing a brown suede jacket for the occasion – was still griping. 'This is *my* business, Chard. You don't even know what you're doing. I saw you trying to burn the house down.'

I turned to Frankie. 'What do you say? Do you reckon we should just boot him off the cliff like we did with Zenia?'

The Man in Black/Sometimes Brown said, 'You didn't do that.'

And the blonde told us who did.

Chapter Twenty-Two

After that we had to get her out of there as fast as we could. My first instinct was to whisk her off to London, but the game down here had not yet run its course. And I needed her for that. So I led her off to my hotel bedroom. I had to hold her hand because she was acting like she was sleepwalking. I even told the mystery man he could join the party. He wasn't happy, but it was the best offer he'd had all day.

I was the perfect host. 'Anyone for sandwiches? How about a drink?'

Yeh, well, apart from you, Frankie.

I got on the phone and rattled off an order for a stack of lagers plus two orange juices for our guests. By this time I'd been introduced to our bleeding friend. His first name was Gus. His second name was his own affair. I sat on the lip of the bath while the blonde slowly washed his bump. She wasn't much cop at it and I had to take over. Even with all my tender loving care, Gus kept on carping.

I said, 'We're quits now. *I* thumped you with a brick, and *you* tried to run me down in your car. Like to tell me why?'

Gus lifted up his head and glared at me in the

mirror. 'I seen you once before. You were snooping around outside the mews house.'

He was missing bits out. He was also looking nasty. I began wishing I'd kept a brick in reserve.

I said, 'The mews? Yep. That was me. But a couple of days back, in Apson, some idiot in a silver Toyota nearly killed me. And that was you.'

Gus screwed up his eyes as if he had a humdinger headache, and I suppose he had. He said, 'If I did, it wasn't deliberate. I never saw you.'

Okay. Maybe he was just another rotten driver. Not in Frankie's class, but still a menace. It didn't matter. I'd survived.

I said, 'That night outside the mews house: who was the woman inside?'

I suppose I already knew the answer. Abigail. But not our very own special Abigail who right now was floating around my hotel bedroom looking semi-detached from reality.

I was starting to grow a headache myself. But I had to nail this all the way through. I said, 'So the mews place was a nest? That's where you stored the Abigails?'

Gus asked, 'It's not your show, man. Why do you need all this?'

Because I need facts. Because I devote my life to the pursuit of truth and justice. But mainly because I want to keep my job.

I said, 'And the mews house – that's where Howard Lanche kept his secret Abigail?'

Gus raked up a smile. 'You guys think you know it all. Does it make you feel good or something?'

I said, 'Or something. But let's just try this again

in plain English. Right here in this room we have Lanche's private Abigail. And he used to go and see her. I know this because I was there one night he called. The night before I bumped into you.'

Gus did something I thought was beyond him. He laughed. He actually laughed. 'She'd already gone. She was long gone.'

I bit on that and gnawed for a while. I said, 'So Lanche went there to see Zenia?'

No argument.

I pushed on, 'And Zenia came up with some Loony Tunes plan to get Lanche and his little Abigail back together. But she didn't tell Eric and that's why he reported her missing.'

Gus didn't bother answering. He just mopped the back of his head with a nice white towel and ambled out of the bathroom. He was still acting one up on me. You know, it really twists me when people start thinking they're sharper.

I said, 'Fair enough, Captain America. You know many things. You even know Abigail's real name. And you think that makes you special.'

Gus didn't quibble.

I said, 'Now take a look at my photographer.'

Gus inched his sore head over to the right. He saw a scrawny, scraggy man in dire need of an emergency tailor. Frankie had his dopey doggy smile hanging off his chin.

I said to him, 'Our chum, Gus, is holding back on a whole heap of stuff. Like he won't tell us Abigail's name. So why don't you tell him what she's really called.'

And Frankie told him.

After that Gus went quiet. Maybe he was sulking. I did the decent thing and cheered him up. I said, 'But there's a lot we don't know. Like where everybody fits in the picture.'

He gave me an under-the-eyebrows stare for a long moment. Then he said, 'This is for your information only. Right?'

Sure. You can tell me anything. I'm a reporter.

And without any further nudging he was off, spilling the lot on Zenia, and Lindy, and the old geezer, and Shernholm, and both Howard and Leonora, and sundry others besides. I didn't even have to ask questions. I just let him chatter on, filing it all away in the back of my head.

When he was through I turned to the blonde. But she was harder-going. She couldn't focus on anything and it didn't take a clinical psychologist to see she was out of her tree on drugs. Barbiturates or such, I guessed. But she said enough for us to work out what really happened that night on the coast path, the night Zenia went off the cliff.

I suppose now was when I should have handed her over to the Old Bill. They don't take kindly to reporters concealing murder witnesses. But I'd already broken so many rules on this job, another one wouldn't matter.

Gus drained his orange juice and said, 'Okay, I've given you what you wanted. Now I'm going, and she's going with me.'

I said, 'I lied about that bit. She stays because we need her.'

He was all set for another ding-dong. The girl shook her head dazedly, as if she'd been the one I'd bopped with a brick. She went and lay flat on my bed. About a heartbeat later she was spark out. Gus stopped in mid-rant.

I said, 'Looks to me like she's staying.'

I sat down in the armchair and swigged lager. I also stuck a knee up and sniffed my trousers. They still smelt of petrol, but only just. I risked it and lit a Bensons. I began taking an interest in our dormant guest. Her face was a shade more washed-out than I'd expected, without even a hint of make-up, and her long hair could have done with a clipping. But it wouldn't have taken much to turn her into a right honey again. Physically anyway. It might take longer to unscramble her head.

Gus was standing like a rock in the doorway, only you don't catch many rocks glaring. He said, 'Why do *you* want her?'

At least he was asking questions instead of flexing his muscles. He even listened without yapping while I rolled it all out for him. I wound up and waited for him to chip in with the objections. He said, 'And I'll be with her the whole time?'

'Right by her side.'

'And when you're through, she stays with me?'

I said, 'You've got it.'

He was still hedging. 'How do I know you'll keep your word?'

I sighed. 'Look, Gus. As you know, I'm a hack, a reporter. All that matters to me is the story. If I had it in the bag now, you could heave her over your shoulder and I'd open the door for you. I need two hours. Not much after all this time.'

Frankie who was wandering round the bed,

snapping Sleeping Beauty, joined in, 'Yeh. The sooner we have what we want, the sooner we're out of here.'

Gus liked the sound of that. He said, 'Go over the final details again.'

And when he was largely satisfied, I got on the phone to Alex Hartiwell. 'Alex! Ed Stonelight again. Just checking you're okay for four o'clock.'

He was.

I said, 'By the way, can you get a message to Howard and Leonora for me?'

He wasn't sure of that one. He'd give it a shot anyway.

I said, 'Tell them I've got something big for them. But I need to see them face to face to tell them.'

That made him even less sure. He asked, 'If you can tell me, I'll do my best to pass it on.'

I took over all conspiratorial. 'It's a bit messy, and I really don't think you'd want to get involved.'

'I see, I see. Well, they're not at home at present, but I have an idea where they might be. I'll let you know if I've had any success.'

Good for him. I picked up the phone again to ring the office. But I hesitated and called Belker's home number instead. He opened with, 'I warned you not to—'

'Tony,' I broke in. 'I have a story ready to roll. Want to hear it?'

He grizzled but went quiet. I gave him everything I had so far, laying a lot of emphasis on the photographs so he knew I wasn't making the whole thing up. He puffed for a while, then, 'Okay. Let's have it. But I'm not making any promises. The Editor's very pissed off with you.'

That made us even. I took a breath. 'I've told you what I already have. And it all hangs together. But give me a couple of hours and I might be able to deliver a story that's ten times as good.'

'No dice. Miranda wants you fired, as of now. I'm fighting your corner because I don't like to see a reporter getting dumped on.'

Phooey. He was fighting my corner in the hope I'd help get his flubbery bum back in the Exec. Ed. seat again.

I played on that. 'Listen, Tony: the stuff I have now is good, but not good enough to help you. Are you with me?'

Much beating of bushes but he caved in. I pushed the phone away, feeling more chirpy than I ought to. We had an hour to fill before meeting Hartiwell. I used it to squeeze all the fine detail out of Gus, for this was one story I had to get bang on the button.

At ten to four we woke the blonde. Gus rinsed the bloodstains out of the flannel and wiped her face with chill water. She sat up groggy and frightened, and it took a bit of soft-talking by Gus before she was with us again.

We helped her downstairs and into the back of Frankie's motor. Whoops, off she went to sleep again. I could only hope he'd be able to get her functioning when her time came.

Frankie parked in the driveway of Red Gables where we were out of sight of Hartiwell's place. He did a systems check on his assorted cameras while I chewed a biro and swore softly to myself.

'Ready?' he asked.

'Half an hour ago.'

There was a maroon Jag lounging in Hartiwell's driveway. Lanche's? I had my fingers crossed on that one.

I jabbed the bell and Hartiwell opened up. 'Ed! Frankie! Great to see you again.'

So far he hadn't noticed the cameras.

He led the way into the living room, and there they were: Howard and Leonora, parked in adjoining armchairs by the front window. Hartiwell, his back to us, said, 'Well, as you've probably guessed, I passed on your message, Ed.'

There was one other inmate. The pale specimen who called himself Simon. Apart from Hartiwell, nobody seemed delighted to see us. I wanted to get this over quickly. I said, 'My name is Max Chard and I'm a reporter. Frankie's other name is Frost, and he's my photographer.'

Hartiwell turned slowly round. 'A reporter?'

I said, 'Yup. And a photographer.' Without waiting to be asked, I sank down in the centre of the three-seater sofa.

Howard Lanche unclamped his jaw. 'You have something to tell us?'

His wife had the end of her nose dunked into a coffee cup. I said, 'You're looking well, Leonora.'

A polite lie, that one. She had her hair pulled back in a sort of bunch and it made her face longer, sharper. Also she looked like she'd been missing her beauty sleep for a week or more. She was in a long green frock with darker green hoops around the bottom. She perched on the edge of her seat, eyeing me like the queen of the vultures. Let's just see how long that held out.

Hartiwell bleated, 'A reporter? Why are you here?'

I stared at Simon. 'You have any ideas?'

His flat eyes skitted away. I said, 'Sit down, Alex, and presently all will be revealed to you.'

This is hard to credit, but first he had to go through the routine of offering us coffee and bikkies.

I said, 'No thanks. Now, if you had gin on the menu, I might change my mind. But then you don't drink, do you?'

'No.' Hartiwell went around switching on every table lamp in the place before he took up position in a chair the opposite side of the fireplace from Simon. So now we were ready.

I lit a Bensons and began. I was talking at the far wall. 'A couple of weeks back Howard took a call from a man – or maybe a woman – whose name I'll never know. The caller was one of those faceless freaks who slink through the sewers of party politics. The message was: "A hack called Max Chard is out to dig up your secret affair with one Zenia Evans." Is that how it went, Howard?'

Leonora chinked cup on saucer. 'This is a waste of time. You have nothing to say to us. We're leaving.'

I looked at her levelly. 'I'll make you a deal. I won't ask questions if you just hear me through.'

She batted that one across to her husband. He was still making up his mind. They stayed.

So I went on. 'The first thing you have to understand is how a tabloid reporter works. It's dead simple. He gets a brief from his News Desk, sometimes even his Editor. Then he goes out and lassoes the story. Or tries to.

'My brief on you, Howard, was muzzier than most.

First I had to make absolutely certain that you and Zenia were up to mischief. I reckoned I had that pinned down on the very first night. You arrived at her mews place at eight twenty-six on Monday the twentieth of February. You left at three thirty-nine on the Tuesday morning. And it wasn't a one-night stand: the way you walked up to the house, I could see you'd been there before.'

I paused to see how this was going down with the congregation. The only one showing any expression was Hartiwell who had a toothy smile wrapped across his face. I puffed on the Bensons and cranked on. 'But then later on that Tuesday I saw you with Zenia in a trattoria down Queensway. This must have been before you were tipped off that I was doorstepping you, for you were so wrapped up in an argument you didn't even notice me. Remember that?'

He did. But he wasn't saying.

I said, 'Zenia was telling you, no she was *ordering* you not to see some other woman. Naturally I glued that all together and worked out she was warning you to keep away from Leonora.'

Leonora looked like she wanted to dive in hereabouts, but she eased back and let me get on with it.

I said, 'You see, Howard, I was simply following a brief: you were having naughties, Zenia was your piece of sport. That was the big story. That was the *only* story. But . . .'

'Yes?' Alex Hartiwell prompted. He was liking this.

'But I was so fixed on my briefing, I'd already walked right past the real yarn. I knew there was something flaky about this from the off. Yet I just filed that away as another of life's little curios. Nothing to do with the big picture. But back to that Tuesday. I checked out the mews again that night. There was a woman inside, but no sign of you. I rang your flat, and got relayed on to another number. So maybe you were in Zenia's drum after all. It doesn't matter. For she wasn't there. She was here. Right next door, up in the tower room.'

'No!' Alex Hartiwell rolled his eyes in shock.

I wasn't fooled. 'Come off it, Alex. You knew that. You even gave her the key, because Howard asked you to. So, let's leave Zenia out of the action in London. Who then was the woman in the mews house?'

I squidged my cigarette in the ashtray. I said, 'Let's call her Abigail. She was just one of many Abigails. And she was what this whole thing was about. I couldn't see it because I was still scouring the metropolis for Zenia. And then later still that very same Tuesday night a bloke called Eric Shernholm rings the police to say Zenia has gone missing. I tracked him down to the Royal Lancaster where he blurted out a load of bull about a little baby called Abigail. His story had so many holes in it you could have used it as a fishing net.'

Leonora broke in. 'You are merely reiterating the outrageous story you spun us. I've had quite enough of—'

'Just this once I agree with you. I'd got it completely back to front. And I might never have sorted it, but for the fact that somebody topped Zenia.'

Hartiwell said, 'You mean she was *murdered*?'

'That's about the size of it. Now I was looking at a different story: MP, or wife, or rival, or whoever, kills MP's mistress. You've got to admit, it was a juicy one.

Especially when I found Leonora's nasty letter, telling Zenia to buzz off. Plus I had both Howard and Leonora withholding evidence in a murder trial. It was getting hotter all the while.'

I broke off to flash Leonora a chilled smile. 'By the way, you stitched me up rotten by blabbing to the police after we'd struck a deal. Nasty but nice.'

There was a sharp little gleam in her stony eyes. Yes, she'd enjoyed that bit. I said, 'And then you did something even sweeter: you got a solicitor to draft Howard's resignation. But how were you to know he'd cock it up?

'Anyway, here I was investigating a strange death, a sex scandal and all the rest. You'll enjoy this; at one point I had Tom Davies down as the killer. Not just because he hates you to the core, but because you once killed a kid called Melvyn Davies in Birmingham. And that's roughly where Tom hails from too. But then I remembered this rumpus about the new road. I'm making a guess here, Howard. Being a politician you told Davies what he wanted to hear – that you supported the road plan. He has a garage right on the route, and if the road was built, laid, or whatever you do with a road he'd be quids in. Then he finds you lied to him. He had a small dream and you took it from him. That's why he hates you. But not badly enough to murder your girlfriend.'

Lanche said, 'It was not the way you make it out.'

Who cares. I said, 'I was still chasing the wrong end. I was so wrapped up in the Zenia story I forgot about Abigail. And then by chance we bumped into her, or she bumped into me: a Chinese girl pushing an old bloke in a wheelchair. You, Howard, half jumped out of your seat when I told you Abigail was in town. But as soon as I said she was driving a minibus, you almost laughed out loud.'

Lanche was looking at his shoes. I stared at him and waited. But his head stayed down.

I said, 'Then Frankie struck lucky. He found another girl called Abigail and guess what? She was a wheelchair chauffeuse too. Odd that. Next thing – and I'm not going to bore you with how I worked it out – I discovered that Abigail was another word for a maid. It's biblical or something.

'But who these days keeps a whole string of maids, all of them called Abigail? Only one person. The bearded old duffer in the wheelchair. So let's have a think about him. Somehow I didn't see him trundling along the cliff path and hoofing Zenia to the fishes. But he's surrounded by a bunch of loons who might do the dirty deed for him. Then you wonder why he'd want her dead. Think of it: this was Zenia's first time in Harding. I knew that because Howard had to draw her a map.'

I looked around the audience again. Leonora was watching me steadily. Alex Hartiwell was wagging his head about in bafflement. Simon had his gaze glued on a distant seascape, and Howard Lanche was frozen up inside himself.

I said, 'Don't worry, I'm nearly there. My problem was I was still hooked to the Editor's original brief. Here's something you don't know: the tip-off about Howard's sex adventures was anonymous. A plain sheet of paper with a few dozen typewritten lines. But they revealed so much about the writer.'

Simon, at least, looked interested. I said, 'And

301

here's something else you don't know: everyone has his or her peculiar way of talking. Like Leonora. She uses "quite" every chance she gets. And you, Alex, your every other word is "probably".'

A chuckle from Hartiwell. 'It probably is.'

I said, 'And our mysterious source used "probably" four times in one short note.'

Hartiwell stopped chortling. 'I'm sure it's a common failing.'

I was watching Lanche. He had his head up now and he was looking straight at me.

I said, 'Then there was one word in Howard's resignation letter, a word that didn't belong. But I'll come back to that. My problem was making a connection between people down here and Zenia. I had to *drag* that connection out of you and Leonora, Howard, and even then you lied about it. Zenia was dead. I bet you guessed it wasn't an accident, yet you still kept quiet.'

Leonora made a big production out of sighing. 'How many times must we have to go over the same ground?'

'Just once more. The next move caught me way out. Howard chucked in the towel as an MP. Why? I mean, half the MPs in the land are flying their kites with stray women. The rest are otherwise inclined. So just because you're caught out bed-hopping doesn't mean you have to quit. That meant you'd resigned for something more important. Murder?'

I stood up and started wandering idly around the room, looking at book covers, paintings, photographs. I stopped in front of the snaps. 'You like yourself a lot, don't you Alex?'

'No more than the next man. No more than the next.'

I picked up the photograph of him and Lanche together. I said, 'A strange shot, this.'

He was still smiling fat as a cat. 'Oh, I don't know. Howard has a copy too.'

I said, 'Correction. His shot shows two men on a boat. Yours shows one-and-a-half men. All of you, and half of him.'

He put on his puzzled face. 'It's just a picture. I don't see what all the fuss is about.'

I stood in front of him. 'It's about this. "The hard slog is done by the election agent . . . the MP takes all the credit." Now, who told me that?'

He said, 'I was not speaking about Howard. I was talking generally.'

I left it there. I was walking back to the sofa, not looking at him. I said to no one in particular, 'Here's another funny thing. When we showed up, pretending we wanted to buy Red Gables, Alex welcomed us like the proverbial.'

I turned about and looked at him. 'Then you showed us through the dump. You shot so fast through all the rooms you probably left skid marks on the scrubbed pine—'

Hartiwell said, '—Well, I had other things to do—'

'—until we reached the tower room. Then you damn well *insisted* I inspect it in all its hideousness.'

Hartiwell said, 'It has a wonderful view. I thought you'd be interested.'

I smiled. He'd earned it. I said, 'Yes indeed. It *had* a wonderful view – of Zenia's rucksack. And you knew I'd see it. You were even betting on me coming back

303

and having a poke through it. For you knew all along
I was a reporter. And just in case I missed the connection, you let me know this was Howard's house.'

Alex Hartiwell stood up. 'Really. I don't know why
we're listening to this. Would anyone like more coffee?'

Nobody had their mouths open.

I said, 'And then there was the stuff you left out
and I had to get elsewhere.'

Hartiwell was standing by the chair, trying to act
like an indulgent uncle.

I said, 'Like Mitch Thrimble telling me you were a
solicitor who handled all the top people hereabouts.
Like Tom Davies saying you'd flogged your uncle's
place to the Jordan House lot.'

Leonora Lanche said, 'You are telling us nothing
which we don't already know. We are leaving.'

But Howard plopped his hand over hers. 'Wait.'

I said direct to Hartiwell, 'I'm going to make a
simple statement and you tell me what's wrong with
it. Right? Here goes: Unbeknownst to most people, San
Diego is quite a small place.'

He floundered before he came up with anything.
'It might not be particularly small.'

I said, 'And that's not the correct answer. The deliberate mistake is the word "unbeknownst".'

Puzzled frowns all round. I said, 'Think of it: who
on earth goes around saying "unbeknownst"?'

They thought, but they couldn't come up with anything. I helped them out. 'I know only three people:
the person who tipped us off. He said Howard was
having a fling "unbeknownst" to his wife. That's one.
Two is you, Alex. When you were prattling on about
the new road, you said that "unbeknownst" to the

planners, the local folks were against it. And the third is you, Howard. In your resignation letter you said that "unbeknownst" to you, the cliff fall victim was in fact someone you did know.'

There was a certain stillness in the room.

I said softly, 'But you didn't write that letter, did you Howard? You got your solicitor to do it for you. Right, Alex?'

He didn't feel like speaking. I let the silence flood back while I sparked up another Bensons. Over by the corner Frankie was leaning against the wall. He was waiting for it.

I said, 'So let's put the phantom tip-off merchant and Alex Hartiwell and the author of the resignation letter all together. What do we get? We end up with you, Alex.'

He blew out his lips, shook his head and generally made it known that I was talking rubbish. I let him get it off his chest before I went on. I said, 'Another thing you notice if you're a hack is odd coincidences with letters, that's letters of the alphabet, I mean.

'Like take this morning. I was hanging around in the hall of Jordan House looking for items of interest. All they had on show was a wonky purple and silver cross with underneath it three letters. U and L and T. I was trying to figure out what it stood for. I started playing with what that: Underwear, Lingerie and Trousers? Unlikely. How about Use Less Timber? No. Even dafter. So what did it mean? And then I remembered where I'd seen the same group of letters, even in the same colours.'

Howard Lanche ground out, 'Ultimate Love Therapy.'

'That's right. Ultimate. Does anyone here know how to reach the ultimate?'

Apparently not.

I said, 'That's strange, Alex. Way up there on your shelves is a purple and silver book called *How to Achieve the Ultimate.*'

He came back with a fairly feeble one. 'I've never read it. Somebody gave me that. Can't remember who.'

I got up, collected a photograph from his collection and said, 'That's okay. I'll tell you who. It was the bloke who owned this.'

The snap showed Alex Hartiwell on the deck of a boat called the *Ultramarine*, registered in Santa Ana, Calif.

He said, 'So?'

'So Santa Ana is just along the coast from San Diego. Then there's that U-L-T thing again. Am I making the connections here?'

Howard Lanche said, 'What . . . he . . .?'

I said, 'That's right, Howard. Alex is the guy who got himself tied up with the ULT people in California. He's the one who gave them a base in England. Right in your own back yard.'

Alex Hartiwell said, 'This is preposterous beyond words.'

I was looking straight at Lanche, 'He was the bloke who tricked *your* Abigail into ULT.'

Hartiwell said, 'There is not a scintilla of truth in this.'

Wrong. But I was all out of words. I called across to Frankie, 'Let's bring on our mystery guest.'

He was gone two minutes. I sat and smoked and waited. Leonora Lanche and her husband were tensed up in their chairs. Silent Simon had his eyes half closed. But Hartiwell, he was jinking his head back and forth. Just like one of Frankie's unhappy rabbits.

And then she was in the room.

Lanche was first up out of the chair, his arms wide open. 'Darling!' he shouted.

'Daddy!' screamed Eva Lanche.

Frankie started whacking off flash shots as fast as his skinny fingers could hit the buttons. Momma Lanche was drooped all over her baby daughter weeping real salt tears. In the doorway the guy called Gus stood big and square and looking wired for trouble. Alex Hartiwell had backed off from the main event and was halfway down the room sweating through his smiles. Only Silent Simon was keeping out of this. He got up without a word and walked out.

I hung around picking up the grand reunion quotes.

'Oh, Daddy, Daddy . . .'

'It's all over darling. It's all over. We're here.'

'Mummy, take me home . . . please take me home.'

Sounds of sobbing and kissing. Not much more in the way of words. I'd just have to make them up.

Alex Hartiwell couldn't help himself. He chimed in. 'Eva! I'm so happy.'

Whereupon Eva Lanche tried to jump into her dad's pocket. 'Keep him away, Daddy. He murdered Zenia.'

There was a magnificent middle-class Englishness in what happened next. Hartiwell blustered and blinked and smiled his head off. 'Eva, you poor girl. You must be . . .'

He wanted to say 'off your chump', but the best he could manage was ' . . . very . . . upset.'

Leonora hoicked her nose in the air and squashed up her lips. Lanche didn't even look at Hartiwell. But Eva, clinging to her dad, put one hand out as if to ward Hartiwell away. The Gus character folded his arms and acted like a rock star minder. Our host was still doing his damnedest, but nobody was listening. The Lanches left in a clutch, with Gus playing tail-end Charlie.

Now there were just we three and Hartiwell had packed away his smile. Frankie snapped him looking dour and sour. Off in the background I could hear Simon on the phone. 'Yes . . . understood . . .'

Hartiwell sucked in air and puffed up his chest. 'Would you mind leaving my house.'

I said, 'On our way.'

He let us open the door ourselves. He stood in the hallway watching. I was about to bang the door shut, but I couldn't resist a last shot.

'Unbeknownst to you, Alex, this has probably been just as bad for me.'

I don't think he appreciated it.

Two steps out the door and I was already on the mobile to Belker. For once he let me do the talking and after I'd given him only the top five lines of the story he said, 'Great. Absolutely *terrific*, Max. How did you know Lanche's daughter was in this Jordan House place?'

I said, 'That was Frankie. He'd taken snaps of all the photos in Lanche's living room. There were several of Eva. He recognized her as soon as he saw her at Jordan House.'

'Well, pass on my congratulations. Now, I want you to get on to Copy and I want every cough and spit. Leave nothing out.'

Off he went to explain to the Editor what a news story was. Frankie and I rocketed back to the hotel and I rang in and waited for a copytaker whose ears worked. I got Tweety-pie, who not only looks like a canary, but talks that way too.

'What are you calling this?' she trilled.

'Cult.'

'*What?*'

I spelt it and she relaxed again. I said, 'This is for Tony Belker only, and mark it "Legals Must".'

That meant our lawyers would have to do a word-by-word check on it. As directed, I threw in the whole nine yards. Here's a taster:

The secret heartache behind a top MP's decision to quit was revealed last night when we freed his beautiful daughter from a sinister cult.

Blonde Eva Lanche wept tears of joy as she flung her arms around her Labour backbencher dad and begged: 'Daddy, take me home.'

And still terrified by her ordeal, she told how she witnessed the murder of a young woman sent to rescue her.

As her mum, Leonora, hugged her tightly, Eva branded a close family friend as the killer.

Only a day earlier, popular MP Howard Lanche stunned colleagues with his shock resignation.

None guessed he had sacrificed his political career to

save his 23-year-old daughter from a bizarre religious sect known as Ultimate Love Therapy.

Eva, her hair unkempt and dressed in the cult's dowdy clothes, said murder victim Zenia Evans was thrown over a 200-ft cliff when the two women tried to flee.

And she said: 'The man who killed her is a monster. Even the mention of his name makes me shudder.'

Police in Harding, Dorset are now waiting to take a statement from Eva who fell into the clutches of ULT while studying marine biology in California.

Clinging to her dad she spoke of how the man she regarded as an uncle lured her into the sect.

Eva sobbed as she said: 'He introduced me to people who seemed kind and friendly. But they led me into a nightmare world.'

Her dad, also close to tears, added, 'I may have thrown away my career. But we have our daughter home and that's all that matters.'

And her mum vowed, 'We will keep you safe, darling.'

ULT, headed by a shadowy American nicknamed Moses, hunts out raunchy young girls to serve as 'Abigails' – maids – for its randy male leaders.

Zenia, an ex-member, pretended to rejoin the cult to get Eva away from the sect's Jordan House headquarters.

She arrived in Harding with a tearful tape-recorded message of love from Howard Lanche to his daughter.

Zenia confided her plans to a local man she thought was a trusty friend. But she was unaware of his links to the secretive group.

And when she and Eva fled in their underwear from the sect's cliff-top mansion, he was lying in ambush . . .

I think that's all you want to hear. Though there was an awful lot more, most of it background on the ex-ULT members like Zenia, Eric and Gus who were trying to de-programme the several Abigails. I also ran a line about the (unnamed) killer telling us to get out of his house.

Tweety-pie twittered, 'Why didn't her dad just call the police?'

I said, 'He thought he might never see—'

'—Hold it, Max. Miranda wants a word.'

Crazy Horse came on dripping bile. 'This is a mess.'

I said, 'Which word don't you understand?'

'I'll find somebody to re-write it properly.'

Maybe I'm biased, but I thought it ran okay. Except for that line about Lanche's shock resignation stunning his mates. Shocks usually do that. I said, 'You're the boss.'

She didn't even get the joke. She just went away and I got back to Tweetie-pie.

And after that I had a long deep breath. And a Bensons. And seeing I was back in the hotel, I reckoned a monstrous gin might be in order. No, that would have to wait. I still had loose ends by the drove. Top of the list was Jordan House. I went and hammered on Frankie's door, but he was too busy playing with his monkey machines. So I went alone. The place was dark and void. They'd legged it. But not in the minibus. It was still out the back, hunkered down on its four flat tyres.

Back to the hotel and a call to the Lanches. Howard answered. 'I have no comment to make.'

Not even a thank you. On to the Old Bill. It's not like London, out there in the darkness. The wooden-tops clock off about four. I had to go all the way through to county HQ and finally some inspector rang me back. I whizzed him the story and he said, 'The Incident Room is closed now, but I'll pass this on to them, Mister Sherd.'

I said, 'Chard. Possibly we have a bad connection here. I have just given you the name of a murderer. If he flees the country tonight I'll have a great story on how you let him get away.'

His brain tick-tocked. 'You say you're at the Reen Court? I'll have someone there within half an hour.'

Do they have to *fail* an exam to join the police down there? I said, "The eye-witness to the murder is Eva Lanche of The Maltings, West Kerrow. The man she says is a killer is Alex Hartiwell of Maidmont Road, Harding. This is just a suggestion: mightn't it be better to talk to them first?'

He said, 'Someone will be in touch.'

Yeh. No sooner had I clicked off than the mobile went. Belker. 'Max. You've done a splendid job.'

But?

He said, 'There are pressures I can't explain at the moment, but I just want you to know I appreciate your efforts.'

But?

Belker lingered awhile. 'I thought you should know there's a complete re-write on the story. This is down to Miranda, and, ah, well there are some legal problems.'

And?

He said, 'I know you've given it your best. If it's any consolation to you, the Editor has told me to let you know he's torn up your resignation. You don't have to worry about that any more.'

And that was it.

I took myself off to the bar and set up a large one. In all honesty I can say I didn't enjoy a single sip. I'd delivered a smack dab splash story. People should have been phoning me, patting me on the back, yodelling my praises. Yet Belker had rung to *commiserate*. Even the news that I still had a job came as a consolation prize. They'd read my story and they'd reached for the Spike button.

I stared across the bar at my reflection in a chopped up mosaic mirror. I looked more zonked out than Eva Lanche.

Frankie came bounding in like a rogue kangaroo. 'Hey! We pulled it off. What a team.'

I didn't have the heart to break it to him. I bought drink instead.

I was lining up the second bracer when he said, 'I've got to hand it to you, mate. You sussed it was a cult. How'd you know that?'

'You noticed it yourself, Frankie. All these people who didn't drink.'

He sluiced Glenmorangie through his picket fence teeth. 'Yeh. Right. Weird.'

'Seriously weird.'

Chapter Twenty-Three

The Law made a nuisance of themselves first thing on Monday morning but it was nothing we couldn't handle. I talked to an inspector with dimples and he nodded a lot, as if he already knew the score. Then I phoned News Desk and told them I was coming home to London. Aaah London. Isn't that sheer music to the soul? News Desk said fine.

But it wasn't fine. I'd already seen the paper. The vile Miranda had fed my story on to one of her wet-nosed features pets. And it went like this.

The runaway daughter of a senior political figure was last night reunited with her family following our assistance in tracking her down to an obscure religious group.

I read it again on the way home to England as Frankie laid waste to the landscape. I'd like you to read it again too.

The 'runaway' daughter. She wasn't a bloody runaway. Also, she was young and blonde and tasty. None of that featured. And what in the name of all that's merciful is a senior political figure? Ten? Nine Zillion? Oh, dear me, I could go on and on. But the story didn't. It lacked a couple of minor points, such as Eva unmasking a murderer. They even left out the bit about raunchy young girls recruited as Abigails.

Worse, far worse, it was by-lined Gretchen Hollander and Max Chard. Gretch the Grouch had top billing over *me*.

I tried to cool down. Okay, so some changes might be due to night lawyers with quivery trousers. But the major redecoration was ordered by Crazy Horse.

Therefore I was in a grimmish mood when I wound up on Rosie's doorstep early Monday afternoon. It was raining too. She opened the door and she was wearing a big yellow smock thing and you could see it was short because there were yards of black leggings poking out underneath. She also had a paintbrush in one hand. She slung her arms round me and I thought two things: it's great to be home, and, has this crazy woman just painted the back of my Burberry?

Rosie is absolutely ace. I can tell you that right now. She took me by the hand and led me straight to the best sofa in the kingdom. Before I'd got my coat off she had the Gordons bubbling away. Other women should take note of this.

Then she sat down beside me and she said, 'I've missed you. Tell me what you've been doing.'

But I was still fascinated by the yellow smock and the black leggings.

And so we talked of other things instead.

It would be great to have a happy ending just about here. But newspapers don't like happy endings and bad news is good news. We had that by the lorry-load. The Law down in Harding pushed the Hartiwell allegations on to the Crown Prosecution Service and some nitwit in there deemed there wasn't a *prima facie* against him, mainly on the grounds that the sole witness, Eva, was too drugged up to know who did what to whom and where and when and why and all the rest. Therefore Alex Hartiwell got away with bloody murder. No evidence, no charges, no nothing. Though the party decided to look elsewhere for Lanche's replacement. Lanche let it be known, by way of a new solicitor, that he was sticking by his decision to quit. And that's got to be a first for a politician.

The ULT lot had a sudden urge to re-base in California. Off they went, with Eric, Gus and Co. in hot pursuit. Cutting this short it meant I'd blown away so much effort for sod all. Actually it was worse than that. Crazy Horse was still holding the reins and she had scalped my expenses by half. I reckon I made only about a hundred quid on the deal.

Belker was still way out there grazing the frozen tundra and I was still copping a grim time from her. Sooner or later something had to give.

It gave on the second of April. I would have preferred a day earlier, but there you go. I was munching away with Rosie in our neighbourhood tandoori and they were just about to sling us out when Mac, my police informer, gave me a call.

'Got a yarn and a half for you here, boy, but you'll never use it.'

I said warily, 'If it's one of your jokes, I don't want to know.'

'Joke? This is too funny to be a joke.'

Knowing Mac's jokes, anything is funnier. But I indulge the man. 'All right, let's have it.'

He did it in his usual tommy-gun style. 'Right. Two people. A guy and a bird. In a car. This was down in

Kensington tonight. Okay? The guy sticks his hand up her sweater. She puts one hand on the wheel. You with me? So they're *both* steering. But they get a bit carried away. Next thing is they smack into the car in front. And guess what? It's a police car.'

I said, 'Is that it?'

'You haven't heard the half of it yet. They might *both* be done for driving without due care and attention.'

I said, 'Mac. I am falling asleep.'

He ripped out a cackle. 'Well here's something to wake you up. The guy's name is Dornaby. Phil Dornaby. Doesn't mean anything to you, hey?'

Not a thing.

'How about the girl then? She's called Miranda Briel. Isn't she a big noise in your paper?'

I sat up faster than a jock on a thistle. I said softly, 'Mac, I will pay you five hundred quid for that. Run it past me again.'

'Five hundred? You wouldn't ever use the story.'

I said, 'That's why it's worth five hundred.'

I took down every detail, even the names of the coppers involved, and when I had the whole biz I rang Belker. He let me know he didn't like being called around midnight.

I said, 'Tony, I have a problem. I need fifteen hundred quid to hush up a crime story about one of our executives.'

He asked the right question. 'Who?'

'Crazy Horse.'

Belker said, 'Crime? What's she done?'

And I told him everything. I could hear him licking his lips.

He flecked away the foam. 'It will cost us fifteen hundred to keep this out?'

I said, 'I'm with a couple of the lads right now. They wanted two grand but I beat them down. But they want it in cold cash.'

Belker said, 'Tell them it's a deal. I'll call the Editor.'

I went off to have a good gloat. Rosie was mystified. 'Why didn't you pass it on to all the other papers? That would really show Miranda up.'

I explained, 'They'd use it only if Crazy Horse was some sort of celebrity. She's not. But the Editor and Belker and so forth think any exec on our paper is a household name. That's why Miranda will fork out good money to spike a rubbishy story.'

She was still puzzled. 'Why are you so happy if it's not going to appear?'

'Because right this very moment Belker is grassing her up to the Editor. And the Editor is going to be more than a bit cheesed off. Remember, he and Miranda sometimes play house together.'

Rosie said, 'Will he sack her?'

'Nope. What he *will* do is blacken her name up and down the street. By this time tomorrow, the story will have grown into Crazy Horse entertaining half the men in Kensington, wearing nothing but her war paint.'

'And you're paying a thousand five hundred pounds for *that*?'

I said, 'The Editor is paying up front, but he'll make sure Miranda pays it all back. Mac, by the way, is getting only five hundred. I'm taking the thousand quid.'

'Why?'

'Why? Because Crazy Horse slashed my expenses. I'm just claiming what is rightfully mine. And the joy of it is she'll be paying me out of her own money.'

Rosie said, 'You crime reporters are bigger crooks than the people you write about.'

I said, 'We like to think so.'

As predicted, the story of Miranda's misdeeds was all over the office next morning. And I suppose I made sure of that. I got into the office before her, and I thought it only decent to sympathize. So I left a one-line message on her screen.

Sorry to hear about your bang in the car – a well-wisher.

Crazy Horse was unusually muted that day. She walked around with her head down pretending people weren't grinning at her. A week later she was even quieter. That's when the Editor shuttled her off to supervise the circulation drive. On the way down the ladder she met Belker crawling back up to his rightful place as Executive Editor. The very first thing he did was to lop twenty quid off my previous week's expenses. It was just like old times.

And things got back to normal. Now I had more time to meet mates and wallow in Hamptons. But there was one little bit of business from the Howard Lanche affair still outstanding, which is why I phoned Jim Graham, our lobby correspondent and invited him out to play. I wanted to know if he knew something I didn't.

He suggested six-thirty in Annie's Bar. That's the main oasis in the Commons. It's an all right place, and I've sunk a few there on occasions, but it's heaving with MPs, and I'd had enough of them for the duration.

Therefore I tried to switch venues to the Red Lion, which is part of the real world. But he was nailed down to the Commons in the wild hope somebody might say something interesting.

I tidied up two bitty news stories, but I was doing them on auto pilot. My brain was otherwise engaged in the Lanche thing. But come six o'clock I slipped out of Docklands and hightailed it for Westminster. Annie's Bar was spilling over with MPs. Jim was late so I had to stand myself a tall Gordons.

He finally showed, all tousled and crumpled. That's his natural state. I screeched out for a double Scotch and started raking through office politics which, believe me, are an awful lot more interesting than the other kind. Then I got down to the job.

I said, 'I suppose the Party suits are a bit narked with us for doing over Howard Lanche.'

Jim took a wary look round before replying. 'Not really. They're more upset about losing Alex Hartiwell. They had high hopes for him.'

'Who's they?'

Jim swung his glass over to a corner where three blokes were sitting. 'See the man in the middle? He's Rayleigh Colwyn.'

That didn't mean much. I knew he was an MP and that was about all. Jim filled in the gaps in my education. Colwyn, he said was not only a Government whip, but a King Kong cog in the Party machine.

Jim asked, 'Ever talked to him?'

'No. I've been lucky that way.'

'He's a devious type, part of the dirty tricks department.'

Colwyn was sitting face on. His two chums had

their backs to us. Then one of them turned slightly and I caught his profile. It was the Simon character I'd last seen in Alex Hartiwell's house.

I said, 'I have this sudden urgent desire to meet Rayleigh Colwyn.'

We didn't rush it. We waited until Colwyn was brushing past our table en route to the gents. I stood up, 'Mister Colwyn. I'm Max Chard.'

Jim added, 'Hi, Rayleigh. Max is the reporter who exposed Alex Hartiwell.'

Colwyn paused in front of us. 'Alex? Ah yes.'

He gave me a very cool going over. Then he said, 'Good story. We might have made a blunder, there.'

Maybe they should give me a Cabinet post.

I said, 'I left out a lot.'

Colwyn raised his tufty eyebrows.

I said, 'If you've got a few moments, perhaps you'd like to join us. Jim, do us a favour and get a round in.'

Colwyn said, 'Actually—' His eyes flicked over to where he'd been sitting. Simon and the other bloke were still there.

I said, 'I'd like to thank you for tipping us off to the story.'

'Me? I'm afraid I can't claim any credit.'

Jim said, 'A glass of white, Rayleigh?'

Colwyn smiled thinly. 'All right. A *dry* white.'

He sat down and straightened the creases on his navy suit. It must have cost him a few bob. He had a chin two sizes too small and the smile looked painted on.

I said, 'I did you *two* favours. I also got rid of Howard Lanche for you.'

'Howard?' Colwyn could pitch his inflections perfectly. I bet he rehearsed them.

He said, 'We were very upset when Howard stood down. He was a highly valued MP.'

I said, 'Bollocks.'

Jim, returning with the glasses, gawped. He's not used to unparliamentary language.

Colwyn settled for the smallest of frowns. 'We had no idea about Howard's private situation, regarding his daughter. Otherwise . . .'

I frosted my teeth in a smile, 'Otherwise you wouldn't have fed us a fake story.'

Colwyn kept cool. 'As far as I can gather, you were led astray by Alex Hartiwell.'

You can turn on TV any old night of the week and watch politicians pump out lies by the gallon. You can live with that. But when they do it in your face, it gets to you.

I said, 'You're a Government whip. Yeh?'

He hadn't touched his glass.

I said, 'So you can dish the dirt on any MP who gets out of line.'

Colwyn oozed an easy smile.

I said, 'And Howard Lanche was well out of order when he kicked the Party line over the fishing quotas. You wanted rid of him. Hartiwell gave you the ammunition. And you promised Hartiwell the job. Right?'

Colwyn looked at me over his wine glass. 'Hartiwell started a rumour. A scandalous rumour – that Howard Lanche was having an affair. I imagine it gained currency somehow.'

I lit a Bensons and said, 'Tell me about the "somehow".'

He looked first at Jim, who was still on edge. Back to me. He was giving nothing away.

I said, 'My Editor is a dope and a dullard, but even he knows better than to send a senior reporter to chase a flaky tip-off in an anonymous letter. That meant somebody with a bit of clout pushed him into it. Someone like you.'

He sat for a moment measuring me up. He said, 'Max – it *is* Max, isn't it? Possibly someone leaked it. That's all.'

All? A man's career had been destroyed. They'd set him up for the chop. They'd even planned the chopping ground. And they'd handed me the axe.

I said, 'I bet you even knew the story was all about Lanche's daughter. There never was a sex scandal. But that didn't matter, just so long as you conned us into turning Lanche over. And I did just that. But all the while you were telling the Editor to hold back on publication.'

Colwyn looked as if I was talking about someone else.

I said, 'So Hartiwell was all lined up to take over. You even sent your snotty little aide, Simon, to groom him for stardom.'

Colwyn stretched out the fingers of his right hand and admired them.

I said, 'And as soon as I pulled the rug from under Hartiwell, Simon got on the phone to you.'

That was just a guess. Colwyn's eyes flickered. It was the right guess.

I said, 'And you knew the story would never make the paper. I was writing straight for the Spike. But the only thing that mattered was getting us to roast

Howard Lanche. And I did a hell of a job for you, Rayleigh. How does that make you feel?'

I waited. Colwyn was figuring out how to spin it. Finally he said, 'I don't think you understand how things are in politics. There was a rumour about Howard. Secretaries gossip, researchers gossip, MPs simply *love* title-tattle. Just *words*. It's not real. It's only politics.'

I gave him a crooked smile. 'Try this one for size, Rayleigh: "Labour Whip Behind Smear Campaign to Oust MP".'

Colwyn hit that straight back on the volley. 'I know your Editor. I know he would be *most* reluctant to run a story on those lines.'

I said, 'But the *Telegraph* or the *Mail* would lap it up. I'll lay you a clear fifty right now that they'll have the story within a week. They'll chew you up.'

He looked mildly amused. 'I fail to see why the *Telegraph* or indeed the *Mail* should become interested. They do not have the inside track.'

I said, 'But these things leak out somehow. Don't they Rayleigh?'

He put down his glass.

I said, 'Maybe you don't understand how things are in newspapers. Secretaries gossip, editors gossip, reporters simply *love* title-tattle. Just words. It's not real. It's only newspapers.'

Colwyn had lost his smile.

I stood up, leaving my gin half-finished on the table. I turned away and got back to the real world. I was on the mobile before I hit the street.